D.A. Dwinell

Bloom of Secrets

Guardian of the Stone
BOOK FIVE

D.A. Dwinell
Bloom of Secrets
This book is a work of fiction, and the events, incidents, locations, and characters are products of the author's imagination or are used fictitiously. Any resemblance to actual persons, living or dead, businesses, companies, organizations, events, or locales is entirely coincidental.
Copyright © 2023, D.A. Dwinell
Self-published

Scripture quotations taken from The Holy Bible, New International Version® NIV®
Copyright © 1973 1978 1984 2011 by Biblica, Inc. TM
Used with permission. All rights reserved worldwide.

This novel is dedicated to my friends and family who have supported and encouraged me. I appreciate the support of my father and brother, along with friends and followers like Charles, Simon, Linda, and Chelly, who keep persuading me to continue the series. God truly blessed me when he put you in my life.

Special thanks go to Audrey, Mark, Bill, and Deborah.

One

Is tomorrow really graduation?

The past four years had flown by. I thought about all that had happened since moving to Louisville. The Bloom Keepers managed to put the Granaldi crime family behind bars. Except for Tony and his family, who were still under house arrest. Tony had become a true man of God. It was amazing how the Lord could transform a person. He had become quite a gardener as well. Rosina, his wife, still homeschooled their daughter, Stefania. The Italian Chief and I continued to meet periodically. I teleported him to the house to keep Tony's location secure. As promised, he kept the Bloom Keepers a secret.

The Bloom Keepers continued training with Akio and Asahi in Japan to develop our skills. Let's just say we never knew who would be face down on the mat at the end of a fight. There was one exception, Mechelle. While she had only had the basic skills, she was continent with her knowledge. No one would want to meet her in a dark alley, but she was not ready to take on a group of villains.

She and Austin's relationship continued to thrive, which thrilled me. He tried hard to balance his relationship with her, his schooling, and his work on the farm. When he was busy and she had nothing to do, she had me take her to the villa in Italy.

Mechelle had been a big help with Leonardo and Isabella. Unfortunately, Leonardo's health continued to decline. He and

1

Isabella agreed they did not want me to heal him. They wanted God's will to be done. Leonardo's frail body led me to believe he would not be with us for long. Isabella told me Mechelle had mastered Italian. I was so proud of her.

With the information the Bloom Keepers provided, Chief Bianchi tracked down Marshall Blaise aka Louis Dupont and he was arrested the previous year. To Austin's disappointment, things remained quiet. He eagerly anticipated being able to participate in some action.

With everyone having received an income from my scholarship, we were all able to concentrate on our education and strengthening our skills both in martial arts and working as a team. In fact, Jacob and I will be graduating cum laude. His degree in Computer Science with a minor in Computer Forensics. I graduated with a degree in Criminal Justice.

Greg and Juliet will be graduating in the top 25 percent of the class. Juliet with an Accounting Degree and Greg with a Business degree. Austin obtained his Business degree also. Mechelle's degree would be in Hotel Management. She would need it to take over the Villa.

With everyone receiving an income from the scholarship it had helped us to have time to concentrate on our education and strengthening our skills both in martial arts and working as a team. It amazed me that Jacob had done so well because he practically ran a small business repairing computers for other students.

Phyllis and Hal married a few weeks before graduation day. Hal would officially move in after my mother leaves with Mechelle's parents. Mechelle's parents and Mom are expected to stay here during their visit.

I was not sure how it would work with him underfoot. Thankfully Hal worked a lot.

Mom had settled into her new home and position in Florida. She still had no idea about the Bloom of Dreams. We had not seen each other since the winter break, as I had been busy with my schoolwork and trying to work on the steps to establishing my business. I've missed her immensely.

There was so much to do to get the business up and running. With that and my schoolwork there was little time for anything. For now, I needed to focus on preparing the house for everyone to arrive. Mechelle and I had been trying to keep everything clean, but we still needed to tidy up the house.

I teleported to the pantry to ensure no one would see me; I opened the door. The sounds of glass breaking shot through the air. Mechelle stood in front of the shattered glass on the floor.

Mechelle's body jerked. "You really need to stop sneaking up on me!"

"I'm sorry. Stay there," I said as I snatched the broom and dustpan from the laundry room. I swept up the glass and discarded it.

Mechelle dampened a paper towel and ran it across the floor to pick up any small shards that I may have missed. She said, "I'll finish up in here. I think the only thing we have left to do is to dust and order the food."

"The food's been taken care of. I ordered Caesar salad, lasagna, garlic bread, and tiramisu," I said. I picked up the duster and made my way to the sitting room. As I removed the miniscule dust, I thought about Leonardo.

Why won't he let me heal him?

I understood he wanted God's will to be done, but God gave the stone it's power to be used for good. It was then I ran conversations through my head on how to approach Leonardo with the topic again. Isabella would be heartbroken, and he was much too young to be going through this. Not to mention, he was an asset to the team.

Mechelle found me in the dining room. "The kitchen is clean. How are you doing in here?"

"I'm just about finished. We still have two hours before we need to be at the airport," I replied.

Mechelle informed me she would shower before we needed to leave. I had to do the same. As I was putting the duster away, I received a text from my mother.

MOM: Just landed. Surprise. No need to get us. We have a driver.

What?

I dashed upstairs and I texted Mechelle to inform her of their pending arrival as I undressed. This was possibly one of the quickest showers I had ever had. As I dried my hair, I wondered when Hal and Phyllis would arrive. It was as if I was in a panic to get ready. I stared at my closet trying to figure out what I should wear.

Just grab something, Brooke!

I selected sundresses and sandals and nearly dropped them as I raced to my bathroom to get ready.

Knock. Knock. Mechelle called out, "Brooke. Can I come in?"

"Yes," I shouted from my bathroom as I attempted to apply my makeup in record speed.

Mechelle sauntered in wearing an outfit she had purchased on one of our shopping sprees in Italy. Stunning was the best way to describe her. She brushed her hair behind her shoulder. "They should be here any minute," she informed me.

I applied my lip gloss. "We'd better head downstairs."

Mechelle seized my arm as she had become accustomed to popping around the house with me. It certainly beats rushing down the stairs.

"We should walk downstairs," I advised. I snuck one more peak at my reflection, picked up my compact mirror, and slipped it into my bra. Mechelle released her grip, and we sauntered down to the first floor. Carrying the mirror with me everywhere was now a habit. I did not want to be caught without it like I was when Greg and I were being shot at.

As we approached the landing in the foyer, muffled voices drifted from the kitchen.

Mechelle and I picked up our pace and rushed toward the noise. Greg, Mom, Peggy, and Jim were hauling their luggage inside. Everyone greeted one another. Greg and Jim picked up the suitcases and brought them upstairs, while Mom explained the reasons for the change in their flight plan. Apparently, her boss, Tim, had a friend with a plane, who graciously made the small detour as a favor for Tim. Mechelle, and I prepared drinks for everyone and carried them to the sitting room.

When Greg and Jim sauntered over, Greg kissed me on the forehead. He asked, "Are you excited about tomorrow?"

"Yes, but honestly I'm more excited about our trip," I said with a smile.

Mom interjected, "Tell us about your trip."

Everyone settled into their seats and just as I was about to start, Phyllis and Hal entered the house through the front door. Everyone congratulated them on their marriage, and they immediately told us about their trip. Greg helped them with their bags, while Mechelle and I brought a couple of chairs from the dining room.

As I listened to Phyllis and Hal tell their story, I could tell they were very happy. I tried to listen but found myself wondering how things would work with Hal being here. We had become accustomed to using the stones powers in the home. He knew nothing about it, and it was best it stayed that way. When the food arrived, we moved to the dining room and with the change in location, came a change in the discussion.

"Brooke, we want to hear about the trip you and your friends have planned," Mom asked.

"We are going to Florence, Italy. We are going to stay at the Villa Grandma stayed at," I explained.

"The resort is amazing," Mechelle added.

Peggy asked, "Oh, and when were you there?"

"Oh, I haven't been. Brooke has shown me pictures and I did a little research online. It's adorable. Mom, it's the place I'm going to be working at. Everyone's going with me to help me get settled in," Mechelle explained. Her eyes darted in my direction.

I held back a smile.

Good recovery Mechelle.

The rest of the evening was spent catching up on everything that had been happening. Our parents, Hal, and Phyllis turned in early. Greg and I went out to the back porch.

"We've a long day tomorrow, so I'm not going to stay long. I just wanted you to myself for a little while," Greg said.

His romantic side always made me feel warm and loved. We snuggled up together. Greg rubbed his fingers gently through my hair.

"I can't wait to enjoy some nights like this in Italy," I said as I ran my fingers between his.

Greg kissed the top of my head and squeezed me lightly. "It'll be fun hanging out with everyone, but I want lots of moments like this."

I gazed into his eyes. He placed his lips gently on mine. They were so comforting and warm. Greg pulled his mouth from mine and took a deep breath. "I need to go before this gets out of hand." He stood up and reached his hand out to help me up. We kissed again before he went home.

As I laid in bed, I thought about how my life had changed since I moved to Louisville. That chapter of my life was about to end. I wondered how the next chapter would go.

Two

Beep. Beep. Beep. My alarm sounded. Just as I was about to hit snooze, the thought of my graduation day popped into my head. My grin stretched across my face as I heard the birds chirping just outside my window. I flung myself out of the bed trotting out of my room for breakfast, but slammed myself into Hal as I entered the hallway.

"Good morning," he said as he noticed my pajamas.

"Morning," I replied feeling my cheeks turn red. I retreated to my bedroom and put on my robe to cover up because I didn't want to dress until after my shower.

It surprised me when I entered the dining room that everyone was already up and dressed. Phyllis had a coffee station set up in the corner of the room. I made myself a cup, making sure to add the cream and sugar. I plopped down in the dining room chair. The warmth of the coffee along with my extra clothing caused me to sweat, but I continued to sip. Hal seemed unsure what to do with himself. He scurried to the kitchen.

He soon returned with a Ham and Brie Strata. Phyllis followed with a fruit salad. Everything was fantastic. Hal and Jim had begun talking about Greg and Jim's adventure at the range. Hal seemed interested in the conversation but did not comment. Mom, Phyllis, and Peggy conversed about the wedding. While Mechelle and I discussed our outfits for graduation. We helped clear the table, but Phyllis insisted she clean up the kitchen. She thanked us for getting the groceries she needed for breakfast. I retreated to my room to get ready.

I scurried across the tile floor leaving a trail of water on the bathroom tile. I wiped the steam from the mirror with a towel. My reflection stared back at me. It was as if I was expecting some miraculous change because it's official, from that day forward I would have to start adulting. The image of myself did not show a transformation to alert others of the change from college student to unemployed adult. While drying my hair, I prayed the day would go well.

Off to the closet.

I perused through my clothes for the perfect outfit.

What am I feeling like today?

I shuffled through my clothes and decided on the knee length, cap sleeved white dress.

My beige heels would pair with it perfectly.

I dumped the contents of my makeup bag on the counter. My mind was bombarded with a list of things I needed to take care of to become a Private Investigator, obtaining a license was a priority. It would permit me to have a flexible schedule as well as an excuse to leave situations on the spur of the moment. My newly gained skills could be used and easily explained to others if needed.

My plan was to have the Bloom Keepers work for me, which would be a fantastic cover for all of us. Too bad I wasn't sure everyone would be interested, and I was still researching the idea and praying about it. Leonardo and Mr. Thomas were working with me to figure out some of the financial details and the requirements for such a venture.

At this point, only God knows my future.

I applied my makeup slowly to ensure it was perfect. As the blush brush gently stroked my cheek, I was startled by my phone alerting me of a text.

GREG: How's my love doing?

Fortunate was the best way to describe how blessed I was to have him in my life.

BROOKE: Smiling now. I'm nearly ready. I am not sure about Mechelle. I'll text you when we are ready.

We would be riding to the graduation together. Jim and Peggy would ride with Mom and Phyllis. Hal could not make it due to his work.

I snatched my heels from my closet, I sat on my gold chair. My Imperial Topaz painted toenails peaked out of my open toed shoes. I glanced at myself in the full-length mirror.

You look marvelous.

I winked at myself in the mirror before sliding the compact mirror, and lip gloss into my pocket. It became a habit selecting clothes with pockets. My phone case had a compartment on the back of it for my ID, credit card, and a little cash, so there was no need for a purse.

The phone buzzed.

MECHELLE: I'm ready when you are.

I texted her back to tell her I was on my way downstairs. She and I met on the way down. After confirming with everyone where we would be meeting after the ceremony, I texted Greg. We needed to arrive much earlier than our parents. Phyllis handed us our caps and gowns which she had pressed for us.

Greg waited for us next to his truck in front of my house. He opened both passenger doors of the vehicle before opening the iron gate for us. He greeted Mechelle with a quick nod. She snatched my gown from me and hung it in the truck.

Greg gently hugged me. "Wow, I don't think anyone could be more beautiful," he said as he twirled me around. "Breathtaking."

It reassured me. Like everyone I could be insecure. I lowered my head and raised my glance at him in a flirty way and smiled. When he held me, I never wanted him to let go. Greg's embrace was soothing.

He helped me into the truck before shutting the doors. I had not noticed how sexy he was until he strolled to the driver's side of the car. His red tie gave him a distinguished and powerful presence.

I would be embarrassed to tell him in front of Mechelle, so I texted.

BROOKE: You're mighty sexy.

Greg slid into the driver's seat. When the phone alerted him, he read the text, turned toward me, and winked. During the ride, we discussed how the four years had flown by. We didn't discuss Bloom Keeper's as often during the last year. This was likely due to the lack of action we had seen in the past few years, but we still trained regularly.

While we put on our gowns by the truck, Austin ambled up and greeted us. He and Mechelle told us they would catch up with us after the event.

Greg turned to me. He held me by the waist and pulled me to him. "I hope you realize the only reason I haven't kissed ya yet is because I don't want to mess you or I up," he informed me.

"I assure you; I am restraining myself too." I helped him with his cap.

When we entered the building, the staff immediately separated us to our assigned areas clear across the facility. This seemed more organized than my high school graduation. Perhaps because there were not immature young adults who didn't want to follow the rules.

I became bored and watched graduates socialize or wander around trying to figure out what they should do. I tried to mind my own business and just observe, but when this guy yelled at his girlfriend who appeared to be on the verge of tears, I stepped in. The idea of persuading criminals to do my will was easy. They were on the wrong path. This young lady should have been on cloud nine because of what she had accomplished. I concentrated on him and forced him to apologize to her. This was followed by him giving her many compliments about her appearance before he wandered off. Deep down I knew I should not have become involved, so I asked God for forgiveness.

My eyes surveyed the area. One man was picking his nose.
Gross.

There was a young lady that appeared to be having a problem with her shoes, bothering her feet.
Poor thing.

To the left of me were two staff members. They flirted with each other. Just next to them were a few guys helping another young man tie his tie.

JULIET: Are we still meeting for dinner tonight?

BROOKE: Yes. We are eating lunch with our parents and dinner with the gang.

Is it wrong of me to wish this was over?
I was ready to move on with my next new adventure. I thought about how to approach everyone with my proposal at dinner. Greg

was the only one who knew my plan. He felt everyone would be on board.

I found myself trying to compose the conversations in my head. Before I knew it, the ceremony had started. I waited patiently for my name to be called as I watched many people cross the stage before me. When called, my biggest fear was tripping. As I crossed the stage, a small group of people holler at me. I shook the hands of those on the stage before making my way back to my seat. Once I returned to my chair, I continued to cheer for my friends as they strutted across the stage.

Regrettably, I didn't know the graduates sitting around me. Once the ceremony concluded, I spoke with a few of the graduates and professors as I made my way out of the building. I hurried to Greg's truck. Suddenly I felt someone grab my hand. I turned around swiftly ready to strike and saw Greg ducking.

"Hold up! I just wanted to hold ya hand," Greg announced.

"I am so sorry!" I clutched his hands. "You startled me."

"Ya would think I'd know better," Greg laughed. He lifted my hands and wrapped them around his waist. He pulled me in, and gently kissed me. "Well, we did it. Now we need to start adulting," he joked. He released me and clicked the key fob to unlock his truck. "Austin is able to join us for lunch, so Mechelle is going to ride with him."

Mom had reserved a private room for us at Brendon's Catch 23. The room was gorgeous. One wall had wood planks along it with a couple of black and white photos. Fresh flowers were displayed in the center of the table. Jim, Peggy, Mechelle, and Austin sat at one end of the table. Mom, Phyllis, Greg, and I sat at the other. Everyone perused the menu before breaking out in conversation. It was apparent we were all famished. Everything sounded amazing. I ordered the grilled wild caught halibut, with grilled asparagus and fresh berries.

It wasn't long before everyone asked us what our plans were since we had graduated. Everyone was aware that Mechelle would be traveling to Italy at the end of the summer to work at the villa.

Austin stated he needed to stay local to help his father out when he needed assistance. He had not planned on searching for a job until mid-summer. "If Pops has his way, I'll work on the farm the rest of my life," Austin said as he rolled his eyes.

Mom asked, "What about you Greg?"

Greg laughed. "I think Bill wants me to work on the farm, too," he joked.

We all had a good laugh.

Greg shifted to a serious demeanor. "I have something in the works, but I still have a few things to work out before I am ready to share the details."

I knew he was referring to the detective agency.

Peggy asked, "What about you Brooke?"

I pointed at Greg. "What he said?"

Mom glared at me with one eyebrow raised higher than the other. It surprised me she did not comment.

Jim must have picked up on my mother's obvious confusion. He changed the subject and commented on how nice the ceremony was. This was the topic of discussion until the food arrived. Afterwards, everything reverted to talks about the amazing meal.

When the meal concluded, Phyllis helped Mom pass out her gift bags to each of us. "You may all open them together," she instructed.

The paper rustled as each of us pulled the tissue paper out of our bag. We all gasped simultaneously. Each bag contained a framed picture of the Bloom Keepers. Although Mom did not know about the Bloom Keepers, she knew we were the best of friends. I suspected Phyllis had some say in this gift. We also received gift cards for Parkour. After we thanked Mom for the gifts, she explained she had one for Juliet and Jacob also. She wanted me to give them their gift bag when I saw them for dinner.

The remainder of the time in the restaurant was spent talking about our trip to Italy. Two weeks before Mechelle was to start working, the Bloom Keepers would be going on a vacation as a graduation gift. Mechelle's parents would arrive the week before she started work.

The conversation moved to what types of things we would like to do while we were in Italy. Our lunch ended early because Austin, Mechelle, and her parents had to leave for Austin's family small celebration at his house. Mechelle and Austin would be meeting us later for a late dinner. Greg, Mom, Phyllis, and I spent the rest of the afternoon at Greg's house with his family. Joann had ordered a cake for us. I was grateful, we would be eating late because I was stuffed and needed a short nap before going to dinner.

Three

Greg picked up the gift bags and followed me into the private room I had reserved in the restaurant. Jacob and Juliet were already sitting at the table. There wasn't any point in waiting for Austin and Mechelle before handing them their gift bags. As expected, they liked the framed photos. They called my mother soon after to thank her.

If the restaurant had been quieter, I might have thought everyone could have heard my pulse pounding. My hands became clammy. Greg must have noticed my nervousness because he put his hand on mine and winked at me.

The server came by and asked for our drink order. I glanced at my watch. Austin and Mechelle were only a few minutes late. Jacob sat quietly while Juliet told us about their afternoon. About ten minutes later, Mechelle and Austin came in and provided us with a brief description of the ordeal to have one of his relatives move their truck because it blocked Austin's vehicle from leaving.

Everyone perused through the menu to determine their meal choices. I opted for a burger. Once the server was done taking our order, Greg knocked me with his elbow on the arm, his signal to me to address the Bloom Keepers with the idea of them working for me.

I nodded to Greg. He proceeded to take his knife and tap the side of his glass to get everyone's attention. Everyone stopped what they were doing and turned their attention to Greg. "Brooke has something she would like to discuss with us," he announced.

I focused my eyes on the napkin in my lap trying to remember where I wanted to start.

Okay Lord, I need you to help me through this.

"I have been pondering the idea of starting my own business and well..." I announced. I gazed at each of them. "I want you to be a part of it. I've put a lot of thought into how this will work and even had Leonardo, Isabella, and my attorney, Mr. Thomas, work with me on getting established and for advice. I don't have a name for the company yet either," I said nervously.

Jacob spoke up, "What kind of business?"

Greg jumped in before I had time to answer. "She's getting to that. Go on Brooke."

In a hushed voice I said, "This business will be a great cover for the Bloom Keepers. In the beginning Mr. Thomas will grant me some of my funds for starting cost. We don't want any unusual funds coming in that could flag the government for suspicious behavior on our accounts. This means in the beginning my company will likely be unable to pay you."

Austin interrupted, "Brooke, ya know my situation. I can't come work for free and neglect the farm."

"I certainly wouldn't expect you to. In the beginning, things will be slow anyways. However, Leonardo and I came up with an idea. As you know my account with him is a substantial amount. My company will be international and with that come some banking restrictions and tax implications, but they are working all of that out. You'll be paid from that account until the company can pay you properly."

I gulped down some water. "Once I can provide you with a paycheck, the funds from the other account will slowly be paid back. Your paycheck will be for working for my company as well as the Bloom Keepers. Well, that is if you except the position to be a part of the team," I said. Inhaling a couple of deep breaths to relax me as I waited for their responses.

Juliet asked, "What do you mean if we are a part of the team?"

"At some point you may decide you no longer want to take the risks associated with being a member of the Bloom Keepers or working for me," I whispered.

Juliet scrunched her eyes up. "Risks? What type of business are you opening?"

"A Private Investigator Agency," I said. Everyone talked at once about what a great idea that was.

Austin asked, "How could we help ya with that?"

I smiled. "Each of you have the skills I need to make it a success. Mechelle will be working in Italy dealing with all our behind-the-scenes stuff." I made quotes with my hands. I continued, "Jacob has a Computer Science degree with a minor in Computer Forensics. I'll need him to continue with the type of work he does for the Bloom Keepers and before you ask Jacob, you can continue your side business, but I will need to ask that our cases take precedence over your other customers."

Jacob nodded in agreement.

"Juliet, you have an Accounting Degree. You will obviously be our accountant," I informed her. I pointed to Greg and Austin. "Both of you have degrees in Business. You can help me make sure we are running a tight ship. I think its best we figure out who'll be working doing the marketing, dealing with clients, scheduling, and other things."

Greg replied, "Austin should oversee scheduling. He is a whiz at it."

"Thanks, man," Austin replied.

At first, I could not tell if they liked the idea. I asked, "What do you guys' think?" They each took turns telling me they loved the idea.

Jacob asked, "Brooke, I know Juliet's parents are not going to like the idea. What about health insurance and other benefits?"

"I totally forgot. Health benefits will be provided directly from the Bloom of Dreams," I joked. Everyone rolled their eyes at me.

I smiled. "Seriously, we'll provide that as well but through Leonardo until the company can afford it. You will even have funds contributed to a retirement account."

Everyone started talking to one another about things they or others should be taking care of. It never occurred to me we should have something to take notes with. I excused myself and went to the restroom to pop out to my room for a pad and pen. When I returned, they were still deep in their discussion. Mechelle peeked up and motioned for me to hand her the paper and pen. Immediately, she started writing as I sat back trying to take everything in.

Greg gently squeezed my hand and said, "I think they like the idea."

I listened for a bit. They were discussing office equipment, tossing around who should have what responsibilities, to suggestions for a company name. I clanked my glass with a knife. The conversations abruptly ended. "There's one more thing. I need to complete the Private Investigator Exam," I added.

Greg commented, "We'll give ya the details about that as soon as we have them. For now, we need to come up with a company name for the paperwork Brooke is going to need to set the business up."

Austin shouted, "Hidden Deceptions Agency or wait for it… The Secret Witness Agency."

Jacob chimed in, "Shared Tears Agency."

Juliet offered, "The Privateer Team or TLC Detective Agency."

Greg added, "Garrison's Investigative Services."

I asked, "Mechelle are you writing all these down?" She provided a thumbs up.

Austin started with some new suggestions, "Bloom-A-Do Agency or Bloom Keeper's Agency."

"I would like to stay away from anything related to the Bloom Keepers or the Bloom of Dreams," I commented.

Mechelle raised her gaze from the paper. She said, "These are great suggestions, I wrote down the ones we discussed earlier also. Brooke, do you have any suggestions. Lillie Davis Investigative Services or Davis Investigative Services."

When the food was delivered, there was a break in the conversation. The topic was switch to our Italy trip by Mechelle. "What do you all want to do in Italy?"

"As many times as I have been there, I would like to see all the touristy things we haven't seen yet," Greg spurted.

"That's a great idea," Juliet commented.

"I've no clue what I would want to do. I'll leave that up to ya'll," Austin said.

I scarfed down my burger. While everyone ate their dinner, I told them we needed to have an official meeting to work out what everyone's responsibilities would be. I instructed them to email me with a list of things they would like to do and anything else that came to mind that we should take care of.

We discussed what we should tell our parents as the plates were cleared from the table. We agreed that until the business was set up everyone should appear to be searching for a position. We will meet to discuss what other responsibilities need to be addressed.

Listening to everyone made me more excited about opening my own business. My fear was finding clientele.

After dinner, we all agreed it had been a long day and everyone made their way to their homes. Greg and I spent the drive discussing everything that had happened. Once he pulled in his driveway. Our conversation ended. Greg kissed me and I felt my body melt like butter in his arms. His gentle kisses sent tingles down my side. There was no way I was going to give in to my desires when we had been good for so long. Yet, I found myself running my fingers through his hair. His cologne was intoxicating to me. I found myself wanting more. My body tried to get closer to him as his lips found their way to my neck. Each kiss sent chills down my body. The temptation was hard to resist.

Greg lowered the seat and repositioned himself. My body screamed for more, but my mind told me to stop. Who would win the battle, my body, or my mind. Who would win? Greg's hand ran along my neck and slightly pushed my shirt toward my shoulder. His lips gently caressed my skin.

Suddenly we were interrupted by Greg's father knocking on the window. We both nearly jumped out of our skin. Greg pulled himself off me.

Thank you, Lord, for stopping us.

Greg rolled down his window, while I put my chair into its proper position.

"Your Mom made an apple pie," Andrew informed us.

I politely declined. Greg informed his father he would be in soon.

"I think God had something to do with that," I commented.

"It's so hard not to get carried away with ya. I think I should take ya home," he said.

The night air was still warm. Lightning bugs could be seen in the distance. "I'm sorry for earlier. I have a hard time resisting ya."

"Obviously, the feeling's mutual," I assured him.

He gently kissed me. I watched him until he closed the front gate. As I replayed the scene in my head, I found it difficult to go to sleep because I longed for his touch.

Four

Over the last few weeks, we have ironed out the details about each of our positions. After taking the exam, I waited for the results of the Private Investigator Exam.

Mom was not happy about my decision. Thankfully she was back in Florida when I told her. She felt I would be better off going to law school or teaching. Phyllis was on her about how she should be supporting me and be proud that I am motivated to do something because so many young people don't have the drive to even get out of bed. Oddly enough I was having a problem that morning. The day before, was the first day in a while doing parkour. Every muscle in my body was hurting.

After dressing, I ambled downstairs, and the smell of chocolate drifted up the stairs.

Perhaps chocolate pancakes.

I strolled in to see Hal and Phyllis kissing next to the stove and quickly covered my eyes.

"Sorry I just need some coffee," I said as I peeked out through my fingers to find my way to the coffee.

"Okay, little missy. Now you know how I feel when I stumble in on you and Greg," Phyllis spurted.

"Touché," I responded.

I carried my coffee to the back porch to avoid listening to their mushy talk. In my rush to escape, I neglected to find out what she was cooking but I was sure I would find out shortly.

Cardinals flew about the garden while other birds could be heard in the distance. As I drank my coffee, the aroma comforted me. I paused a few moments from watching a butterfly flutter across the flowerbed to thank God for blessing me with the Bloom of Dreams and was compelled to open my Bible app on my phone. The verse of the day was from Deuteronomy 31:6 Be strong and courageous. Do not fear or be in dread of them, for it is the Lord your God who goes with you. He will not leave you or forsake you.

Wow! Powerful. Thank you, Lord.

The verse soothed me. As I ventured out into the adult world by opening my new business, it was comforting to know God wants me to be courageous.

The back door opened, and Phyllis popped out holding a muffin in her hand. She placed it on the table and kissed me on the top of my head.

"Are you okay with Hal living here?"

Did she just ask me that? How do I answer? Yeah, I want everything as it was. I can't do that. Do I tell her the truth? I hate feeling like I need to dress to move around my own house. No, I could tell her the truth. This was our home.

"It's just going to take me a little while to get used to a man in the house. I adore Hal," I replied. Phyllis kissed me on the head again before going back inside. She seemed pleased with my answer.

The smell of the chocolate chips was comforting. I pinched a small piece off. The steam flowed out. The warm muffin tasted fantastic. With each bite, I composed a list of the things I need to accomplish to open my business. I quickly devoured the muffin and sauntered back into the house.

Phyllis and Hal were not around. I rinsed my plate and went into the pantry to teleport to my room. I made myself comfortable on my bed with my laptop.

What should I work on first?

I worked on the forms I needed to create.

About thirty minutes into my design of the Confidentiality Agreement. A strange ringing noise interrupted me. I scanned the room.

Where's that coming from? Behind my dresser? Oh no.

I swiftly leaped from my bed to answer the phone hidden behind my dresser. My cousin, Allison had given it to me. It is a secure line to use when talking to her. Because she works in intelligence, it was important we be extra careful when communicating.

"Hello," I answered.

Allison whispered, "Brooke, I hope you're not too busy. I need your help. Can we meet?"

"Of course. Where and when?"

"Pulcinella Ristorante in McLean, Virginia. It's just outside of Langley. I'll meet you in the restroom at 6:22 pm," she said. The phone went dead.

I rushed over to my computer to find a picture of the place.

It's Italian. Pul-sin-ella? How do you spell that?

I started punching in Italian restaurants in McLean, Virginia.

Found it!

I searched for a picture of the restaurant. The pictures of the restaurant showed a hallway that probably led to the restrooms. I would need to arrive there invisible. The more I thought about Allison having a mission for us, the more excited I was. I closed my computer and changed to go for a run. I was about to call Greg but remembered he was helping Austin on the farm. Mechelle flew back with her parents and wouldn't be back for a few more days.

I descended the stairs quickly and nearly ran in to Hal as I approached the landing.

Hal scrunched his eyes and asked, "How in the world did you get upstairs?"

It was that moment I remembered I should not be teleporting around the house if Hal was home. "I woke up about thirty minutes ago," I said. His eyes squinted as he tilted his head to the side.

"I was … I was right here," he said pointing at the desk next to the stairs.

Think quick, Brooke.

"I passed quietly, because I didn't want to disturb you."

Hal lowered his head with a puzzled expression on his face.

I asked, "Would you mind letting Phyllis know I am heading out for a run?"

Hal said he would as he strolled toward the back of the house. I went out the front door and stretched. The rays of the sun peeked through the trees making a beautiful view for me. I remembered my mother telling me it's God's light peeking through the sky. That always comforted me. As I ran, my muscles loosened up from the stiffness of doing parkour. The neighborhood was quiet because most people were on their way to work. My thoughts were consumed with the past. Would Eleni Kostopoulos ever return to our lives? How was Tony Granaldi and his family doing? It had been a long time since I visited them. Oddly, even Chief Bianchi had not contacted me in a while. Did Grandma have periods like this where life seemed normal?

It felt great to have the fresh air filling my lungs. With graduation, starting the business, and testing, there had been little time to work out. It was my mission to ensure I worked out at minimum of four days a week. I turned the corner and saw a German Shepard running toward me with its leash dragging behind him. The owner was screaming in the distance as she tried to catch up with him.

I concentrated on the dog whose name was apparently Thor. Without hesitation, I told Thor to stop, which he promptly did. I reached out and petted Thor.

An out-of-breath owner stopped and picked up his leash. "I thought for sure he was going to attack you. He usually doesn't like strangers," she said breathlessly.

"He's just a protective boy. Right Thor," I said as I patted him on the head. Using telepathy, I instructed Thor to be friendlier to others unless he senses danger. It was funny when he barked at me. I believed he understood. We said our goodbyes and I jogged the short distance home.

I went to the attic to complete my workout. It wasn't the same without other people to spar with. None the less I continued for another hour.

It wasn't until I was done with my shower, I realized I could have gone to Japan and trained with Akio and Asahi.

I really need to take the gang over to spar with them some.

That always proved to be a learning experience.

The day felt like it was dragging as I waited for the clock to be 6:22 pm.

Why 6:22 pm and not 6:15 or 6:25?

Me and my laptop went to the library to work on the long list of things I need to complete before my business could open.

Where's my brain?

The Bloom Keepers have a meeting tonight. Not knowing why Allison wanted to see me, I suspected I would be back in time. Just in case I was late, I texted everyone to let them know they could start without me if I had not returned. I told Greg where I would hide a key. Phyllis will set us up in the library. I also reminded them Hal would be home.

My stomach growled. I was surprised Phyllis had not called me for lunch. I meandered my way to the kitchen. She and Hal were nowhere to be found. There was a note on the counter.

22

Brooke,

  I went with Hal to his doctor's appointment. He and I will be having lunch afterwards. After lunch, there are a few errands I need to do. I'll be back to make dinner around 6 pm. I'll make something quick. There's egg salad in the refrigerator.
Love, Phyllis

I texted Phyllis.

BROOKE: Thanks for lunch. Don't worry about dinner. I won't be home till about the time the gang comes over. Why don't you guys have a date night.

PHYLLIS: Thanks

I made myself an egg salad sandwich. A little of the egg salad oozed out of the bread. I pinched it up with my fingers and licked it. The crisp dill pickles were delicious. I brought my lunch and a water with me to the library to continue working. The time flew by as I plugged away at my paperwork. In need of a break, I checked the mail.

  Flipping through the junk mail I noticed an envelope from the state of Kentucky Department of Professional Licensing. My heart raced.

  Do I open it? Should I wait till after my meeting?

  If it's bad news, it could change everything about my future. On the other hand, if it was good news, it could reaffirm my decision to become a Private Investigator. I gazed across the neighborhood and saw a few of the people wandering around.

  I should open it inside.

  I dropped the other mail on the entrance table before sitting on the sofa in the sitting room. The beat of my heart was strong. I found myself staring at the envelope. Negative thoughts entered my mind. They were telling me I failed.

  Not today, Satan!

  I ripped open the envelope and pulled out a letter and behind it was a certificate with my name on it. My eyes filled and I felt like there was something in my throat. I was overcome with my emotions.

  I did it!

I passed and was officially a Private Investigator. I wanted to call someone, but everyone was likely busy. Regrettably, I would need to keep this to myself until the Bloom Keepers Meeting. I returned to continue working.

The certificate motivated me to get everything done to open the business. Before I knew it, it was 5:30 pm. I needed to eat before meeting with Allison. Knowing no one was home, I teleported to the pantry. I glanced at the items there before searching for the refrigerator. There was a small bowl of pasta salad and a grilled chicken leg.

Perfect!

I sat at the bar and ate them while I scrolled through social media.

I noticed the time. It was 6:07 pm. I tossed the dishes in the sink and teleported to my bathroom to brush my teeth quickly. A quick check of my breath to ensure the garlic smell was gone.

I'm good.

I put my phone on the charger. As I peered into the full-length mirror, I could see the hallway in the Pulcinella Ristorante. I concentrated on arriving invisible and stepped through the mirror. The sounds of a busy restaurant could be heard. I peeked down the hall and found the ladies room. I sneaked through the door and went into the farthest stall where I reappeared visible. I waited there until someone came in.

I stepped out of the stall. Immediately, Allison came toward me with her arms open.

"Princess. It's good to see you."

I hugged her.

"Congratulations on the graduation and on becoming a Private Investigator," Allison complemented me. "Now to business. I'm going to take you out and introduce you to a co-worker of mine. I have explained to her you are very young but talented. We need some help from you regarding a case. You'll be working with her. For obvious reasons, I was vague about your work, but I assured her you can be trusted."

I nodded as I followed her out of the restroom to a table in the back of the restaurant. There sat an attractive woman who appeared to be about forty. She was a thin woman with her straight blond hair in a bob. Her blue eyes twinkled a bit in the dim lights of the restaurant.

Allison motioned to me and said, "April, this is Brooke. She's the Private Investigator I spoke to you about." She turned to me. "Brooke this is April, a coworker of mine."

April examined me with her eyes before I sat. April leaned over to me and in a quiet voice asked, "You're very young to be a P.I. Are you some type of prodigy?"

Does she have an accent?

Using telepathy, I asked Allison what my response should be. I went with her advice.

I replied, "Yes, you could say that."

Allison motioned to the menu in front of me. She said, "Please join us for dinner."

Yep, British.

Knowing I needed to return home for the Bloom Keepers meeting, I tried to have her get to the point. After thanking her for the offer, I said, "I really cannot stay long. What is it you need from me?"

April cleared her throat. "I have a case in the UK. More specifically Plymouth. It's a port city in southwest England. We have been trying to find out what Mark Cooper is up to. He's known for dealing in the arms trade among other things. We suspect he'll be bringing a shipment in to that port and our sources tell us he plans on taking out our Vice President on his next visit to the UK. We just don't know when the shipment will be here. He's a master of disguise. This is who we believe he truly is," April stated. She pulled a photo from her purse.

Mark appeared to be in his early fifties. He had glasses, gray hair, and a goatee. His hair was short on the sides and a little longer on the top. The photo said his height was six feet and weight was 180 pounds. I asked, "Do you know where he hangs out or where he was last seen?"

April leaned toward me. She whispered, "He frequently hangs out at the Cornwall Street Fish Bar. It's in a rough area. Anyway, we lose him when he' goes in. We have people staked out front and out back and somehow, he disappears. He has revealed little to us. He will meet up with people inside the restaurant and sometimes one will come out but usually they both disappear. Allison thinks that you have skills to help us establish how he escapes the building and possibly determine when the shipment will arrive."

I nodded and replied, "It's possible. I would be glad to help."

April's whole demeanor changed. "Fantastic!" She gave me a phone and said, "We'll use this phone to communicate. Please keep it with you. My number and Allison's are the only ones in the phone." She tapped her fingers on the table. "How soon can you make it to the UK?"

I estimated the flight to be seven to nine hours. It was already late in the day. I replied, "I'll need time to make the arrangements and pack. I believe I can be there the day after tomorrow at the latest. I'll contact you when I get there."

She held out her hand, "Thank you Brooke. I look forward to working with you." She motioned the server over and they provided their orders.

I stood. "I really need to be leaving," I informed them.

Allison said, "Let me show you out."

She followed me out the door and led me to her vehicle which was parked away from prying eyes. She opened her trunk and pulled out a small bag. She instructed, "Put the phone in this." She handed me a Faraday bag. "It'll prevent anyone from tracking you. Only pull the phone out of the bag when you are in England or working on the case. It's important to make sure you place the phone back in the case before teleporting. They'll know all your moves. We don't want you to have to explain how you move from one place to another in an instant. Also, make sure you consider how long it would take you to travel from one point to another using normal means before taking the phone out of the bag."

I put the phone in the bag and thanked her. She surveyed the area and motioned for me to climb into the vehicle. "I won't be with you on this case. Stay safe," she said as she shut the door.

Immediately I teleported back to my room.

Five

I tucked the phone in my dresser drawer and inhaled before sauntering to the library. Despite the shut door to our reserved room, I could hear muffled voices. When I entered, I found everyone in their usual spots.

"Mechelle tried to call you. She can come if you get her from her room," Austin informed me.

I nodded and pulled out my mirror. "I'll be right back." I seized Mechelle's shoulder and returned to the meeting. "Sorry I was late, but we have a mission," I announced. I told them the details I knew and inquired to see if anyone could join me.

Austin spoke, "Greg and I've already committed to working with Pa tomorrow." Greg nodded.

"I've an appointment with a kid from the university tomorrow. His computer crashed and he's lost his thesis. I'm not sure how long I'll be helping him," Jacob answered.

"I know you're not asking me this question," Mechelle commented as she tucked her head toward her chest and leaned back.

Juliet smiled, "I guess it's just you and me."

"I can't believe there is finally some action, and I can't go," Austin said. He lowered his head and exhaled.

"Honestly, I think we're just going to be there to observe and collect information. It can be time consuming and quite boring," I assured Austin. I glanced around the room. "What did I miss?"

"Not much. Everyone is nearly done with the assignments. Jacob has put everything on a flash drive for you," Greg advised me.

Jacob added, "Yah but, we need to get you a secure computer. Can Leonardo get you one like mine?"

"I don't see why not," I said assuring him.

"I've some news. I'm officially a Private Investigator," I announced.

Everyone congratulated me. We discussed the documents everyone had been working on. About thirty minutes later, Mechelle informed me she needed to arrive before her parents did. After I dropped her off, I spent the remainder of the evening discussing our to do list for the agency.

Before the meeting ended, we agreed to meet the next evening for some sparring. Greg stayed while everyone else left. I asked him to give me a minute. I went to my room and teleported to Japan to see if we could spar with Akio and Asahi. They agreed to it. We would be in Japan at 8:00 am, but it would be 6:00 pm our time. It had been a while since we had trained with them.

I returned and did not mention it to Greg. It was important they did not expect what Asahi and I had a plan.

Minutes later, I found Greg sitting in the middle of the sofa in the library. He gave me that come here stare. I smirked at him before straddling him and planting a kiss on his lips.

"Now this could get us into trouble," he announced. He pulled me closer to him and gazed into my eyes. "I like that we can have fun with one another like this, but we can't let it go too far. I can only restrain myself so much."

He pushed my hair behind my ears. Ran his hands across my cheeks and pulled me to him. Greg laid the most sensual kiss on me. It sent chills down my entire body. I wrapped my arms around his neck and reciprocated the kiss.

Voices came from the stairs. Immediately, I swung myself off Greg and snuggled up to him. He wrapped his arm around my shoulder. We glanced at one another knowing we were nearly caught. We both smirked.

Hal and Phyllis entered the library and asked about our day. We provided some details including telling her about my certificate.

Hal stared at us with his chin down and said, "Perhaps you should put a Bible between the two of you." He turned and exited the room.

Phyllis stayed. "Please forgive him. He doesn't know you that well. He's trying to protect your virtue Brooke," she assured me.

"I appreciate his concern. Perhaps we need a reminder about our actions from time to time," I said.

Phyllis waved to us and followed Hal. Greg and I agreed we should call it a night. After locking up, I meandered to the kitchen for a snack before retiring for the night.

With so much work to go review from the meeting last night the day passed quickly. There were only a few minor changes to the documents everyone sent me along with a few questions I needed to ask my attorney, Mr. Thomas.

With some time to spare I teleported to Italy to speak with Leonardo and Isabella. I found them sitting in the dining room reviewing the staff schedule. Leonardo face had lost its vibrance and appeared to have aged.

I requested computers for everyone. They would be used by them at the agency but could be used for the Bloom of Dreams. He said that would be fine, but we needed to save my company files on a server and have computers for them in the event of an audit or something. He assured me he would work with Mr. Thomas to make sure I had all the equipment we needed.

He had lost weight. I leaned over to Leonardo. "Please let me help you," I pleaded. Tears formed in my eyes. I glanced at Isabella with a watery gaze. She appeared to be on the verge of crying as well.

"Look at the two of you. You'd think I was on the verge of death already," Leonardo said in a weak voice.

He must have seen it in our eyes and said, "I'm considering it. I need to pray about it some more."

A smile sprung across Isabella's face. At that moment I was tempted to persuade him, but I knew God would not want me using it that way. I kissed them both before returning to get ready for the sparring match.

I opted for my camo workout clothes. Secretly I knew it might give me a slight advantage. I waited downstairs for everyone to arrive. Hal was in the sitting room reading the current issue of Bassmaster. I had forgotten about him.

How am I going to explain our going upstairs and suddenly disappearing? I know, we were abducted by aliens. No, Peter Pan came and flew us to Neverland.

I retreated to the kitchen to find Phyllis.

She was frying okra and did not react to me coming in. "Phyllis," I called out to her.

She peaked over her shoulder at me. "Are you sure you don't want to eat with us," Phyllis asked.

She knew how much I loved fried okra. I popped a few pieces she had cooked in my mouth. They were still super-hot, and I nearly burnt my mouth, but they were worth every bite.

I announced, "Everyone's coming here to work out." I whispered to Phyllis, "We're going to work out with Asahi." I widened my eyes. Phyllis tilted her head. "We're going to his house."

Her eyes widened. She whispered back, "I see."

From behind us we heard Hal say, "You see what?"

Phyllis turned and responded to Hal, "Brooke and her friends are going to be training in the attic. She asked that we not disturb them because they will be practicing being unobserved."

He asked, "How do you do that?"

"Stance is important when you sneak around. We need to work on our crouching, sneaking around on squeaky floors, grabbing furniture, and crawling through things without being heard," I said shrugging my shoulders.

He scrunched his eyes and asked, "Are you expecting to be in a lot of situations that require this skill?"

"We really need to be prepared for any situation," I advised.

Hal turned his attention to Phyllis and asked, "I can't understand how you're okay with her choosing this as a career path. It's not safe for a young lady."

"Brooke has more skills than you are aware of. She has been training for a while," Phyllis assured him.

Hal took a deep breath and poured himself a sweet tea.

I opened the refrigerator and picked out a few grapes to tide me over. As I popped the last one in my mouth, the doorbell rang, and I left the kitchen to answer the door.

Jacob and Juliet came in and informed me that Greg and Austin were right behind them. I told them to head on up to the attic as I waited for Greg and Austin.

Austin seemed excited to be here. I chuckled knowing what was in store for him. Greg gave me a quick peck before he locked the door behind him. Hal came out and said hello to them. He started to ask us if he could come and watch us, but thankfully, Phyllis told him dinner was ready.

When Greg and I entered the attic, we found everyone stretching. We joined them. Once we were done. I locked the attic door. "We'll be on teams for this mission. Jacob, Juliet, Austin, and I will be one team,"

Greg interrupted, "Two years ago that would have been fair, but I don't want to take you guys on by myself."

I giggled. "Oh, you won't be. You have Akio and Asahi on your team. The goal is to retrieve the other team's flag. Greg's team has a red flag, and our team has a blue flag," I said moving my attention toward my group.

Juliet asked enthusiastically, "We're going to Japan?"

"Yes, I'm going to drop Greg off and will return for my team." I clung to Greg and dropped him off at Asahi's hut.

"I'll give you time to get to your area. I'll bring my group shortly," I said.

After, making sure to grab our blue flag and the whistle, I brought my team to the heavily vegetated area of the island. Everyone recommended putting it up in a tree. My first thought was to teleport to the top of the tree, but that would not have been fair. Austin volunteered to place the flag up there. He climbed up the tree like a squirrel.

Before we searched for their flag, I emphasized I was not permitted to use the power of the stone other than if it alerted me of danger. The stone had never alerted me when we sparred so I felt confident I should not be using it at all.

Our team agreed to allow someone to stay near the flag to protect it. Juliet volunteered. Jacob, Austin, and I hurried in the direction I knew the red team would be starting. "Stay vigilant," I advised.

My senses were on high alert. Every little sound I heard; I was ready to act.

"Crack!"

I pivoted toward Austin who had stepped on a branch. I moved my finger to my mouth to remind him to be quiet.

We spread out a bit. Jacob put his fist up and we held our position. He waited a second and pointed off toward the west. I motioned for Austin to circle around from the east and for Jacob to circle around from the west. I moved toward the sound.

When something rustled ahead of me, I tucked myself behind some foliage and peered through it to see who was coming.

Suddenly, there was a great deal of noise ahead. I glanced around the bushes in the direction of the noise. Whatever it was, it wasn't too far away. There was a tree about ten feet from me. I scanned the area and saw no one.

I scurried up the tree to get a better view. Jacob was in a battle with Asahi. I watched them for a moment.

You go Jacob!

He was able to counter everything Asahi threw at him. Austin quickly approached them. Sadly, Greg came up behind Austin. I scoped out the area past them to see where they were coming from.

Where are you Akio?

I hadn't spotted him, but I did see their flag. It was on top of a large bush. I searched the area for Akio but could not locate him. I quietly made my way down the tree.

Okay, which way Brooke?

I opted to go to the west of Jacob. There was too much risk going in the direction of Greg and Austin.

I moved stealthily through the forest.

What was that?

I stopped in my tracks and listened. Like me, the noise halted. I surveyed the area trying to figure out which direction the flag was in.

Am I close?

I found another tree and climbed.

What felt like hands pulled me from the tree. I saw the top of the tree as I fell backwards and plunged to the ground. Akio kicked me in the side, but before the next blow I rolled out of his way and jumped to my feet.

He put his palm up and motioned for me to come toward him. I lunged forward as if I was going toward him but diverted myself toward the tree. I placed my leg on the tree and pushed off it to come down on him with an elbow strike. Regrettably he darted out of the way.

Akio charged at me with a multitude of strikes I was able to block. When I started throwing punches, he avoided them. He lunged toward me with a front kick, but I dodged right to avoid it.

I stepped on his thigh and jumped up to wrap my leg around his shoulders. I tightened my thigh around his neck followed by an elbow punch to the top of his head. He dropped to the floor in a choke hold and nearly passed out.

I surveyed the area but could not locate the flag. I scaled the tree and was able to see the flag in the distance. I jumped from the tree and went southwest toward it with little concern for anything else happening around me. I located the flag and lunged toward the top of the bush for it. The whistle was attached. I blew the whistle enthusiastically multiple times to let everyone know the flag had been captured.

We won!

I was a bit giddy for a moment.

Akio!

I remembered how I left him. When I returned to him, he was sitting up nursing his head. I moved his hand from the top of his head and placed my right hand there. His hair felt wet from perspiration. The Bloom of Dreams was clutched in my left hand as I healed him. The stone heated up.

"Thanks Brooke," Akio said.

I opted to say nothing. Once the stone cooled, I helped him to his feet. Voices could be heard in the distance. Jacob, Asahi, Greg, Austin, and I found one another and discussed the battle. Jacob was so excited about how well he did, he didn't notice Juliet was not within the group. I popped over to our flag to search for her.

Juliet must have seen me appear. She popped out from behind a tree. "Brooke, you're not supposed to use the stone," she announced.

"We captured their flag."

Juliet narrowed her eyes and asked questioned, "Do you mean to tell me I did not get to participate in any of the action?"

Knowing she was disappointed, I just shrugged. "Sorry."

She lowered her head, took a deep breath, and lifted it back up. "At least we won," she said with a smile.

I retrieved the flag and whistled before tossing the flag to Juliet and gripping her hand and pulling out my mirror. We teleported back to the group. They were still patting themselves on the back for their extraordinary skills. I glanced over at Juliet who appeared disappointed. She needed to be relieved of this torture. "I hate to break this up, but I need to get back. I'm starving," I said.

We returned to the attic. Everyone collected their things and chugged down some water. Jacob gulped so loudly he had everyone's attention. I lead them downstairs, where we were met by Hal.

"I wanted to peek in and see your workout, but the door was locked," Hal informed us.

"I'm so sorry Hal. We really do not like to be disturbed when we are working out. It's about focus," Greg advised him.

I was grateful for Greg's quick response. I turned to Hal and said, "One day we'll let you sit in and watch us when we are doing some regular sparring," I promised.

We said our goodbyes.

Six

I glanced at my clock. 8:18 am, I stretched my arms and pulled myself out of bed.

Juliet should be here soon.

I strolled down to wait for her. She would be joining us for breakfast. On my way to the kitchen. I received a text.

GREG: Sorry I can't join you today. Stay Safe.

I loved how he was always thinking about me and how he could keep me safe. Muffled voices drifted from the kitchen. Immediately, I tried to figure out how to get around Hal when we would have to leave and return from our missions.

My car needs to be moved. Where would I put it?

To my surprise, Hal was not in the kitchen. Juliet chatted with Phyllis. I asked, "Where's Hal?"

"He's back to his normal schedule now. He should be home around 5:00 pm," Phyllis informed me. She returned to her pan. "Grab a couple of plates for me please." She held out her hand for them. "Hal and I are going to be at my sister's house for the weekend. There will be some meals for you both in the refrigerator. All you need to do is heat them up. I'll tidy up around here before we leave."

I kissed her on the cheek. "You do so much for me, but I don't want you worrying about me. I'll fend for myself while you're gone and make sure we try to keep everything clean," I assured her.

Phyllis plated the omelet she had cut in half for Juliet and me to share. "Just don't burn down my kitchen," she snickered as she placed some pink grapefruit slices on each dish.

Juliet and I ate at the bar in the kitchen, while Phyllis cleaned up. We enjoyed each other's company a bit too much because we were cutting it close to our appointment in Plymouth. Phyllis motioned for us to be on our way. We returned to my room for a quick glance at the Cornwall Street Fish Bar. The restaurant had British flags on each side of the sign. The character on the window of the restaurant, had a large man with his dog. His shirt was adorned with a British flag. There were a few tables outside. Juliet and I agreed to arrive invisible and see if we could locate April's team before revealing ourselves.

It was best to be elevated to get the best view of her team. We landed on the roof of the building with the phone still secure in its bag. I assessed the back of the building while Juliet had the front. We agreed to use telepathy to communicate. I told her there were two men in a vehicle who appeared to be watching the back door.

Juliet said she found one on the roof of the building on Cornwall Street along with one on a bench in front of the building. Another one sat in an unmarked vehicle across the street.

I moved to Juliet's location. Juliet seemed to be watching someone. She pointed to her head, which told me to use telepathy. Juliet found a woman who appeared to be talking on her phone as she paraded around.

I explained to Juliet the lady was my contact April. I teleported us to the sidewalk near the restaurant. We remained invisible. An African Food Store was to our left with very few people inside. I pulled us through the door into an empty isle and made us visible.

"Come on. We need to hurry," I said to Juliet pulling her inside the back of the store. We rushed to the front. I pulled the phone from the bag and placed it back in my pocket. A quick glance revealed the clerk never even noticed us because her face was buried in her phone.

We exited the store and made our way to the Fish Bar. I showed Juliet the picture before we reached the bar. Using telepathy, I reminded her he was a master of disguise. April and I made eye contact just before Juliet opened the door. April nodded at me.

The restaurant was relatively busy. We had a plan. I exited the restroom and Juliet ordered her food while I made myself invisible. Juliet pulled a book out and appeared to be reading it while she peaked around the restaurant with me searching for Mr. Mark Cooper.

The restaurant smelled of oil and fish. The black and white checkered floors reminded me of a pizzeria back home. I quietly made my way around the room searching for any man that was six feet tall. One man came in and paid for his pickup order. I didn't suspect it was him. April said he comes in and never leaves the building.

Oh Brooke, where's your brain?

I whispered to the stone, "Reveal any secret passageways." I examined the room and saw nothing.

There must be one here.

I made my way to the kitchen trying to dodge the staff as they chattered and clanked their cooking equipment. The smell was stronger here. I stared at the fish wishing I could eat a piece.

One man seemed to be restocking for the cooks. Out of nowhere a man with a large box rushed to the counter. I dodged him to avoid being hit. I asked the stone again to reveal a secret passage. Still nothing.

Really? Mr. Cooper, how are you getting out of here?

Suddenly, Juliet was in my head. "I think he just came in. He's not in a disguise. He went straight for the men's room," Juliet advised me. I teleported to the door of the men's restroom. I snuck through the door and scanned the room. There was no one there.

I concentrated on Juliet and asked if he left the restroom. She assured me he had not come out. I shook my head. I inhaled and concentrated. I asked the stone again to reveal any secret passages. That time, a glow came from the wall.

Got ya!

I told Juliet to come to the men's room. Thankfully she did not argue and came quickly.

"Where is he?"

Not knowing how to open the door I gripped her hand and made her invisible. I yanked her through the wall. There was a small platform, then a flight of stairs heading down. We descended into an underground tunnel.

Juliet tapped me on the shoulder to stop me from proceeding.

Telepathically, Juliet said, "Put the phone in the bag. If they chase after us, we'll never discover his plan."

She was right and I stored the phone away. The tunnel was long, and a Whooshing noise could be heard from the distance. Rather than moving swiftly through the area. I teleported us to the furthest point I could see to try and catch up with Mr. Cooper.

There was not much farther to go in the direction we were headed, and the sound grew louder in this area. It sounded as if we were under a highway. As I thought about the map I had seen before coming to Plymouth, I remembered there was a highway not too far from the restaurant.

At the end, the tunnel made a ninety degree turn to the left. We teleported to the end of the path. In front of us were two directions we could head. Juliet shrugged her shoulders. We were both clueless about which way to go.

Lord, please help me here.

It was as if I heard in a light gentle voice say, 'ask the stone'. In a hushed voice I said, "Bloom of Dreams which direction is Mark Cooper."

A light illuminated the pathway, much like the one that reveals secret passages. Not thinking about being quiet, I pointed at the path and said, "Isn't that amazing."

Juliet moved her head back and forth with a confused expression. I suspected she could not see it. I pointed in the direction the stone was sending us. The path seemed to be a bit narrower than the ones we had been down. At the end of the path was a stairway leading to a platform. To prevent making noise we teleported to the top. There was a rather small door. Mr. Cooper must have crawled through it. Rather than crouch. I stuck my head through the wall. I still could not see. I moved farther. Still nothing.

Surely this wall ends soon.

I scooched forward some more. Finally, a bedroom appeared. There was a twin bed in front of me on a wood platform with inexpensive pink bedding. A desk was pushed up against the wall to my right. On the left was a window with boxes next to it. I leaned forward some more and saw stones surrounding my head.

Am I in a fireplace? I was.

I backed out of the room and told Juliet what was going on. We both agreed to enter the home invisible and try to discover more about our mysterious Mark Cooper.

We entered and immediately inaudible voices came from another room. I peered out the doorway to the right where there was a door. To the left was a hallway with two more doors at the other end. The voices came from the left. We moved toward the two doors. One appeared to be the front door.

I stuck my head through the door.

Is this the living room? Why would they have a door between the living room in the front entrance.

The room was small. Smaller than the bedroom.

Is this normal in England?

The door to the kitchen was open.

Another strange place for a door.

It appeared there were two people in the room. Juliet and I snuck closer to understand what they were saying. They were out of our view from the doorway.

A woman said, "Here have a cuppa." Pots clanked.

A man's voice said, "Are they still there?" There was a pause. "They should leave once they know I'm gone. Tell him to stay there a little longer. I'll be back once they've gone." What sounded like a chair dragged across the floor. "He says the coppers are still there."

The female said, "I made Toad in the Hole. Do you want some?"

Ugh. That sounds disgusting.

I wondered what they were really eating.

Who would name a dish Toad in the Hole?

I shook my head.

Juliet's eyes were scrunched up and she pretended to throw up.

I bit my lip trying not to laugh.

"Amelia, you know I can't resist your cooking," the man said praising her.

"You should come by tomorrow. I'm making Beef Wellington."

Now that sounds yummy.

"I ain't going to miss out on that," the man informed her.

"Be here at 6:00 pm," Amelia instructed.

His phone rang. "Yes…Tell him I'm on my way," the man announced. The chair moved. "Amelia, thanks for the meal. I've work to do."

Mark came into view. He was swiftly moving toward the back rooms. Juliet and I pivoted out of his way. He entered the room with the secret passage. I glanced into the kitchen to get a glimpse of Amelia. She had short gray hair, black glasses, pale skin, and had similar features to Mark. They could be related.

I pivoted back to Juliet and clutched her hand. We teleported back to the tunnel just outside the secret passage to the men's room.

My best guess was he was heading back to the restaurant. I instructed Juliet to stay there and let me know when he arrived. I teleported to the hallway.

A large man was telling everyone they had a family emergency, and their meals were covered. The staff was packing the orders for those who were waiting for their food. I noticed April was gone.

Once the last customer left, the man who seemed to be in charge asked the staff to head back and clean the kitchen. He wiped the tables.

I popped back to Juliet. We continued using telepathy to communicate. I informed her about my findings within the restaurant.

Juliet pointed to Mark who was swiftly moving in our direction. I motioned with my head for her to follow me into the restaurant. We found a spot along the wall out of the way.

I teleported to the roof to see if all of April's men had left. Those in the vehicles were still there. I returned to my position next to Juliet.

The large man seemed satisfied with the dining area and went to the kitchen.

He asked his staff not to disturb him and turned on some music. He returned to the dining area. A few moments later Mark exited the men's restroom.

The two nodded and sat at a table. Mark leaned back against the chair and said, "I wasn't expecting you to send your customers packing. How is your business going to make money? By the way, where's Richard?"

"He had to finalize the shipment. The special fish you wanted," the owner stated as he winked at Mark.

Mark leaned forward. "Go on Alfie," he said.

"The shipment will be here Saturday at 3:00 am. Victoria's looking forward to it," Alfie said scraping something off the table with his nail.

Mark said, "Everything is covered? You said Victoria, right?"

Alfie nodded. "Yes, boss. I have some amazing cod coming in from Alaska." He winked at Mark again.

Mark nodded. He rose and shook Alfie's hand before he said, "Now, I'm anxious for that fish. Are you going to open back up?"

"I best not. They may have someone out there I'm not aware of. I'll send the staff home early and I'll pay them anyway."

Mark nodded, "You're a good man. I'll take care of you." He retreated to the restroom.

Alfie moved toward the kitchen. I snatched Juliet's arm and we returned to the African food store. Once no one was near we became visible. I pulled the phone from the bag. There were numerous missed calls from April. I called her.

"Where have you been? Don't answer that. We need to meet me. Grab a taxi and meet me at The Morley Arms," April demanded before hanging up.

We did as she instructed. On the way over Juliet and I discussed what had happened with Mark. We wanted to make sure we had all the important details needed for April.

Juliet asked, "Who do you think Amelia is?"

"Not sure, but she could be related to Mark. Perhaps a sister or cousin. We also need to figure out who Victoria is. One thing I know, Mark seemed happy about some fish arriving. Somehow, I bet it's lead poisoning," I joked.

"Good one. That must be the guns."

I agreed with Juliet. The taxi stopped. We strolled in and scanned the area for April. Juliet found her sitting in a section that gave the appearance of a green house. Several walls and the ceiling were made of glass. "April, this is my associate Juliet," I said.

After the introduction, April did not hold back anything. With her southern drawl she said, "What's wrong with you?"

I started to answer but she held her hand up as if to say that was a rhetorical question.

April continued, "I give you a phone to be able to keep track of you for your safety. Yes, your safety and you prevented me from tracking you. Do you have any idea how dangerous Mark Cooper is?"

I started to answer and was shushed again.

She leaned in and said in a stern voice, "This is my case and despite Allison being my superior and thinking you're the cat's meow, I'm not going to let some young ladies keep me from doing my job. This is my career. Do you understand me?" She paused a moment to before inhaling.

Can I talk now? Dare I try?

April leaned back in her chair, "What do you have to say for yourselves?" Her eyes shifted between us.

Juliet motioned for me to speak.

After steadying my breath, I said, "I understand your frustration. However, I don't work for you. We are here as a favor to Allison. She asked me here because she knows you need my skills."

April scrunched up her eyes and asked, "Brooke, what exactly are your skills?"

I knew she was wondering why she had to deal with me. As far as she knew I had no experience.

Be patient with her.

41

"I've a way of doing things, special skills that make me unique. Skills that I prefer not to disclose. You're full of questions but you're not asking the right ones." I leaned in closer to her. "What should you be asking? Were you able to find anything out? The answer to that... is yes. We know how he is leaving the restaurant undetected, but until we discover more, we'll keep that to ourselves. I don't need one of your team members messing up my work. I'll disclose that when I am certain I'm done helping you." I peeked over at Juliet. Using telepathy, I told her to tell her what we knew about the shipment.

Juliet smiled at April. "The shipment is coming on Saturday at 3:00 am. Someone named Richard is coordinating it. Oh, and someone named Victoria is excited about it. We do not know who Richard is, but he was at the Cornwall Street Fish Bar today. He left around the time the customers cleared out of the building. The shipment might be a cod shipment. That should help you to determine which ship it will be," Juliet stated.

"Alfie, the owner of the fish bar, is the middleman between Richard and Mark. I will be at the pier on Saturday to assist you. I'll find you when I arrive," I informed her.

"Victoria probably means Victoria Wharf," April paused for a moment. Her eyes bounced back and forth between us, "Fine. We'll do things your way," April said. She tossed some money on the table. "You better not screw this up for me. Have a nice evening." April stood up and marched toward the entrance.

"I don't think she likes working with us," Juliet stated.

"I agree, but if they're bringing weapons here, something big must be planned. We need to figure out what it is."

Juliet asked, "How do we find that out?"

"I don't know but we only have a few days. I need to be back here for the dinner he's having with Amelia. Come on, let's get out of here."

As we entered the ladies room, I felt as though someone was watching us. Juliet touched my arm. I shook my head. "Let's get a taxi out of here," I said to Juliet. She tilted her head with one eyebrow raised but followed me out of the bathroom.

As we exited the restaurant, I still had the feeling someone was watching. When no one was within ear shot, Juliet asked, "What's going on?"

I said, "I'm not sure. It feels like we're being watched." I glanced around.

"They could be anywhere," Juliet stated.

She was right.

Lord, what do I do?

It hit me.

In a soft voice I said, "Bloom of Dreams reveal to me anyone who is watching me." A line with a blue glow to it appeared and pointed in the direction of a vehicle in the distance.

"Come on. We need to lose them." The vehicle was facing toward our left, so we ran to the right. "We need to get somewhere we can teleport."

We ran to the building ahead of us that looked like it sold tires. Since no one chased us, I pulled out my mirror and reached my hand out to Juliet who backed away. In a stern voice I said, "We need to go!"

"No. That phone needs to be in the bag," Juliet said sternly.

She was right. I tucked it away before teleporting us to the safety of my room.

Seven

Mark's dinner with Amelia was at 6:00 pm, which meant I needed to be there at 1:00 pm. I did not feel I needed anyone else on this mission because I was simply trying to obtain information.

I spent the morning working on my future business. Mr. Thomas had sent me a list of things I needed to complete. At 11:30 am, I realized I never had breakfast. I teleported to the pantry. When I opened the door to the exit, I found Hal sitting at the counter reading the paper while Phyllis cooked.

What's he doing at home?

My heart began to race.

Stay cool, Brooke.

He lifted his head from his paper and asked, "How long have you been in there?"

Phyllis spun around with her eyes wide and mouth wide open. She asked, "Yes, how long have you been in there?"

Think of something quick.

"Not long. Both of were busy. I didn't want to disturb you," I said.

Please believe me.

Hal shook his head and returned to his paper.

Phyllis said, "I guess those stealth skills you've been working on are working."

I laughed and tiptoed over to her and said, "I'm starving. What kind of cuisine are you making for lunch?"

"Hal's not feeling well…"

I interrupted, "This means Phyllis's famous chicken soup. Yum."
I pulled a glass from the cabinet. "I'm sorry you're not feeling well." I
poured myself a glass of sweet tea.

"Lunch will be ready in 30 minutes," Phyllis advised me.

"See you in 30 minutes," I said before taking a gulp of my drink.
I left it on the counter and exited the kitchen. Once out of view, I
pulled out my mirror and teleported to Grandma's secret room below
the stairs.

I really need to spend more time down here.

I pulled a journal from the shelf and read.

November 22, 1963

I was blessed to be on the streets of Fort Worth, Texas with
our wonderful President John F. Kennedy. I was there because I
was supporting him for his possible re-election. My plan was to
try to find a way to meet him. I was standing outside the hotel
where they had stayed for the night. No one cared about the
light rain, me included. The President came out and made some
remarks. He commented on his wife organizing herself. I
thought that was adorable.

He traveled to Dallas. The procession traveled through town.
I dashed over there to see him again. There were several
thousand of us waiting for just a glimpse of him. I was standing
with some lovely ladies. Cheers filled the air as he and his wife
passed by us. The next thing I knew, gunfire could be heard in
the distance. Everyone was running toward us from Dealey
Plaza. It was impossible for me to go see what was going on. I
returned home to later find out he was shot and was
pronounced dead. My heart grieves for this country.

November 23, 1964

Every news media is talking about the horrific assassination
of John F. Kennedy. I kept replaying the incident in my head to
see what I could have done to prevent it. The entire country is
mourning his death. I continue to pray for his family. Jacqueline
must be beside herself. If only I knew a way to help her.

I had never heard my grandmother tell me about this. I suspect
she could not tell us because she should not have been there.

There is so much I do not know about her.

She had mentioned in her letter the stories she told me were true. Memories started pouring in. She had rescued a princess who had been kidnapped. There was a kid driving the car down the road in reverse. I teleported to the piano invisible to insure no one was there before appearing.

I thought about keeping some distance between Hal and myself because he was sick.

Why?? The stone heals me.

Hal wasn't very talkative and went to bed when he was done eating. Phyllis and I transferred everything to the kitchen.

In a hushed voice, she said, "Hal being here is a bit of a problem, isn't it?"

As much as I wanted to tell her he wasn't, I knew it would only be a matter of time before we revealed our secret. "It's difficult, but we'll figure it out," I assured her.

"You've such a good heart child," Phyllis said as she placed her warm hand on my cheek. "We can't let Hal find out. I don't think he could handle it." Phyllis lowered her head. "Honestly Brooke, having him here is more work for me. I don't mean cleaning and things." She shook her head. "There are so many times I have had to redirect him or send him shopping for things I don't need to keep him from discovering the strange things that go on around here. I don't know if you noticed but I try to keep him out of the house when the Bloom Keepers are over."

I knew this was a burden on her. "What do you suggest?"

"I have no idea what to do. Hal has rented his house out," Phyllis said and let out a sigh.

Lord, I need an idea.

I scoured my brain trying to come up with something. "I've got it! I will buy you a house near here. That way you can work here during the day and be with him at night. What do you think?"

"We can buy a house..."

I interrupted, "I know you could, but I can buy an investment property. Only, I'm going to rely on the housing market to make a profit. That means it would be part of your salary as a fringe and I'll pay the taxes for you."

"I don't know. This is an expensive neighborhood, and these houses are too big," she informed me.

Ah, she's considering it.

"I insist. I'll talk with Leonardo and discuss the budget. We'll figure this out," I assured her.

"How would you explain to your mother about the house? She has no idea how much you are worth," Phyllis reminded me.

"You're right. That's a bit of a problem," I said. As soon as it rolled out of my mouth, I snapped my fingers. "We put the house in a trust in your name. When you pass the trust states it goes to my estate. No one will know you didn't create the trust."

"You're brilliant. I'll tell Hal the money was from your grandmother, and I feel obligated to give it to you. He'll still have his house. Oh Brooke, this is perfect," Phyllis said as she hugged me.

"I need to head to Plymouth," I told her as I ambled to the doorway. "One more thing." I spun around. "You're going to have a maid for your house because you don't need two houses to clean."

Phyllis picked up a spoon and teased me like she would spank me with it, but I left too quickly.

I changed into my Bloom Keepers outfit and teleported to Amelia's house. She was in the kitchen cooking. Mark had not shown up. The aroma in the house made my mouth water. A hint of rosemary lingered in the air. Amelia set the table. I expected it would be for her and Mark yet there were three table settings.

Who is our mystery guest?

For someone who lived in a modest home, she took great care of her things. Someone opened a door in the front of the house. I moved out of the way as Amelia hurried to the front door. Two men's voices could be heard. The two men followed Amelia had similar features and could have been brothers.

The mystery man asked, "Well, what's for dinner?"

"Beef Wellington," Amelia answered.

Mark picked up two bottles of Henry Weston Cider and sat at the kitchen table. "Here," Mark said handing it to the mystery guest. I squinted to read the label on the bottle.

Is that beer or apple cider?

Mark sipped his drink. "I've the info we needed. It's coming on Saturday. We're meeting at the dock at 3:00 am. We need to set up a meeting with our buyer as soon as possible," Mark instructed.

"George, would you cut this for me," Amelia asked as she put the Beef Wellington on the counter.

"Amelia, this looks just like Mums," George complemented.

Mark inspected the beef. "George's right. You did a bang-up job. Mum would be proud," he agreed.

Ah, there siblings.

They were right, the Beef Wellington was making my mouth water. Amelia put roasted carrots and potatoes on the table. The final touch was the rosemary bread. I found myself salivating as they ate. Her food appeared as gourmet as Phyllis's dishes.

Their conversation continued about the buyers, but no names were given. Amelia said little. It appeared Mark was in charge.

Mark swallowed a carrot and said, "That American…oh blimey, what's her flipping name?" He stabbed a potato.

Amelia commented, "April."

"Yes, Ms. April's a bit of a pain in the backside, but I'm sure her agency thinks she's worth her weight in gold," Mark commented. He took a swig of his cider. "We need to be cautious. If we're going to get busted, that yank's gonna be the one to do it."

"I'll get the lads out there and take her team out before the shipment arrives. Alfie's crew can take care of the shipment," George stated.

"We need to get the shipment moved quickly. It should only be four crates," Mark said.

"Can you not talk shop at the dinner table," Amelia insisted.

Mark and George lowered their heads as though they had been scolded before. The rest of the evening did not provide me with helpful information. When Mark was in his car, I teleported to his back seat.

What a tiny vehicle.

Things were very different here than in the states. We pulled up to what I presumed was his home. As he climbed the stairs, I noticed a patio facing the water. I teleported there making sure I remained invisible.

The view was spectacular. He had his own pier. The railing was glass giving you a tranquil view of the water. Three glass doors led to the main living area. The walls were eggshell white. Stained wooden beams supporting the structure were visible. They gave the room an extraordinary design. The furniture was pale shades of brown, gray, black, and eggshell white.

Mark entered his home. He placed his keys on the counter and sat on a sofa that faced the patio. He seemed to take in the view for a moment.

I teleported inside. He slipped his shoes off and held them in his hand as he ambled toward the back of the home. There appeared to be several bedrooms. His room had the same color pallet and wood accents as the rest of the home.

With this memory of his home, I knew it was time to leave. It was nearly 3:00 pm when I returned to my room. I changed out of my uniform into something more appropriate for the villa in the evening and teleported to my room there.

When I exited my room, I nearly ran into a couple of staff members. They peered at me, then at the door to my room. They immediately glanced at one another.

"Sorry Ms. We didn't think anyone was ever in that room," the taller one stated.

The other gentlemen elbowed him. I presume to shut up. He said, "Let us know if you need anything." He pushed the coworker onward.

I couldn't make out which one was whispering but I heard one of them say, "I heard that room was haunted."

I chuckled. There seemed to be a lot of guests and hoped they had time to speak with me. The dining room was filled with customers. I stopped a waiter and asked if they could direct me to Leonardo or Isabella.

He said, "Isabella should be around, but Leonardo's not working tonight."

I thanked him and made my way to the reception area to find Isabella. She was on the phone. Her hair, that was normally well groomed, seemed a bit of a mess as if she had rubbed her fingers through it a couple of times and she was a bit short with the person on the other end of the line. This was not like her. I waited patiently for her call to end.

"Oh Brooke, I'm so glad you're here," Isabella gushed as she hung up the phone. She pulled me in for a hug.

"Are you okay?"

Isabella scrunched her eyes and tightened her lips.

Oh, she's frustrated.

"That man…" She shook her head before continuing, "He needs…how do you American's say…Oh yes. He needs a good swift kick in the pants. He's taken a turn for the worse. I thought for sure he would contact you about…" Isabella canvased the area. She leaned in and said, "you know helping him with his situation."

"Where is he?"

She led me to their room. When we entered their suite, she announced my arrival before bringing me into their bedroom. Leonardo had lost weight. His face was hollow and had aged a bit. Isabella excused herself.

Leonardo provided me with a weak smile.

Oh my.

It pained me to see him this way.

Lord, if it's your will, please give me the words he needs to here to want to be healed.

I sat on the edge of the bed and lifted his hand with mine. He quickly pulled it away. I knew this was not going to be easy.

"Leonardo, you're not very good," I informed him.

"Tell me something I don't know," he said with a chuckle.

"Okay. You're stubborn. Why do you think you're not worthy of being healed? God put you in my family's path for a reason. With that come certain perks," I informed him.

He stared up at me for a moment before rolling his eyes.

It suddenly hit me. I asked, "Do you think because of all the illegal things you have had to do and the criminals you have had to deal with make you unworthy?"

He scrunched up his face and his eyes filled with tears.

Motioning to his frail body, I said, "That's it. Isn't it. You think you deserve this?"

"Brooke, before I met Lillie, I was a horrible person. Lillie saved me. I deserve this," he announced.

I could not believe what I was hearing. I asked, "Is Jesus your Lord and savior?"

Fighting back tears he said, "Yes."

Lord, speak to me.

I replied, "1 Peter 2:24 says, 'He himself bore our sins in his body on the tree, that we might die to sin and live to righteousness. By His wounds you have been healed'. Jesus took our punishment."

He nodded. "You're right." Tears streamed down his face.

I pointed to his hand and asked, "May I?" Leonardo nodded his head up and down. I clasped his hand in mine. I held the necklace to my skin and prayed while the stone heated and healed Leonardo.

Once the stone cooled, I lifted my head and asked, "How do you feel?"

Leonardo motioned for me to move. I stood up and watched a man who appeared as though he could barely move spring out of bed and jump around in his pajamas.

He reached out and pulled me to him for a hug. "This is amazing!" Leonardo spun himself around a few times and wobbled a pit as he tried to stabilize himself. I suspect he was dizzy.

He asked me to leave so he could get dressed. He wanted to see Isabella and everyone at the villa.

"That's not a good idea. You've been very ill. You can't just have a miraculous healing after I enter the room. Wait till tomorrow, spend a few hours out there and gradually increase it. When people ask why you're doing better you'll be able to honestly say Jesus healed you," I recommended.

We talked for a bit about God before moving on to a house for Phyllis. He liked the idea. Leonardo said, "We can't risk anyone finding out about the Bloom of Dreams. It's best to get Hal out of the way. Regarding her having a maid, Hal might find it weird she can clean your house but not her own."

"I know, but now that they are married, they will be co-mingling their finances. Phyllis can only put him off for so long," I stated.

"Yes, that's true. We should pay her for her services. That should divert some issues. I'll talk with Mr. Thomas to set up a trust. He'll provide her with a realtor," Leonardo said. He made himself comfortable on the sofa. "I nearly forgot. Your computers and office equipment are ready to be shipped. Have you found a location for your business?"

I explained, with everything going on, I had forgotten to search for a place. He advised me to have the realtor help me with that also. I went out and told Isabella Leonardo needed her. As I turned away and held back a grin by biting my lip. She was going to be ecstatic to find out he was healed.

As I approached my room, I heard rustling inside.

I bet those boys are in my room.

I tucked myself away from lingering eyes and teleported to my room invisible.

What do we have here? Two staff members think my room is haunted. What shall I do?

I chuckled to myself.

The taller man said, "You know we could hang out here from time to time and no one would know where we were."

So, they're nosy and lazy.

I pinched the shorter one who was sitting on my bed. He checked the room and inspected his arm.

Let's see...

I ran my finger up the back of his neck. This created an immediate reaction. He jumped from the bed and stared at it.

The taller man asked, "What?"

With fear in his eyes, he said, "Something touched me."

With an exasperated sigh the other man said, "Really?"

The shorter man crossed his arms, "Yes. We need to get out of here."

The taller man sat on the bed where his friend had been. He commented sarcastically, "See nothing."

I reached over and ran my finger through his hair. His reaction was the same. I jumped on the bed and bounced on it until they both raced out of the room. It was difficult to keep from laughing out loud.

With a smile on my face, I returned home in time for dinner.

Eight

As usual, dinner was good. Phyllis made a Thai soup because Hal was still not feeling well. He returned to his bed after his meal. This gave me time to tell Phyllis our plan was in the works for her house.

Juliet had arranged for us to have a meeting to discuss the plan for how to recover the weapons. We agreed to meet at Greg's house because Hal was home. Apparently, his mother gave him permission to hang out in her she-shed because she was having a girl's night out.

I went over early. Karen answered the door and informed me Greg was in the shower. She and I hung out for a while talking about her and her relationship with Ty. They were both attending local colleges, but they struggled a bit because of their schedules.

Greg came out with his hair wet and shirt hanging over his shoulder. I couldn't help but admire his chiseled body. He was in great shape when we met but the definition was more pronounced. He noticed me and winked. I fluttered my eyes and winked back. I bit my lip and shifted my eyes away out of embarrassment. Karen had her face fixed on her phone and never noticed our flirting.

I rose because Greg was about to put his shirt on. With one hand I held his hand to prevent him from putting his shirt on. I leaned in close to his ear and whispered, "Your back's still a little wet."

He replied, "Is it?"

I nodded and kept my eyes locked on his as I leaned closer but resisted the urge to kiss him. I slowly moved my hand up his back to catch the few water droplets he still had resting on his skin. The tension was thick. He planted his face on my neck and gave me a raspberry.

Karen's head flung around and said, "You too need to behave."

Greg snickered as he put his shirt on.

Austin suddenly appeared in the doorway. He asked, "I think your doorbell is broken. I've been out there ringing it for a while."

Greg apologized and moved toward the front door.

I sat next to Karen. "It must only work intermittently," I shouted toward the front door.

Without raising her head, Karen lifted her eyes to me. She asked, "How long do I need to wait for you to become my sister?"

I didn't see that one coming.

How do I answer? Greg hasn't asked. Does she know something I don't? My mind was racing.

She flung her head around. With eyes wide and eyebrows up she asked, "Well?"

"I don't know. We're just trying to get our careers started. Not to mention we haven't even discussed it," I responded.

Greg comes in and asked, "What haven't we discussed?"

"Oh nothing," I replied. I turned my attention to Austin. I haven't spoken to Mechelle. How's she doing?"

"I was talkin' to her on the way here. She changed her flight. My baby will be back tomorrow," he said proudly.

"Really? That's awesome," I announced.

Jacob and Juliet wandered inside.

Juliet asked, "Why's your front door wide open?"

Karen jumped up. "Really Greg! The bugs are going to get in," she said as she stomped her way toward the front door.

"I thought it was a perfect way to solve the broken doorbell," he said sarcastically.

Austin announced, "I'm in complete agreement." He and Greg knuckle punched one another.

Karen returned and rolled her eyes. Greg opened the back door and motioned for us to exit.

Karen asked, "Where are you guys going?"

"To the shed and sadly you can't join us," Greg replied. He let me out before shutting the door.

Greg unlocked the shed. Everyone piled in. I made myself comfortable on the couch. Greg sat on the floor next to me.

Jacob set his computer up at the small two-person table. While Juliet sat next to me, and Austin sat next to Jacob at the table.

Jacob pulled up a map of Victoria Wharf and said, "There's not a lot of places for April's team to hide. The tops of these buildings are more than likely where they'll be." He pointed at two structures.

One on each side of the narrow port. "If there's vehicles or other boats around, they could hide there also."

Greg replied, "Perhaps that's another reason Mark's team picked this area."

Austin asked, "Will we be able to be that far apart and still be invisible?"

I replied, "Not knowing the actual distance it could be a problem. We should go there and test it."

"I think we should go now. It's what… midnight or so there," Juliet suggested.

I commented, "Great idea. I only need a couple of you. How about I take Austin and Greg?"

Austin jumped up enthusiastically. "I'm in."

Greg placed his hand on my shoulder. Austin followed his lead. We arrived at a long building on the west side of the port. Greg was left on the south end of the building, and I made him visible. Austin and I remained invisible even after I dropped him off on the north end of the same building. Once they were in place, I teleported to the far side of the building on the other side of the pier. I waited two minutes before retrieving them and returning to the shed.

Jacob and Juliet were entangled in each other's arms with their lips locked together when we returned. They were unaware of our return. Greg cleared his throat to get their attention.

They broke apart. Juliet's cheeks became rosy. Jacob discreetly wiped the lipstick from his mouth. Without saying a word, he returned to his spot at the table.

I asked, "Well, Greg, could you see Austin or myself?"

Greg rocked his head back and forth. He replied, "I could see Austin but not you."

"Okay so we know we need to stay as close as we possibly can," I informed them.

Juliet asked, "How many of us do you think should go?"

Everyone turned to Greg for an answer. "We might need all of us. Those of us invisible need to be aware of Brooke's location, or we could suddenly appear," he suggested.

"We don't know where they're going to be or how they plan on getting the guns out of the area," Jacob stated.

I said, "That's right. Someone may need to go with the guns so we can find where and who they're dealing with. I think April's only trying to stop the shipment."

"They'll just buy from another dealer if this gets stopped," Austin stated.

Greg said, "He's right. We need to let them take the shipment and find out what they are planning and who they are planning to do it with."

Everyone agreed. We finalized our plan before adjourning the meeting. It was determined the next time we would meet would be Saturday night at 8:00 pm. We needed to arrive before Mark or April's teams.

Since it was still early in the evening, Greg built a small fire in the firepit. He instructed me to ask Karen for the ingredients for smores.

Karen seemed annoyed when I entered the house. I asked her for the ingredients before asking her to join us. Her demeanor immediately changed. She trotted to the pantry and handed me the graham crackers and marshmallows. She told me she would be out with the rest of the ingredients soon.

Greg and Austin had their pocket knives out and were whittling sticks for us to roast the marshmallows. Moments later Karen appeared with a bag of supplies. She unloaded bottles of water from her bag. Along with Reese's Peanut Butter Cups and chocolate bars.

I roasted my marshmallow. I let it catch on fire and it continued burning until it was nearly completely charred on the outside.

Karen rushed over and blew it out. She said, "You're holding it too close to the fire."

I said, "I like them burnt." I returned it to the fire to catch another flame. Once the fire burned out, I pulled it off the stick and popped it in my mouth.

Karen scrunched up her face and said, "That's gross."

I snickered at her response.

Karen continued taking her time roasting hers. Once it was golden brown, she placed a peanut butter cup on and the marshmallow on top a gram cracker. She placed another gram cracker on top of it and squeezed it while she pulled the stick out.

My mouth salivated as she bit into it. "Wow! Who ever thought about putting a peanut butter cup on a smore is a genius."

I followed her lead. When it hit my mouth, the crunch of the gram cracker with the soft marshmallow was only made better when the sweet chocolate and peanut butter oozed out. "This is a masterpiece," I commented with a nod to Karen.

We spent the next hour and a half hanging out with her until everyone started going home. Karen went inside and left Greg and I to enjoy the firepit which was nearly out.

Greg snuggled up next to me on the bench. He asked, "How are things going with getting the business started?"

"Good. We are nearly done. I'll be going with a realtor to find a property soon. Mr. Thomas should be sending me their information soon," I informed him.

He smiled. "I'll be glad once we are up and working. I'll like working with Bill on the farm, but honestly…" He shrugged his shoulders. "He doesn't smell as good as you."

I groaned loudly at his corny joke.

He gazed into my eyes and said, "Seriously, I miss being with you. At least during school, we would run into each other."

I nodded. "I know what you mean. I miss you too," I admitted.

Greg caressed my hand. He inhaled deeply. His eyes met mine. He softly said, "One day, we will be together forever."

Is he thinking about getting married? Is it too soon? We need to get the business going. Yes, that needs to be my focus. A family can wait for now.

He wrapped his arm around me and pulled me closer.

We could manage a family. Couldn't we? Brooke, you just graduated college. There's plenty of time.

He said, "I know one day you and I'll be man and wife. I hope you feel the same. I think you do."

I peered up at him. "Yes, I want that too. More than you know."

"Yes, one day. I can't picture my life without ya," he said as he leaned in for a kiss.

With each kiss it was as if the bond between us grew stronger. Thankfully tonight the flesh did not tempt us. A short while later, Greg escorted me home.

Phyllis was enjoying the latest Audrey Rich novel in the sitting room. She asked, "How was your evening?"

I told her about my introduction to peanut butter cups in smores and my conversation with Greg about our future. She listened attentively.

Phyllis said, "There's no doubt in my mind you and Greg will marry one day." She patted the cushion next to her. "Come have a seat."

I sat as instructed.

"A Ms. Tonya Greenwood contacted me today. Mr. Thomas gave her our numbers. She was unable to reach you. We have a meeting with her tomorrow at 9:00 am. I explained to her what we are wanting."

I said, "That's great. I left my phone here."

"I figured as much."

59

We talked a little bit about Hal who was starting to feel better, but she did not expect him to be well enough to go to work for a few days. That didn't sit well with me. Tomorrow night the Bloom Keepers needed to go to Plymouth. He needed to start working again. There would be a lot going on around the house until that case concluded.

I told her I was going to my room but popped into their room invisible instead. Hal appeared to be asleep with the television on. I held on to the stone and leaned over the bed to place my hand on his head. The stone immediately heated. When it cooled, I returned to my room.

That should help him get back on his feet.

I showered to remove the smell of smoke from my body before jumping into bed.

Nine

I woke up excited with the idea of shopping for a place for my new business. I dressed and raced down to grab breakfast. Phyllis must have been excited too. She pulled out some yogurt and fruit, while I poured some coffee.

I smiled as I stirred my coffee.

She said, "I hope that's enough. If not, I could make you some toast."

I assured her, "This is fine."

Phyllis rinsed her coffee cup and put it in the dishwasher. She sauntered over and said, "I'm going to finish getting dressed. Tonya Greenwood should be here soon to pick us up. Oh, Hal went to work today."

I scarfed down my breakfast and rushed upstairs to finish getting dressed. About fifteen minutes later the doorbell rang. I ran down to answer it.

Behind the door was a beautiful woman. She had long medium blond hair with hints of gray throughout the curls. It was hair anyone would love to have. Something told me the curls were natural. She wore a rust-colored pants suit with flats.

Phyllis joined us and after the introduction, we piled into her vehicle.

Tonya informed me, "Phyllis said you want everything relatively close to your house. I've come up with a few things for you to see today. There aren't too many homes around here in the price range

Phyllis set but there is one that just came on the market last night. It will go quickly, but luckily, it's only a few blocks from here."

We pulled up to a cute house. It needed some improvements to the lawn. It was mainly rocks but the house was nice. The front sitting room was small but had a lovely fireplace. Windows were everywhere giving the place a lot of natural light. I watched Phyllis's reaction as Tonya joyfully told us about the place. She showed us around the house pointing out details of the historic home. It was apparent she loved her job. The hardwood floors were pristine. They seemed to interest Phyllis also.

When we came to the kitchen Phyllis stopped and seemed to be taking in the beauty of the room. The cabinets were white but seemed relatively new. Phyllis said nothing. Tonya led us upstairs to see the bedrooms. She asked Phyllis, "What do you think?"

Nearly with tears in her eyes, Phyllis said, "It's perfect!"

I asked, "Do you think Hal will like it?"

Phyllis smiled. She said, "He told me he would like anything as long as I was there."

"Well, if you're interested you need to jump on this. It won't be available long," Tonya announced.

Phyllis paused a moment. She appeared to be praying. I asked Tonya to give her a moment. Tonya and I strolled to the front of the house and discussed my needs. In the middle of our conversation, Phyllis pranced up with a smile on her face.

Phyllis turned to Tonya and said, "I'll take it."

Tonya and she spoke about the offer and completed the paperwork needed to make an offer. Tonya's assistant Gracie came by to pick up the paperwork so we could continue searching for a place for my business.

Tonya showed us several office buildings. They were a bit too far away or provided little privacy. I was beginning to get discouraged.

Tonya pulled her car over and said, "I have an idea and it's in the area you like." She glanced at herself in the mirrors and straightened her bangs. In an excited voice she said, "Oh let me just show you."

Tonya turned the car around and drove in the direction of my house. We were only a few blocks away in a lower income area. We parked in front of a small light gray home with a bright red door.

Tonya turned to me and enthusiastically said, "I think you'll find everything you are asking for is here. Keep an open mind." She exited the vehicle.

Phyllis and I turned to one another and shrugged our shoulders as we followed her inside.

Tonya spun around as we entered.

She said, "Now picture this. Over here." She pointed to the living room area. "This will be your reception area. Some sofas in this area for your customers to wait. A table over there for meeting with a client." She rotated around and strutted toward the kitchen. "Break room." She gave us a moment to admire the kitchen.

"This way ladies," she instructed. We followed her to the first of three bedrooms. "Office number one."

The room was a decent size and could easily be used by two people. The second bedroom was similar in size. We followed her to the master bedroom.

"Another office, or Brooke you could live here," she suggested.

I meandered around again trying to picture us using this space. *This could work.*

I spun around to Phyllis who seemed to be examining the kitchen. I asked, "Phyllis, what do you think?"

She glanced around, "Everyone's homes including my new one is close by. This could work. It's not like you're going to have a lot of customers piling in here every day. You're a specialized field. Most people will call and make an appointment."

I agreed with her. The place was perfect. I turned to Tonya.

"I'll take it," I said cheerfully.

We completed the paperwork. Tonya made a few calls before taking us back home. There was nothing left to do but wait to see if our offers were accepted.

Phyllis and I went out to lunch to pass the time. To celebrate, I drove Phyllis and I to Asahi Japanese Restaurant. We both loved the soft-shell crab there.

I asked, "Are you sure that's not too big a property?"

"No. I think with the right decorator, the space could be made functional for all of you. If you work it right, one of you could even live there," Phyllis replied.

"Perhaps," I said.

Who would that be?

I stopped myself from considering it. I needed to figure out where everyone's desks would be first.

Phyllis handed me paper and a pen. I drew the floor plan. While taking into consideration the front bedroom was bigger than the second one, I determined Greg, Austin, and myself could share an office. Juliet and Jacob had very specific jobs and would need more privacy. Their office should be the second bedroom. Phyllis was right, one of us could live there.

I was excited about taking this next step, but I couldn't help but worry if I was doing the right thing. My emotions were rolling like a rollercoaster. Excited to panic in a blink.

Our conversation moved to how Phyllis would decorate her new home. She liked the way our house was filled with antiques. I told her she was welcome to have anything in the storage area of the attic. That put a big smile on her face. She assured me if I needed them, there would be mirrors throughout her home also. We both chuckled at that.

The lady at the next table must have been eavesdropping because she glared at me for a moment, appeared to be scrutinizing me as her eyes moved up and down me. An eye roll followed just before turning her attention back to her husband.

She must think I'm vain.

Phyllis did not seem to notice her.

We went home after lunch. I popped over to inform Leonardo about the new home. He assured me he would take care of the financial side of it. The home would be in a trust setup for myself. The rest of the day Phyllis and I wandered around the house doing miscellaneous chores as we checked our phones for missed calls.

Just before dinner. Tonya called. She informed me the property could be mine in a few weeks if I was paying cash for the property. Per Leonardo, I provided Mr. Thomas's information. Tonya informed me she didn't expect to hear about the home Phyllis made an offer on until the following day.

Immediately, I ran to Phyllis and told her the good news. She was elated. She was not happy to hear she would need to continue waiting.

I decided to wait and tell everyone after I had the keys because anything could go wrong. Leonardo and I worked out salaries for everyone including myself. I would be provided with a loan and would need to pay it back once we were making money. It occurred to me I needed offer letters for the Bloom Keepers. I was excited to tell them they would receive benefits along with a good salary. I was working on Juliet's letter when there was a commotion from downstairs.

I peered down from the balcony and saw Phyllis hugging Mechelle. Austin was holding her suitcase. Without thinking I bolted downstairs to give her a hug.

"Girl, I've missed you," I said as I squeezed her.

"I've missed you too, but I need to breathe," Mechelle laughed.

I asked, "Why did you decide to come back early?"

"My parents are so involved in their social life; I barely saw them. Besides, I miss you guys. Before I know it, I'll be in Italy and I'll barely see any of you," Mechelle said to Austin.

While I looked at them, I thought that I asked a lot of them. I would need to ensure they saw each other regularly.

I suggested, "We'll work out some sort of schedule for you to see one another on a regular basis. Although you can't really be around people that know you when you're together."

Mechelle giggled. "Does that mean lots of dates in foreign countries?"

I rolled my eyes. "That's a possibility," I informed her.

Austin carried her bag to her room. Phyllis provided us with a snack in the dining room. We spent the remainder of the evening discussing what she did with our Florida friends during her visit.

Ten

The Bloom Keepers arrived for dinner and hung out before we returned to Plymouth. Hal and Phyllis had left for dinner and a movie. We reviewed the satellite photo of the area and discussed where everyone would be. We felt our plan was strong. Everyone was to meet at the Thrifty Car and Van Rental place nearby to regroup and I was to pick them up there.

We went to my room because it was less nauseating for them to use the full-length mirror to teleport. Jacob and Juliet teamed up on the roof of the building on the west side of the wharf. Austin and Greg were on the ground. I was on the roof of the building to the east. I had everyone check in using telepathy. Sadly, I was the only one who could hear them. Everyone was within ear shot. That told me they should all still be invisible.

About thirty minutes later, Jacob told me April's team were on the scene. They had parked along the water west of his location. Juliet explained April was not with the group.

Moments later, I saw lights in the distance on the south end of the area I was in. I thought about teleporting there, but I would be too far from the others which might cause them to be visible. It wasn't worth the risk.

Juliet reported two were on the roof and the other remained hidden on the ground. A fishing boat entered the wharf. At the same time, two men entered the area just south of my location. Something hit the roof. I did not want to take a chance by moving to the other end of the building. It would risk the other's being discovered. A man wearing black soon revealed himself.

"Brooke, there are two people entering the wharf just northeast of you," Greg informed me using telepathy.

I watched the northeast. Greg was correct. They hid in the shadows along the wall behind a crane.

The man on the roof was now in the northern most corner of the building. He was lying down peering through the scope of the rifle.

The boat docked. There appeared to be one person on the vessel. They were dressed just as the others were. Teleporting to him would allow me to be closer to the team. The man stayed in the cabin of the vessel when I arrived to find out any information.

The man had a radio in his hand. It was difficult to understand him from the bow. I peaked in the cabin and switched positions had had myself against the back wall.

He held up the radio and asked, "Gamma team, are you in place?"

A deep voice answered, "Roger that."

A familiar voice said, "Now we wait."

April.

I scanned the area.

Where are you?

She was nowhere in sight.

Forty-five minutes later, a voice came across the radio. "Fishing boat approaching."

I couldn't see anything from my location. I teleported back to my spot on the east roof. A fishing vessel was approaching from the east. I watched it move slowly toward the wharf.

Did it stop? Why isn't it coming?

Another vessel was pulling alongside the fishing boat.

I concentrated on Greg. "I think they could be making the swap right now," I informed him.

"I agree. You need to go. Tell everyone they are about to become visible before you leave. We'll meet up with you later," Greg insisted. Once I told everyone, I gave them time to hide before teleporting to the bow of the vessel.

Mark, Richard, and George were on the other vessel. They were tying the two vessels together. Alfie was driving the fishing vessel. Richard and George climbed onto the boat I was on and moved crates to the other boat. I sat and watched from the bow. Suddenly it appeared as though Mark was glaring at me.

Can he see me?

I glanced down into the water to see my reflection.

Oh no! I forgot to make myself invisible.

Mark turned to Alfie and pointed at me. He asked, "Who's she?"

Alfie turned his focus to me and shook his head. Mark told them to keep working. He tossed himself over the edge of the boat and charged toward me. I honestly couldn't say I was bumming a ride or anything because I was in my Bloom Keepers uniform. Fortunately, he could not see my face and had no clue who I was.

Buddy, you don't know who you're dealing with.

I positioned my stance and waited for him to attack. Mark sprang up and seized the bar above him as he approached. He flung himself off to kick me in the chest. I swiftly jumped toward the port side of the boat.

Perhaps you've some skills.

I countered with a back kick.

Mark caught my leg and twisted my foot knocking me over. He dragged me to the edge of the boat but held me at arm's length. I attempted to kick him but was unsuccessful with each strike. He flung a net around my foot and pulled me to him.

Mark hollered, "George, get over here."

George held my arms while Mark tangled my other foot in the net. They threw me overboard. I could see them as they peered over the boat waiting for me to drown. I struggled a bit to free my feet but was unsuccessful. They were saying something, but their voices were muffled. I soon remembered I could breathe underwater. They're waiting for me to drown. I played along pretending I was giving up the fight and became lifeless. Once I stopped moving, they left me.

I was afraid to pull my mirror out while I was in the water. My fear was I would drop it. I worked on freeing my feet. Once free, I swam over to the bow of Mark's boat. I pulled out my mirror and teleported invisibly to the bow. They appeared to be done loading the weapons.

Mark said, "Make sure she's off the line before you leave. Then pull into Victoria Wharf. If she doesn't come off, just dump her and the net. We'll soon get you a new one."

I noticed a puddle of water forming around me.

Not good.

Once they moved into the cabin, I teleported to the starboard side and held on to the fender. I was in for a bumpy ride.

We pulled away from the boat and moved out of the area.

Where are we going?

We rode for a while. My arms were killing me. After what felt like an eternity, we pulled up to a pier. I teleported to a grassy area invisible and watched them.

The three men moved several suitcases to a vehicle in the parking lot. A sign said we were at the Saltash Pier. Richard left in the boat and left when the last case was unloaded. Mark and George carried it to their vehicle and placed it in the trunk. I teleported to the backseat before they entered the vehicle. I was making a mess of the seat. A hot mess is how I would describe myself. Completely exhausted from being pulled through the water and soaking wet. I even caught myself nearly dozing off from the rocking of the car. My mind began thinking about the others on the team.

Lord, please let them be okay.

I felt compelled to check up on them.

I teleported to the roof Greg was on. No one was there. The boat Alfie was on was covered in April's men. Alfie was sitting on the ground handcuffed. I spotted April standing by a police car.

Is that… Austin. It is!

Austin was in the back of the squad car. I teleported invisibly to the side of the vehicle. I glanced inside and teleported to the open seat beside him.

Using telepathy, I told him to lean forward. I concentrated on moving his wrists out of the handcuffs. Austin's eyes widened as he was able to move freely. I told him to keep his hands behind his back.

April was on the phone but frequently gazed over at Austin. I placed my hand on his shoulder and opened my mirror. When she turned away, I teleported us to the meeting spot at the car rental place.

Jacob and Juliet were there. "Thank God," Juliet gave Austin a hug. He could barely stand.

I asked Austin, "What happened?"

Greg and I jumped off the roof. I landed wrong. I told him to go because I couldn't run. I figured he would be here," Austin said a little choked up.

I paused a moment to heal him. "Wait here for Greg. He'll show up. I need to get back," I instructed. Without hesitation, I teleported back to the backseat of Mark's vehicle.

They were parked outside a storage unit. I glanced around to make sure I could return before teleporting to the door of Unit 106. There were three suitcases stacked in the middle of the room.

The two men said nothing and returned to their vehicle. George said, "Drop me off at Amelia's house. I'll use the back way to get home."

Humm, the tunnels must take him to a secret door to his house.

I teleported back to the meeting spot to take everyone home. Greg was not with them. I asked, "Where is Greg?" My heart raced.

It appeared they were holding back something. No one said a word. They just glanced over at one another. Austin lowered his head at the ground and said, "We don't know. They caught me and another guy started chasing him."

I felt like I was going to puke. I asked, "What direction was he headed?"

Austin started shaking his head back and forth.

In a stern voice I said, "What direction?"

Jacob interrupted, "Austin the building ran north and south. The water was to the south end."

It was as though he had an epiphany. Austin blurted, "West. He was heading west."

He must have headed to the marina. "Let me take you guys back, then I'll go find Greg," I told them.

Austin said, "No. I'm going with you. It's my fault we don't know where he is."

"Juliet and I are staying here. He may show up. We'll fill him in," Jacob insisted.

"Fine," I said gripping Austin's arm. "We'll be back every ten minutes or so."

I pulled out my mirror and before I had a chance to teleport, Greg came around the corner of the building.

"We need to go," Greg barked as he nearly collided into me.

"I can't take all of you," I informed him.

"Go," Austin instructed as he let go of me.

I teleported us to my garage. I said, "I'll be right back." Teleporting back invisible, I found Juliet, Austin, and Jacob in a battle with April's men. I went around the corner and became visible. I ran back and removed my mask.

I shouted, "Guys we're all on the same side." Everyone turned and stared at me. Jacob had one of the men in a hold. "Let him go," I demanded. I turned to the man that was released. "Where's April?"

He said, "At the wharf. Are you Brooke?"

I answered, "Yes, and this is my team. Why are you attacking them?"

"Miss, your team never announced themselves. They just ran when we spotted them," he shouted.

I stood my ground. He was not going to intimidate me. "They weren't fleeing from you. They were instructed to leave the area. While you were chasing us down, we were chasing Mark Cooper and his team," I said sarcastically. I relaxed my stance. "See the exchange happened before the boat was in Victoria Wharf."

The man pulled out a radio, but before he could call April, I said, "I'll contact April when we find out more about the sale. In the meantime, I'll keep an eye on the warehouse the weapons are at." I concentrated on persuading them to head back to the wharf. The man nodded and told the other men to follow him. Once they were out of view, I teleported everyone back to the garage.

Greg asked, "What took you so long?"

Jacob gave him a quick explanation.

"We all need to get back to the attic to change. Everyone needs to be extremely quiet. Hal and Phyllis should be back home," I explained.

Mechelle was sitting in the chair on her phone when we entered. She said, "I was beginning to wonder if you guys were going to make it back. What happened?"

Austin explained while Juliet went into the storage room to change.

When Juliet returned, she said, "Brooke, you can't let Hal see you. You look like a drowned raccoon."

I was confused. A glimpse in the mirror told me she was right. Mascara was making my eyes appear as if I was wearing a mask. My hair was in a wet ponytail. It appeared to have many knots. Once everyone was dressed, I returned them to the garage. Greg assured me he would lock the door when they left. I teleported to my bathroom.

I showered and as I dried my hair, I thought about how well the team did despite losing track of Greg. We were placed in a difficult situation and came through it. I chuckled as I thought about how mad April must be. I'm sure she had already left me a nasty message on the phone she gave me. Too bad I wasn't going to head to the United Kingdom to listen to the message. My bed was calling.

Eleven

I woke up to the sounds of birds chirping outside my window. To me this was one of the best ways to wake up. I dressed for church before going down to breakfast. Hal was at the dining room table reading a paper. I greeted him as I passed by.

Mechelle was helping Phyllis with breakfast. I did not want to interrupt them. I poured my coffee and waited for a pause in their conversation.

Mechelle turned and asked, "Guess what we're making?"

I shrugged as I drank my coffee. I answered, "Pancakes."

"No. That was a good guess though. Greek Yogurt Crepes with Berries," she replied.

"Sounds amazing," I informed her.

"Two minutes," Phyllis announced.

I topped off my coffee and helped them carry the plates to the dining room.

The breakfast was a piece of artwork. It amazed me how talented Phyllis was. Hal said grace for us. The tanginess of the yogurt with the berries was scrumptious. I darted my eyes to Mechelle. I asked, "How much of this did you do?"

Phyllis smiled and said, "She made it all. I just plated the food."

"It's superb," I complemented.

The faint sound of a phone chimed in the distance. The ringtone informed me it was Phyllis's phone. Yet she did not move. "Phyllis your phone is ringing," I informed her.

She asked, "Who would be calling me?"

"Perhaps Tonya Greenwood," I suggested.

Without a word, Phyllis sprang from her seat to get the phone. Hal got up and followed her.

Mechelle said, "I spoke with Leonardo. Apparently, he's completely healed."

I smiled and replied, "That's wonderful news."

We both giggled.

Mechelle leaned over and whispered, "I'm so glad he changed his mind."

I nodded.

Hal and Phyllis returned. Phyllis said, "We have some news." She squeezed Hal's arm. "They came back with a counteroffer, and we accepted."

I leapt from my chair to give each of them a hug. Mechelle followed my lead. After congratulating them. We scarfed down our food before rushing to church.

Mechelle and I strolled in and were stopped by Jerry and Kate. They had been married for years. In their sixties and still madly in love. They loved the Lord and wanted everyone else to also.

Kate asked, "Brooke, a little birdy told me you're opening your own business as a P.I."

"Yes, Ms. Kate, I am," I confirmed.

"Well, Jerry and I need your help. When you get your business up and running, we would like to hire you," she said.

"Sounds good. I'll give you the friends and family discount," I commented with a wink.

They both smiled and moved on to speak with a couple that just arrived.

Mechelle and I found our seats. The congregation settled down when the band started to play. As we worshipped the Lord, I was overwhelmed as I thought about the gift I had received.

Why was I deserving? Why did he pick me? Why our family?

The music ended. Our pastor preached on John 8:1-11. The Pharisees were testing Jesus. He knelt and wrote with his finger in the ground. The Pharisees wanted to stone a woman for adultery. Basically, Jesus told them they should only cast a stone if they are without sin.

Only Jesus could cast a stone because we are all sinners. Okay Lord, I get the message. Like the disciples that were chosen, they were sinners. So am I. I look forward to being with you in heaven. Lord, thank you for choosing me with all my flaws to help you. Please lead and guide me to do your will.

Church concluded. As we were exiting, I glanced at my phone.

JULIET: If you're going back. I want to go.

BROOKE: Be over in an hour.

I told Mechelle what was going on. She wished she could go but knew it was best she didn't. We stopped to pick up subs for lunch. It was funny, now I consider the things I eat. To eat or not eat tuna fish, onions, and garlic. I needed to be keenly aware of my breath and scents on my body. I would have to opt for the less scented foods. It was too easy for someone to discover me with lingering odors.

I chose a turkey sandwich, with lettuce cheese and mayo. Sadly, no pickles or onions and a glass of water with lemon. Mechelle and I discussed how much we loved Hal but having him in the house was difficult to keep from revealing our secret.

Juliet marched in while we were cleaning up our mess from lunch. She said, "Where's Phyllis?"

"She and Hal went to her sisters. They'll be back late tonight," I stated.

Mechelle followed us upstairs. I changed into a professional outfit to meet with April. I was going with 'I look older than I am', but I didn't think it worked.

I grabbed the bag with April's phone and teleported myself to the corner of Friars' Lane and Southside Street. Friar's Lane was a narrow road, which was why the vehicles were so small. We tucked ourselves behind the Fayre Trade Fairy Jewelers shop and when the coast was clear we appeared visible. We strolled along the narrow-cobbled road to Southside Street and moved toward the east.

The streets still held what appeared to be the original cobbled streets along the edge of the sidewalks and the narrow roads. The historical area was breathtaking. It appeared old homes were above the thriving shops. I found it interesting that the sidewalk area was larger than the road running through it.

Juliet said, "I believe this is the Barbican area. This is one of Plymouth's most famous streets. Some of these buildings are from the 1800's."

I liked how she and Jacob both loved the history of the places we had been to. For a while, I didn't think the two of them would stop discussing Greek history.

I pulled the phone from the bag. As expected, there were several missed messages from April. To be honest, I deleted the messages where she was scolding me. I dialed her number.

"So, you are on Southside Street," she informed me when she answered the phone.

I shook my head. Sarcastically, I asked, "What, no hello?" I could feel her eyes rolling through the phone.

April cleared her throat and said, "We need to meet. Remain on that road. The marina will be on your left. Continue south. When you get to the Mayflower Museum cross the road. The Mayflower Steps Memorial will be south of there on Pilgrim Way. I'll meet you at the memorial in thirty minutes."

We did as she instructed until we crossed a cobble-stone road. While we waited, we read the dedication signs along the wall. Although interesting, Juliet found them more fascinating. There was a tablet in the walkway that read Mayflower 1620 just in front of an archway to the area the stairs would have been when they boarded the Mayflower to establish the New England states.

We enjoyed the fresh air and view until April arrived. She strutted up by herself. "It's a good thing you are on Allison's good side because I told her I want to arrest you for what went down last night."

I suspected she did not know Allison and I were related. Ignoring her snide comment, I said, "Mark has the weapons in a storage unit. I'll let you know when the sales go down. I'll even have my team stay out of your way. Until then, this is my show. I'll contact you when I have something for you." With only a glare to tell me how annoyed she was, she turned and went north.

"We need to get to the storage unit," I said to Juliet.

She pointed to the marina, indicating that we could teleport from there. She was right, so we shuffled down to the jetty.

"We need a small boat blocked by a larger boat," Juliet suggested.

I nodded in agreement. Something told me to check behind me. I stopped and pretended to tie my shoe. One of the men from April's team was getting on the jetty.

She's having us followed.

I jumped up and told Juliet, "We've got company."

We both scanned the area for another way off the jetty but passing him was the only way. We both nodded in agreement. As we approached him, he stood there frozen for a moment before turning back and getting off the jetty.

I nodded as we passed him. Thankfully, Juliet and I were dressed like businesswomen, but our shoes were made for this work. We jogged across the street. I glanced over at Juliet and pointed up. She knew we were about to get a workout in. The Barbican had the perfect exterior to scale. She motioned for me to go first. I jumped onto the large bricks on the exterior just below the arched window. My hands clasped the decorative accoutrement just below the sign. From there I was able to make it to the roof of the Admiral MacBride building.

We leapt from one roof to another. Unfortunately, he was able to keep up with us. We descended. I tucked the phone back in the bag, while I waited for Juliet to make it down the building.

I noticed the sign on the building, 'Barbican Theatre'. We ran along the cobble pathway. A small sign on the planter showed us we were on Castle Street.

At the intersection of Lambhay Hill and Castle Street was a great deal of foliage. I ran down Lambhay Hill with Juliet close behind. I hurled myself over the fence along the road. We stowed ourselves behind some large thick plants. I peered through the bushes. The man came to the intersection and stopped. He bent over with his hands on his knees trying to catch his breath. His head darted back and forth in each direction. He shook his head; I presume it was because he had lost us.

I placed my hand on Juliet's shoulder and pulled my mirror out. We returned home to change into our Bloom Keeper's uniforms before going to the storage locker.

While I was dressing, Juliet said, "Can you bring those cameras?" There was a pause. "Thanks sweetie. See you soon."

I adjusted my shirt and asked, "Is Jacob on his way over here?"

With her uniform in hand, she came into my bathroom. She hollered, "Yes. He's bringing some cameras. That way we can watch what's going on from here."

Brilliant.

"I hope he's coming with us to install them," I hollered back.

"He hoped you would say that. He wanted to come with us today, but I told him I thought you wanted just me because I've met April," she said as she exited the bathroom.

"That's true," I agreed. I contacted Jacob and persuaded him to let me pick him up. He would text Juliet when he was ready.

Juliet and I went up to the attic to get us each a bottle of water from my mini fridge in the gym. Ten minutes later, Jacob texted. I teleported to his closet and as usual, I fell into his arms when he opened the door.

I asked, "When are you going to clean that mess up?"

"Do you see how small that closet is? Take a gander at my drawers. They're organized. Mom won't let me get rid of anything." Jacob picked up a bag from his bed before we went to the gym in my attic.

After a brief explanation of the situation, the three of us arrived invisibly inside the storage unit. We were the only ones there. Using telepathy, I told Juliet to stay with Jacob. I went outside to keep a lookout, while he went to work.

About thirty minutes later, I popped back to see how he was doing. He held up his hands showing me all ten fingers.

Ten more minutes.

I gave him a thumbs up and returned to my post outside.

After what felt like ten minutes, I returned, and they were ready to go. We returned to the gym in case Hal and Phyllis were home.

Jacob opened his laptop and placed it on the table. "We're all set." He tapped a few keys and said, "Audio and video."

I waited for the audio, but I heard nothing. I asked, "Are you sure it's working?"

Jacob cocked his head and scrunched his eyes. "Brooke, there's no one there to make noise."

Duh.

Annoyed with myself, I said, "Don't mind me, I'm an idiot."

We watched the screen for a moment and suddenly the gym door flung open. Hal rushed in with his arms full of water. "Interesting outfits," he said ogling us.

Thankfully, we had all pulled our masks off before he entered.

Hal started loading the water in the mini fridge. I caught him eyeing the computer.

He asked, "What ya watching?"

Jacob scratched his head. He said, "Oh, it's just some security cameras."

"All that for a few boxes," Hal said shrugging his shoulders. "Well, I need to find out what else is on the honey-do-list."

Once Hal shut the door, we all glared at one another in shock. Juliet asked, "Is it hard trying to keep all this from him?"

I replied, "Absolutely. Fortunately, he and Phyllis are buying a place. They should be out before too long."

Jacob asked," Phyllis is leaving?"

"Oh no. She'll only be a few blocks away. She's going to continue working here. She just won't be here at night, or I suspect much on the weekends," I said.

I had not thought about her only being here five days a week.

Brooke, this is Phyllis. She'll be around when I need her.

"Well, I best get back before Mom puts out a missing persons alert." He held out his arm for me to take it. He tucked his laptop under his arm and held out his other arm for me to take. He turned to Juliet. "I'll see you at dinner tonight," he said, before winking.

Before leaving Jacob, he informed me he would let me know with a text if he saw any activity.

I returned to Juliet.

"I thought my parents were bad. His parents are always checking up on him. They're always trying to see what he's doing on his computer. Fortunately, he's quick about changing the screen when they barge in," Juliet informed me. "Oh, Mechelle told us to meet her in the library when we're done. She wants to hang out."

We joined her after we changed. Mechelle was watching a cooking show on Chicken Marsala.

We chatted a bit about Mechelle moving to Italy. We were bored and transferred some of the things to my room at the villa. She could move them to her new room once she was officially there. We informed Isabella, who assured us she would take off moving them to Mechelle's new room before we come up for our vacation.

After returning, we had dinner followed by facials before turning in for the evening. Greg and I had a quick Bible study before we both crashed for the night.

Twelve

While Hal was at work, Phyllis and I spent the day shopping for furniture for her home. Phyllis's focus was on several antique stores in downtown Louisville. She had purchased several pieces that would be stored in the garage until she officially moved. While she debated on a Victorian walnut side table, I received a text.

JACOB: There's movement.

I texted the Bloom Keepers.

BROOKE: It's time.

"Phyllis, I hate to do this, but I need to go," I whispered.

She nodded. "I'll see you at home later. Thank you for your help."

I tucked behind a mahogany Chippendale style secretary desk and bookcase and teleported to my room. I changed and checked my phone.

GREG: On my way. Austin can't make it.

JULIET: Jacob and I are on our way.

Pleased most of us would be going, I placed April's phone in my pocket and teleported to the bushes I was last at. April answered my call swiftly. I told her I believed it was going down and provided the address. I popped the phone back in the bag and returned home to wait on the others.

GREG: It's going to take me thirty minutes to get there. I'm parked.

I received a similar text from Juliet. I picked up three of them and brought them to the library. Jacob showed us on his computer the status. I pointed at the monitor, "That's George." I watched another camera's video. "That's Alfie and that is Mr. Cooper." I scoured the screens. I asked, "Where's Richard?"

"He must be nearby. I'm sure April's team are there by now," Jacob stated.

"The cameras are still on. That means we can't do anything within the view of the cameras. We are merely going to be watching as April's team takes them down," I advised.

We appeared in a wooded area near the building. I made sure I teleported everyone to their assigned areas invisibly. Juliet was placed on the roof of a nearby storage unit. Jacob stayed where he was as he tracked what was going on inside. I put Greg near the door, and I left to locate April's team. We were all close to one another.

I teleported across the area in hopes of finding them. In my search, I noticed Jacob had moved. Using telepathy, I had asked if he had seen April's team.

He said, "Yah, I had to move because her team was approaching me. They're spreading out now along the back perimeter. They have listening devices aimed at the building. It sounded like they have a sniper nearby."

A sniper? I need to get my team out of there. They could get shot.

A small van pulled in. The storage door opened. I couldn't see what was going on. I moved to Greg's location. He had a good view. Two people climbed out of the van. A man and a woman. She had long brown hair and wore sunglasses.

I could not make out what she was saying. I pulled out my mirror. Greg seized my hand holding the mirror and shook his head. He must have suspected I was going into the building. He tapped me. A tap to his head followed. I rolled my eyes. Using telepathy, he said, "It's not safe."

I told him, "There's something familiar about that woman. I need to get closer." I concentrated on the mirror and moved to the far wall.

Why does she seem so familiar?

She and her partner backed away from the group and whispered to one another. They returned. With a British accent, she said, "Yes sir, we do."

There was something unique about her voice. It was almost as if it was being disguised.

Her partner went to the vehicle and returned with a briefcase. Mark glanced inside the case. He nodded to George and Alfie. They loaded the weapons in the van. I flipped my mirror open and moved back to Greg. I swept his hand in mine, and we teleported to the roof to get Juliet. We needed to leave before anyone got shot.

Where's Jacob?

I moved us outside the exterior wall invisible. Using telepathy, I told them to meet back here. We needed to find Jacob. Just as we were about to split up Jacob came running with his computer from behind a tree. Without thinking, I teleported us back to the attic.

Greg asked, "Why did we leave so soon?"

"There was a sniper on the roof. I thought April's crew would have barged in and arrested everyone," I responded.

Jacob scrunched up his face. He asked, "Yah. Why didn't they?"

"There was also something familiar about the woman, but I can't put my finger on it," I admitted.

"You guys stay here. Brooke lets go back and find out what's going on," Greg instructed.

I did as he requested. Thankfully, we were invisible because the woman nearly ran into me as she strutted by. She removed her glasses but turned her head away before I could see her.

They got in the van and pulled away. I teleported Greg and I back of the van.

They drove out of the storage place with April's men just letting them go. We pulled down an alley. She turned to the driver and said, "I can't believe we did it."

What? No.

I moved a little closer. She must have heard me because her eyes darted toward me.

The driver said, "What?"

"I thought I heard something, but it's all good" she said with a southern drawl.

April?

My mind was all over the place.

She removed her glasses, wig, and pulled off a layer of clothes before changing her shoes. "I need to get back before anyone notices I'm missing," she said exiting the van.

She jumped into a small car and raced off in the direction of the storage unit.

Greg and I teleported back to the front of the storage unit.

George was closing the unit up. Alfie was keeping watch and Mark was nowhere in sight. I teleported us to the perimeter invisible. We needed to know what April's team was saying.

The team members were regrouping. A tall man said, "I'm getting no response from Little Sparrow."

They all said the same thing.

Abruptly, April charged up with her radio in hand. In a nasty tone, she said, "What happened?" Her eyes wandered across each of their faces. "We had them and no one listened to me. Now Mark Cooper and the weapons are gone!"

One of the men said, "Little Sparrow, we have been trying to contact you throughout the mission. You never answered."

She lifted her radio and turned away from the men. Luckily, she was right in front of me.

Without pushing the button, she said, "Testing...Testing."

She turned back toward the men. In an unpleasant voice she said, "What, no one checked the radios?" She banged on the radio and tried it again. This time she pushed the button.

"Testing...Testing." April's voice streamed out of each of their radios. She rolled her eyes. "Get back to the office!" She slammed the radio in the man's chest next to her. "Make sure this equipment is working properly. We can't have this happen again," she ordered. She turned to the taller man. April said, "McCoy, I want a first draft of this incident by the end of the day." She pivoted and stomped off in the direction of her vehicle.

McCoy said, "Before checking the equipment, I need your reports. Now let's get out of here."

I wrapped my hand in Greg's arm and teleported us to Mark's house. He was on his patio. His eyes moved from the water and to his phone every few seconds. Periodically he would pace back and forth.

His phone rang.

Mark said, "Where are you?" There was a pause. "It's unlocked." He put the phone in his pocket and went inside.

Suddenly George appeared. "That went well," George proudly said.

"Did it? I'm not so sure," Mark said as he went to the kitchen to make two cups of tea with milk. He handed one to George.

Why do they do that? Note to self, try hot tea with milk.

George ambled over to the sofa and sat. He asked, "Why aren't you sure?"

"I can't put my finger on it, but it's that woman," Mark shook his head and joined his brother in the living room. "Are you sure we've never done business with Ms. Demeanor before."

"Never," George said before taking a sip of tea.

"That's clearly an alias, you Muppet! Find out who she really is," Mark ordered.

We teleported back to the attic.

Juliet asked, "Where have you been?"

I asked Greg to tell them while I ran to the restroom. When I returned, Mechelle was in the room. Greg was finishing up the details.

"So, now we need to find April and the weapons," Greg informed everyone.

The weapons, that's it.

Without thinking I left them to return to the van because it contained the weapons. The van was empty. I stepped out and found a dirt path that led me to the entrance of a tunnel.

Are there tunnels all over this place?

I peaked in. The walls were brick for a short while. I followed the path for a short distance before I spotted one of the cases left along the wall. What little light from the entrance was nearly gone.

They'll be back for this.

I sat on the suitcase and waited.

A short while later, footsteps could be heard. I stood and noticed a dim light dancing toward me. As it came closer, I realized a man was wearing a headlamp. I followed him deep into the tunnel. He turned left and entered a small room with an iron door. He pulled the suitcase next to the others. There were other weapons in crates along the wall. As he exited, he shut and locked the iron door. I teleported back to the attic.

"Seriously Brooke," Greg said annoyed. "We don't mind ya going off on your own but ya need to tell us where you're going."

"You're right. I'm sorry. I found the weapons. I don't know where April is, but she's not with the weapons. Oh, and it looks like they have been stocking up on firearms. There are more stored in the tunnel. I need to talk to Allison.

I went to my room to grab the phone she had given me. I texted 911. She sent me a picture of an office. I changed into an appropriate outfit and teleported invisibly to what I presumed was her office. To let her know I was there by pushing a few of the papers on her desk.

She canvased her office and rose to close her door. The room had windows and no blinds. She picked up her phone and said, "Brooke?"

I moved closer. "Yes. We need to talk about April," I informed her.

Someone walked by and peeked in the window. Allison waved. "I'm thinking my suspicions are accurate," she said grabbing a pen with her free hand and tapping it on the desk.

"Your suspicions?"

"Yes. Some of the things in her reports don't add up or they contradict her team's reports. It happens occasionally because someone might miss something. Only with her, it happens more frequently. Honestly, I was hoping I was worried about nothing. April is a valuable source with good instincts."

I filled Allison in on everything I knew so far.

Allison leaned back in her chair and put her feet on her desk. She spoke into her phone. "She doesn't know you're on to her. Does she know you were there today?"

"No," I replied.

She sprung up out of her seat and said, "That's good news. Tell her you and your team had another situation to deal with and couldn't make it. I'm interested in knowing what she tells you."

Allison sat at her computer and tapped away at the keyboard. It wasn't long before she wrote something on a note pad and slid the paper closer to me. It read 'Duke of Cornwall Hotel – Room 205'.

"April's hotel information. Follow her and see what you can find out," Allison said as she gazed in my direction. "Brooke, Lillie was right to choose you. I wanted to be the protector, but I can see she was wise in choosing you." She stood. When this is done, I will need a W-9 from you. We are going to pay your new company for your team's service. I'll need details about time spent and travel of course."

"Allison, I can't provide travel expenses," I reminded her.

She chuckled, "Of course you can. Speak with Leonardo, he'll provide you everything you need." She opened her arms and said, "Now give me a hug."

I wrapped my arms around her. We were interrupted by her assistant who knocked and immediately opened the door.

She asked, "Are you okay Allison?"

I could only imagine what she thought. Slowly, I slid down out of her arms.

"My shoulders are a little stiff. I was trying to stretch them out a bit," Allison informed her.

The woman nodded and said, "I'm on my way to an appointment. See you tomorrow." She closed the door.

"It's best you go. Don't forget to check in with updates," Allison said as she returned to her seat.

I teleported back to the attic. They had all changed into their street clothes. After a brief explanation of our new mission. Everyone was starving. We teleported to the garage and pretended we had just returned home. Phyllis was in the kitchen.

She hugged me when I entered. "Mechelle has kept me abreast of the situation. I knew you would be hungry. I have enough chili for everyone. Please dig in," Phyllis insisted. There was a stack of bowls and spoons next to the stove. She carried a pitcher of sweet tea and a pitcher of water to the dining room.

Hal came into the room as we were sitting down. He said, "How was your training?"

I figured Phyllis was covering for us. I said, "It went well. Before you know it, we'll be master P.I.'s."

"I'm in need of one. I seemed to have lost my glasses if anyone finds them," Hal said as his eyes swept the room.

Mechelle giggled. "I know I'm not going to be a detective, but I think I've this one solved. There on your head, Hal."

We all had a good laugh. I think we were all ready to turn in early. I returned everyone to their vehicles, showered and crashed on my bed scrolling through social media.

Mechelle knocked on my door frame. I motioned for her to come in and she plopped herself on the end of my bed.

We chatted for a bit, but I sensed something was bothering her. I tried to read her mind. A moment later, I said, "I'll make sure you and Austin get to spend time together and you will be hanging out with us."

Mechelle bit her lip. Her eyes darted away and filled with tears. "I love him," she said.

"I know. How about this, when we are slow, he can go to Italy and spend time with you. He'll be on the clock when you are, so you'll need to find him something to do. He can stay in my room if the place is busy. Just give me a heads up if he does," I suggested.

She leapt toward me and gave me a hug. "I want to work in Italy and be part of the team, but I want to be with him too. Thank you for understanding. I'm going to give him a call. Good night."

I pulled out my Bible and read until my eyes were too heavy to continue.

Thirteen

I woke up in the middle of the night. After tossing and turning for about thirty minutes I realized I was not going back to sleep any time soon. I rolled over to check the time. 4:08 am. I calculated the time in Plymouth. 9:08 am. I jumped out of bed and got dressed. I could meet April before she had time to move the weapons. With the phone she had given me and left and arrived in a hallway at the Duke of Cornwall Hotel.

I found a public restroom to become visible. Straightening my clothes as I exited before making my way to the reception area. I pulled the phone from the bag and called April.

She answered, "Well hello."

"I'm in the lobby of your hotel. Can we talk?"

She told me she would be down in a few minutes.

April arrived, she motioned for me to follow her to the hotel restaurant. The server seemed to know her well. April said, "The usual and she'll have the same."

"April, I owe you an apology. My team had an emergency we had to deal with yesterday. I forgot to bring your phone. I hope everything went well," I said trying to sound sincere.

We were both quiet while the server brought us coffee. April slowly drank her coffee. "Well would not be the way I would describe it."

I stared at my coffee before sipping it.

Your team might agree but I think deep down it went as planned for you.

She placed her cup on the table. April continued, "We had some technical difficulties with our radios. If we had a sniper, they could have taken out the tires of the vehicle to prevent them from leaving with the weapons."

Oh, but you did have a sniper. Why would you lie about that?

She put more sugar in her coffee. As she stirred, she moved her eyes up toward me. Sarcastically she said, "I mean, Allison thinks you're better than sliced bread."

Our food was delivered. A plate containing a sausage, what appeared to be a hashbrown patty, an over easy egg on a bed of beans and a slice of bacon. A few pieces of toast were placed between us.

While I prayed, April dug into her food.

"Again, I'm sorry. If I can be of further assistance, please let me know," I said. I bit a tiny piece of bacon. Not bad but not what I was accustomed to. "I'll contact Allison and let her know I let you down.

April swallowed. "Thanks." She ate a piece of her hashbrown with a bit of egg. She stared at me while until she swallowed. "Could you find the weapons and the people that seized them?"

I already have.

I asked, "Do you have any leads?"

"All I have is the information for the van that was used. I'll send you the information," she picked up her phone and began clicking. "I just sent it to the phone I gave you."

I pulled out the phone and examined what she sent. "Thank you. I'll get right on this," I assured her before I bit into my eggs and beans. It wasn't horrible but not like southern baked beans. The beans were bland and odd with the egg.

April stared at me.

I wiped my mouth.

She's still staring.

I asked, "Do I have something on my face?"

She lifted her right eyebrow and said, "No. You have work to do. What are you still doing here."

I chugged my coffee down and patted my mouth with the napkin. I said, "Thank you for breakfast." I rushed out of the restaurant and made my way into the restroom. Once a stall was available, I teleported invisibly to the entrance of the restaurant. She was paying the bill when a lady approached her. She had long blond hair with the underside died much darker and dressed well. Her beautiful turquoise jewelry made a fashion statement. I moved to the empty table next to her to hear their conversation.

"She went in the ladies room," the woman told April.

"Don't let her out of your sight," April told her. The woman turned to leave. "Chelly, there something off with that girl. Find out more about who she is."

Chelly nodded and rushed toward the ladies room.

She's going to be there a long time.

It was at that moment I remembered the phone. I snuck a few steps away to put the phone in the faraday bag.

April paid her bill and exited out of the hotel and jumped into her vehicle. I teleported to the back seat of her car. Her driving was what it must be like on the autobahn. I wondered if her vehicle was even equipped with a blinker. It was confirmed numerous times her brakes worked just fine. She really would make a fantastic race car driver.

Quickly, somebody sign her up. Tonight, we would like to introduce our newest star, April who can swerve her way through the winding streets of Plymouth without any concern for other drivers. Is it possible I'm getting car sick.

Fortunately, she parked.

Plymouth Central Library. Really??

I followed her in. The library had accents of blues and greens. She passed a table with several computer stations and continued to the back wall. She picked up a book and pretended to read while she watched her surroundings.

A tall man with dark hair entered the section April was in. I moved closer. April turned to him and asked, "Do you know where I can find a Devon Says book?"

He smirked. The man leaned toward April. With a Spanish accent he said softly, "I am Devon Says."

April's eyes inspected him. She rudely said, "You could pass for sixteen." She rolled her eyes, "I've what you wanted, and you know my price. Where are we going to do this?"

"My boss doesn't want to miss out. He's on holiday, with his kids. Can you wait two weeks?"

April abruptly closed the book she had in her hand and returned it to the shelf. "I suppose but I want ten percent more for securing it another week," she snapped.

Devon pulled out his phone and started texting. "It's a deal. We need a time and place," he said.

"I'll contact you in two weeks with the information," April said before leaving.

Knowing there was nothing more I could do until we knew the location, I returned to the comfort of my bed. I laid there thinking about everything that was going on and what needed to be done. Not just regarding this case. Thoughts about my business led to thoughts about what Kate and Jerry might need me for. The list went on. Eventually, my mind calmed down enough to sleep.

I was awoken suddenly by a light blaring in my eyes.

"Time to get up sleepy head," Mechelle said as she opened the next curtain. "We only have a short time before I'm out of here. We are going to do something fun today."

I pulled the pillow over my head. "Go away," I hollered into my pillow.

"It's nearly 11:00 am," Mechelle informed me.

I did the math in my head. If I estimated the couple of hours I was with April, I would have over ten hours of sleep. She was right, I needed to get up. I flung the pillow to the side and said, "Fine."

"Your coffee is on your nightstand," Mechelle informed me. She sat on the gold chair.

I sat up and blew on it. "Thank you." I asked, "What did you have in mind for today?"

A smirk came across Mechelle's face.

"Shopping it is," I said pulling myself out of the bed.

She laughed and said, "You know me so well." Mechelle pointed to the corner of my bed.

She had laid out an outfit for me. "I get the point, hurry up. Just know I need breakfast," I informed her as I shuffled my feet toward my bathroom.

Mechelle rolled her eyes at me.

"The kitchen's closed. We're going to lunch, but I suppose we could go somewhere you can get breakfast," Michelle advised me.

"A Denny's Moon's Over My Hammy sounds good to me," I hollered. I showered and dressed quickly. Rather than dry my hair, I made a loose braid. I slapped on mascara and tinted lip gloss for a clean inspection.

While Mechelle drove us to Denny's I texted everyone and asked for a meeting. I wasn't getting my work out in, so I asked them to meet us at a local park. I promised subs and cold drinks. Everyone was going to bring their pads for sparring. I texted Phyllis to let her know we would not be there for dinner.

Mechelle seemed a bit disappointed we would not have the entire day to shop. I knew we were getting a late start, but the meeting was important. Shocked I finished everything on my plate, but I didn't regret it.

Mechelle and I were able to get some shopping done at St. Matthew's Mall. We spent hours going through Dillards, Ulta Beauty,

Forever 21, and Hollister. We got great deals on the items we bought. It was nice being able to afford these things. When we lived in Florida, Mechelle would be the one purchasing most of the items. Mom might give me thirty dollars and I would need to make it stretch.

On the way back home, I placed an order with a local sub shop. We needed to drop off our bags and change quickly. Mechelle and I filled our arms and banged on the back door.

Phyllis opened it and saw how much we had and said, "Hal's in the shower. Just teleport up to your room. Phyllis fished the mirror from my pocket and held it for me to use since my hands were full. I dropped my bags next to my bed and used the full-length mirror to take Mechelle to her room before using a mirror in Mechelle's room to return to Phyllis to get my mirror.

After a quick change we jumped in my car to get the subs. Everything was ready when we returned.

Surprisingly, it was difficult to get a parking spot. Mechelle and I had to circle around several times until one became available. The gang had secured a picnic table for us.

As we ate, we discussed everything that was going on with April. Jacob suggested we bug her phone. "Great idea. We'll know when and where they will be meeting. I suspect she had a burner phone. She would not be doing this on her business or personal phone.

Jacob commented, "She must keep the burner on her all the time. I'll need access to the phone. Have you been in her hotel room?"

I responded, "No, but I know what hotel she's in." We determined we would go that night at 10:00 pm. April should have been fast asleep by then.

A phone call came in and I glanced down to see it was Tonya. I motioned for everyone to give me a minute. I answered, "Hello this is Brooke."

Tonya informed me we would be closing on Monday because I was paying cash for the property. She told me the inspection went well and only minor issues were found. The owner would have the items fixed before the closing. I hung up the phone trying to hold back my excitement. I wanted to surprise everyone and right then wasn't the time.

I had a plan.

We cleaned up our trash and were a bit full for a workout. I should have insisted on the workout first, but it was good to have everyone together.

We researched the things we would like to do when we went to Italy in a few weeks a few weeks from then. Jacob jotted everything down and tracked who was interested in what. We were going to try and tackle the items most of us were interested in.

A man came up. His eyes were wide and a bit out of breath. He asked, "Excuse me, my daughter is missing. Have you seen a ten-year-old around here? She's wearing a white shirt with a red elephant on it."

Greg answered, "No but we'll help you look."

We all stood. The man explained she had been on the playground while he cooked them some hotdogs. He called her when they were ready, but she was gone. He told us her name was Annie.

Jacob put his computer in his trunk.

Juliet said, "Jake and I will go with him." They rushed off hollering for Annie.

Lord, please help us locate Annie. Please let me know the best way to find her. Amen.

Austin and Mechelle said they would search the parking lots. Greg told them we would search the wooded area. We moved along the dirt path hollering for Annie.

Suddenly, a bird flew down and nearly hit me twice.

I asked, "Are you trying to tell me something?" The bird hovered in front of me. "Okay, you have my attention."

Greg said, "That is so weird."

He continued calling out for Annie while we followed the bird. Who had taken off through the trees. We picked up our pace. It flew back like it was making sure we were following. It circled around me before it continued in the direction it was heading. I dodged tree limbs but foliage along the path slapped me in the shins. A man was about to get into a van a short distance away. The bird shot off toward the man and attacked him.

Greg hollered, "Just go!"

I pulled out my mirror and teleported to the side of the van. The least of my worries was someone seeing me. The bird flew to the top of the van and rested. The bird stared at me and squawked.

The man looked at me and asked, "Where did you come from?"

It seemed to be a rhetorical question.

As soon as he opened the van door, the bird attacked him. He tried to shoo the bird away. "Stupid bird."

I raced over to the van door to prevent him from shutting it. I asked. "You haven't seen a girl wondering around here by herself, have you?"

"No. Now let go of my door. I need to go," he insisted.

Greg caught up to me and pulled the door wider.

The man pulled back and asked, "What is your problem?"

I asked, "Would you please open the back of your van. We just want to confirm she's not inside.

He scrunched up his face and moved it toward mine and said, "I don't have to do anything. Now move out of my way before I call the cops."

Greg suggested, "Why don't you call the cops?"

The man tried to peel Greg's hands off the door.

What if she's in there?

Using the power of persuasion, I told him to open the back door to the van.

He stopped fighting and I motioned for Greg to move out of his way. He shuffled to the back of the van and unlocked it. When the door swung open, a young girl was curled up in the fetal position with her mouth, hands, and feet taped.

Greg flung the man to the ground and tossed me his phone. He hollered, "Dial 911."

"Sweetie, we are here to help," I said trying to let her know this horrific incident was nearly over. The 911 operator answered. I told her what was happening. After she said vehicles had been dispatched. I was given permission to remove the tape from her. Before doing so I snapped a quick picture for the police.

I climbed in the vehicle and tried removing the tape from her mouth. Unfortunately, the tape was caught in her hair. As I pulled, she squeezed her eyes shut.

"I'm so sorry little lady." Once removed, it revealed a small piece of rolled up cloth was shoved in her mouth as well. She said nothing and just stared at me while I untied her hands. Sirens could be heard in the distance. Once her hands were free, she sat up and hugged my neck. Tears streamed down her face.

I held her until the officers showed up. She did not want me to release her. I rocked her as the officers cut the tape from her legs. They tried to ask her questions, but she just held on to me. Greg pulled his phone from my pocket and called Jacob to tell him where we were. He said they would bring the father over and let the others know.

I wiggled to the end of the van and held her until the ambulance driver asked us to come to their vehicle. I tried to calm her down as they checked her vitals.

Greg could be heard telling the officers how we discovered her. He left out a few details about the bird and me teleporting to prevent him from leaving. He simply told them; we noticed a man by himself closing the back of his van. We asked him to allow us to see inside and he refused.

A few minutes later Jacob pulled up with Juliet and Annie's father. Her dad eased her out of my arms and consoled her. An officer approached me and took my statement. The officer thanked me for taking the picture that Greg had provided to them.

Once the commotion ended and Greg and I were released. Everyone gathered in my backyard and hung out by a small fire until Jacob and I needed to leave for April's hotel room.

Fourteen

Jacob and I arrived invisibly at the hotel lobby. A man stood behind the reception counter playing on his phone. I suspected he did not have many people wandering in at this hour.

On our way to her room, we came across an intoxicated couple. The lady dropped her purse and Jacob politely picked it up. I believe he had forgotten he was invisible. The woman backed into the wall with her eyes and mouth wide open. She appeared to be in shock as she fell to the floor. It was at that moment I believe Jacob remembered because he told her, "I'm the ghost of Christmas past…"

With the back of my hand, I slapped his arm gently.

The man laughed and said, "You've gone and made a ghost mad." He continued laughing as his attention was drawn to the purse.

The woman appeared to be trying to focus on her floating purse. She blinked her eyes a few times and flung her hands up. Her gaze moved to the man. She managed to spurt out, "Come help me get up." He ignored her as he focused on the purse.

Jacob reached down and tried to help her up. He turned to me and said, "She's dead weight."

The drunk man asked, "Who said that?" He spun himself around and nearly fell over.

I caught the woman under one arm and Jacob had the other. We managed to get her back on her feet. Her head wobbled as her eyes darted around. "Thank you, Mr. Ghost."

Jacob tried to hand her the purse. After a few tries she grasped it. At that point, I yanked Jacob's arm and pulled him away. Neither of us could hold back our laughter.

Suddenly, the door next to us flung open. A man inspected the area and noticed the intoxicated couple stammering toward us.

He said in a loud whisper, "Quiet down."

The woman shushed her friend.

We picked up our pace. Once we were at the door to Room 205. I went through it and pulled Jacob in behind me. I moved my finger to my mouth to remind him to be quiet. I told him using telepathy he needed to work quickly. Jacob nodded.

He located April's phone on her nightstand. He went to work setting up the tap on her phone. While he worked, I searched her room. She had amazing taste in clothes. Her computer was on the desk. Using telepathy, I told Jacob he might want to check it. Next to the computer was a notebook.

I brought it to the window to use the moonlight to be able read it better. It appeared to be a field journal and contained details about her team, but the rest was vague information like dates, times and a few names, nothing that seemed familiar. No mission information was disclosed. I flipped through the pages to see if there was anything of value.

What's this?

Tucked in the back of the book was a note with a bunch of numbers on it.

1-20-20-6-10-9-8- -6-10- -10-12-10-21-6-3-6-9-12-10

I stared at the numbers. There seemed to be three groups of numbers.

What does this mean? I need a key.

Suddenly, a glowing key with the alphabet and some numbers appeared on the page. I found a pen on her desk and deciphered the message as I wrote on the palm of my hand. The 1 represented an A, 20 was an L, 6 was a I, 9 was O, and 8 was an N.

Allison?

I continued until I had the message deciphered. It read, 'Allison is suspicious.

She knows. But how?

I wracked my brain trying to think who might know.

Perhaps her secretary or someone on April's team.

I needed to talk to Allison. I tucked the note back in the book and continued searching. Before Jacob returned the phone to her nightstand, I rummaged through it. April's handgun, some receipts, lip gloss, and another phone were in the drawer. I showed Jacob the phone. He nodded. I moved to the bathroom. There was nothing of significance there.

A soft voice said, "I'll get them."

I returned to Jacob. It appeared April had talked in her sleep but stopped abruptly and rested quietly with a small amount of drool coming from the corner of her mouth.

Jacob worked on the phone found in the drawer.

While I waited for Jacob to finish, I peaked at the view from her room. The streets were quiet in what I considered a beautiful city. The little pieces of history scattered throughout the area made it charming. Historical Williamsburg or parts of Saint Augustine were the closest I could compare but this place had more appeal.

Jacob tapped me on the shoulder and gave me a thumbs up. He locked his arm in mine, and we returned to my room. We took turns changing before teleporting to the garage.

Juliet and Greg were the only ones still there. I asked, "Where's Austin and Mechelle?"

Juliet leaped up. "Austin went home, and Mechelle went to shower and go to bed. I'm going to follow her lead. Goodnight." She seized Jacob's hand and strolled off toward Jacob's car. Jacob waved as he left.

I cuddled up next to Greg. "Are you tired too?"

Greg kissed me on the forehead and said, "Surprisingly, I'm wide awake."

"I'm not either," I said softly. I watched the flame lightly flicker and dance around.

Greg sat up and removed his arm from around my shoulders. He seemed to be searching for something on his phone. "I'm hungry. How about a trip to Sydney, Australia?"

I was surprised by his question. "Really?"

"Why not? It's nearly 10:00 pm here. It must be about 4 o'clock over there," Greg said reaching out his arm for me.

I placed my hand in his and I hopped out of my seat. We went into the garage and put our phones on the top of my car. Fortunately, I had the credit card Leonardo had given me to use. For that night, I would be Lillie Watchman.

We appeared just outside the restaurant invisibly. The restaurant had a breathtaking view of the Sydney Opera House. Greg led me into the Aria Restaurant. A quick glance at all the well-dressed men and women screamed we were underdressed. Greg gave me sad puppy dog eyes.

I squeezed his hand and pulled him back outside. We were still invisible as we strolled around. Enjoying the beauty of the area. Tourists stood by the Opera House snapping pictures. We tried to find casual restaurants but there did not appear to be any in the area. Suddenly, it started to rain, and I raised my head and welcomed the rain on my face. This made me smile. I loved the rain.

Greg turned his gaze to me as a spun around. He returned the smile, but his eyes quickly widened, and his mouth flew open. His head pivoted left toward a group of people.

What are they doing?

Greg's eyes nearly popped out of his head. He whispered, "We need to go."

Confused I said using telepathy, "Why? I'm having fun." I twirled again.

He answered, "Brooke, were invisible." His eyes widened.

"I know. What's the problem?"

He pointed in the direction of a few people snapping photos. "Brooke, the water must be making a silhouette of us," he said in a panic.

What? No!

I clutched his arm, and we arrived in the garage.

At first, we were both rattled. Unexpectedly, Greg started laughing. I followed his lead. Once we calmed down, we both decided to turn in for the night. We gathered our phones and locked up the garage.

He pulled me to him, "This is going to be a day to remember." Greg gently pressed his lips to mine, and they lingered for a moment. "I love you." He kissed me again. "Now off to bed," he said as he released me.

"I love you too." Greg watched me as I entered my home. I noticed through the window, Greg stayed until I locked the door.

I cleaned up before sliding into bed. My phone received a reminder about the closing.

How could I have forgotten?

I will be getting my office building the following day. It became hard to fall asleep because my mind was racing with everything that needed to be done.

My alarm woke me up and I fought the urge to go back to sleep.

Why did I set the alarm?

I opened my eyes. Suddenly, I remembered the closing was that morning. I leapt from my bed and dressed for my run.

There's no time for a full workout.

I waved to the neighbors I occasionally passed. My routine frequently changed for safety reasons. I was focused on my breathing for a while, but my mind wandered. I ran different conversations in my head about how to surprise everyone with the office opening and already having a case.

I turned down a street I rarely chose and saw two ladies, each trying to hold back their large dogs as the dogs barked and tried lunging at one another. The women struggled to keep their pets apart. I slowed my pace and focused on calming the canines down. The dogs relaxed.

Without asking I crouched down and said, "Now, you need to be nice. No one is here to hurt you." I patted them on the head.

The lady with the German Shepard said, "How did you do that?"

"I just have a way with animals," I said before I sprinted away.

After I showered, I perused my closet for a professional outfit. There weren't many. I needed to go shopping. I dressed.

While applying my makeup, someone knocked at my door, and I hollered, "Come in."

Mechelle strolled in. "Would you mind dropping me off at the villa again?"

I did this on a regular basis because she grew bored when Austin and I were busy. "Absolutely. Just give me a minute to get dressed. I settled on white slacks and a blue and white striped blouse."

Mechelle asked, "What are you getting all dressed up for?"

"Phyllis and I have an appointment," I replied. Mechelle knew me well enough to know not to ask additional questions if I was vague. When I exited the bathroom, Mechelle sat on my bed.

She asked, "Are you ready?"

I nodded and told her I would get her before dinner.

Okay, one last look.

I peered into my full-length mirror to approve my outfit for the day. I hurried toward the kitchen. I browsed the pantry for a snack. Since Phyllis and I were going to lunch after our meeting, I selected a granola bar. I ripped it open.

Phyllis pulled the pantry door open wider. She asked teasingly, "What are you getting into?"

I consumed it quickly because it was nearly time to leave. On the way to Mr. Thomas's office, Phyllis and I discussed how things were going with the closing of her house. She explained it should still be a few more weeks.

As I approached the law office, I was reminded about the first-time meeting Mr. Thomas. That was the day my life changed. Just as he had done that day, he greeted us and led us to the conference room. Mr. Thomas introduced us to the current owner and their attorney who sat at the far side of the table.

We chose a seat and finalized the sale of the building. Everything went so smoothly.

Thank you, Jesus.

As they handed me the keys, I realized the responsibility was now being handed to me.

I can do this.

I held back my enthusiasm until Phyllis, and I were in the car.

"I can't believe it! Phyllis, I own a business," I boasted.

Phyllis let me carry on for a while as she drove us to Doc Crows, which had the best Shrimp Po-Boy in town with its mouthwatering remoulade. I savored every bite.

We had some time to kill before meeting the interior decorator I hired for the office. Phyllis helped me select some professional outfits since I was the proud owner of Davis International Investigative Service.

I had chosen Davis in honor of my grandmother.

We pulled up to the property a few minutes early and found two people peaking in the windows.

I called out to them, "Can I help you?"

A beautiful Spanish woman turned around. "We're here to see Brooke Garrison," she said with a bit of an accent.

I introduced myself.

She smiled and said, "I'm Angela and this is Juan. We are the interior decorators."

I spent the next few hours explaining the needs for the spaces while they tossed ideas at me. They came prepared with samples of fabrics, paint colors, and various types of granite and tiles. They also had plenty of examples of flooring. Once we reviewed a few sketches, we discussed fabrics, colors, and styles and we developed a plan.

After more discussions, we agreed on a price. I explained there would be a hefty bonus if the project was completed within the following two weeks.

I told her I would trust her vision. I knew from her website I had liked her style and felt comfortable with leaving everything to her. She would be sending me a contract the following morning.

As exciting as it was working with them, I was exhausted. I told Phyllis I would meet her at home. We decided to order Chinese after I returned.

Before leaving, I glanced around trying to picture the rooms when they were done with it. The bare space would soon be transformed into an amazing space. I smiled as I captured a mental image before teleporting to Italy.

I set off to find Mechelle. Leonardo was talking to a guest and nodded at me when I passed by him. Mechelle was behind the front desk checking a customer in. She had no idea I was watching her. I lifted the Bloom of Dreams from my neck to confirm my suspicions. Mechelle was speaking Italian to the guests. She had accomplished a great deal in a short amount of time. I could not believe how well she was doing already. A moment after she made a call, a young man showed up, picked up the guest luggage and led them to their room.

Mechelle saw me and said, "I can't believe it's time to go. Give me a minute, I need to tell Isabella I'm leaving." She turned to the phone and made a call. I perused through the brochures of the things to do in Florence while I waited.

Mechelle called out, "I'm ready to go, but we need to stop off at the kitchen before we leave."

Chef Giovanni greeted Mechelle and I when we entered the kitchen. He said, "Ms. Brooke, it's so nice to see you here."

After a brief conversation about how much he loved working with Mechelle, he informed his staff about an order that needed to be packed up.

I figured Mechelle needed to take it to a guest's room, but when he returned, he said, "Enjoy."

I asked, "Is this for us?"

Chef Giovanni replied, "Yes. Spezzatino made with lamb."

I thanked him. Mechelle snatched the food from him. As we entered my room, I asked what Spezzatino was. She informed me it was stew.

We returned home and enjoyed our meal. Phyllis was thankful she had not needed need to cook or order Chinese. It was difficult keeping the events of the day a secret from Mechelle.

Fifteen

I was awakened by a call from Jacob. In a groggy voice I asked, "Isn't this a little early for you?"

I know it is for me.

"I was alerted by a text April received on the second phone you found in her room. Somethings about to go down. She texted that she was in the U.S. and would call after a meeting with her boss. Did you talk to Allison?"

Immediately, I sat up and was wide awake.

How could I have forgotten?

"No. I forgot." I noticed the clock. 6:30 am.

I need to get dressed.

"She didn't say when the meeting was, but it sounded like this morning. You need to tell her," Jacob urged.

"Yes. I'm on it," I blurted before hanging up. I texted Mechelle and told her to let Phyllis know I needed to leave. I jumped in the shower and wore one of my professional outfits because I didn't know if she would want me in the meeting or not. I teleported upstairs to get a granola bar from the gym. Phyllis always made sure I was prepared.

I waited for her to arrive as it was 7:18 am. For the first 15 minutes I stood.

I need coffee.

The next ten minutes were spent leaning on Allison's desk. My body needed caffeine. I plopped myself into the desk chair and put my head down. Seconds later the office door flung open causing me to jerk back in the chair.

Allison nearly spilled her coffee. She shut the office door and whispered, "Brooke?"

"Yes. We need to talk," I answered as I moved out of her chair and to the opposite side of the desk she was approaching from.

Allison plopped her things down on the corner of her desk. "Where are you?"

"In front of your desk," I answered. "It's my understanding April is coming here to meet you today."

"Yes, she'll be here at 8:30 am," she sipped her coffee.

"She's leading you to believe she's on your team. I don't know how to tell you but she's the one that met up with Mark to buy the guns," I explained. I continued telling her everything I knew.

"I'm going to tell her I invited you to the meeting. You can't just appear here. This building has a great deal of security." She flipped through her phone. "This is my building. You can appear over here. She pointed to some bushes on the side of the building. I'll call security and tell them you're expected. You'll need an ID and dress professional," she instructed as she turned her computer on. "Be back here no later than 8:30 am."

An ID.

I teleported home to grab my ID and some coffee. Phyllis and Mechelle were chatting as Mechelle poached some eggs.

"Good morning," I said as I poured a coffee cup.

"We weren't expecting you back so early," Mechelle said pulling a piece of toast from the toaster. "Do you want breakfast?"

"Only if it's quick. I need to be back at Allison's office in a few minutes.

Mechelle placed the poached egg on top of the toast which was covered with guacamole. She added salt and pepper. Phyllis picked up the plate and placed it in front of me with some silverware and a napkin.

"Looks delicious," I said after a quick prayer.

Mechelle continued making breakfast for her and Phyllis while I tried to fill them in between bites on the mission of the day. I thanked them for the meal and teleported myself back to my bathroom to brush my teeth and touch up my lip-gloss. One final glimpse in the mirror before grabbing my ID and teleporting to the bush by Allison's building.

Once the coast was clear I appeared and confidently strutted into the building. I was greeted by a security guard.

He sternly said, "ID."

Well, hello to you too.

I presented my ID. "I'm here to see Allison Dunara."

"Tenth floor," he said handing my ID back along with a guest pass.

There's a man that doesn't seem to like his job.

I put my ID in my pocket and hurried to the elevator. It was packed with people, but a handsome man moved to allow me in. I glanced at the buttons and noticed the tenth floor had been pushed.

It was a relief when people exited. As I escaped the packed elevator I was greeted by a receptionist.

"Ms. Garrison please follow me," she instructed before she headed down the hall. We made our way to Allison's office where I was handed off to Allison's personal secretary.

She leered at me before opening Allison's office door. "Ms. Garrison is here to see you."

I was barely in the door when the secretary closed it.

Allison smiled and said, "Have a seat, Brooke. April is on her way up now. Do you want a coffee or anything?"

I assured her I was fine. We talked about how things were going with my business until April was announced. Once we made eye contact, she seemed rather surprised I was there. She sat and waited for Allison to address her.

"I'm disappointed in the outcome of capturing the arms dealer. I expected more from both of you," Allison said firmly. She turned to me. "Ms. Garrison, thank you for keeping me updated on the situation that kept you from being at the exchange. I understand somethings are just unavoidable."

I gloated a little knowing Allison's story was a ruse.

"Now, we've received some intel that might be credible about a homeless man coming across what we presume are the weapons in a tunnel." She handed both of us a file. Allison continued, "This contains information on how to find the location they are being stored." I expect you both to do whatever is necessary to get those weapons off the streets and to catch those trying to sell them. I don't expect you to work together but I do expect you to keep each other aware of anything you discover about the people moving them."

We both nodded and perused through the folder.

"Ms. Duncan, I expect you to be back in Plymouth within the next two days. I'm interested to see the explanation of why your mission was unsuccessful. Have it on my desk before you leave today. Now, you may go," Allison said.

April stood up and squinted at me before quickly turning away.

Allison turned to me. "Ms. Garrison, I would like you to stay for a minute," Allison instructed.

I straightened my shoulders and lifted my chin. With her folder clutched in her hand, April turned and swiftly exited Allison's office.

After the door shut, Allison said, "Have your team keep an eye on her. You're the only person I trust to help find the mole in this office," Allison said encouragingly. She tapped a pen on the desk a couple of times. "Try to find out who she's working with also. I need a strong case against April." She turned to her monitor. A s she focused on her computer she said, "You'll need to go back out the way you came."

I strolled out of the office with the folder in my hand and my head held high. If I was going to continue doing work for Allison, I needed to show those in the office I was a confident young woman. Several eyes were on me as I moved toward the elevator. When the elevator door opened, April leapt in with me.

As soon as the door closed, she said, "I'll check out the tunnel, you concentrate on finding the homeless man. See what he knows about who stowed the weapons there. We need detailed descriptions of the people." She hit the button to the fourth floor and hopped off. As the door was closing, she said, "I'm counting on you."

I'm sure you are. You're counting on keeping me busy with a homeless man while you move the guns. I'll make sure we find the homeless man while I keep an eye on what you're up to Ms. April. You may be able to pull one over on Mark, but I know who you really are.

I exited the elevator and dropped off the guest pass I had been given. Something told me April might be watching me, so I moved quickly to a nearby parking garage and teleported from a bush beside it.

Before changing, I texted everyone about a meeting for dinner at my house. Juliet was the only one not available.

What am I going to do until the meeting?

I texted Mechelle.

BROOKE: I'm home. Where are you?

MECHELLE: On the upper balcony sunbathing.

I changed into my turquoise bikini and joined her. I filled her in on the meeting with Allison and April. Mechelle told me about a double date she and Austin had with his parents.

With all that had been happening with the business and helping Allison I had not relaxed much. I enjoyed laying in the sun listening to the chirping coming from the nearby trees and the distant voices of children playing. My body gave in to the peace and I dozed off lying on my stomach.

"Brooke...Brooke, you need to wake up," Mechelle urged.

I woke up to drool on my cheek. Without moving I responded, "Why?"

"We both fell asleep. Our skin was red like tomatoes."

I tried to rollover, but the Bloom of Dreams was caught in between the straps of the chair. With a light tug it moved from its position. I rolled over and sat up. "I can't believe I was so tired." The stone heated up, which woke me up immediately. I peered over the balcony to see if someone was approaching the house. There was no one.

Something's not right.

Mechelle, stay here," I said sternly. Suddenly the stone cooled.

What is going on?

I shrugged it off. "Never mind," I said.

Mechelle rolled her eyes and picked up her things. I snatched my towel from the chair and followed her in. "Wow, you are burnt," I commented.

"Wait till you see your back," Mechelle giggled.

I went to Mechelle's bathroom and inspected my back. There was nothing more than a golden tan. "You need to get your eyes checked," I said loud enough for her to hear me in the other room.

Mechelle rushed in. "Let me see."

I turned around and displayed my back for her.

"How is that possible? Brooke, your back was burnt a few minutes ago," she said with her eyes scrunched up.

The stone.

I chuckled. "The stone wasn't touching my skin when I was asleep allowing me to get sunburned. When I sat up, it healed me It wasn't alerting me of danger." I shook my head at my stupidity.

"That's incredible! You have an amazing tan now," Mechelle pivoted exposing her back to me. "Do me," she belted out.

I rolled my eyes and placed my hand on her back. When the stone cooled, I sarcastically announced, "There you're done. That'll be $25 for Brook's perfect tan."

Mechelle rolled her eyes. She spun around trying to see her back before moving to a mirror. "Brooke you're fantastic. Now be gone. I must shower," she said poshly before a smile appeared and she snickered.

Jokingly I raised my eyebrows and dropped my mouth open. She and I both laughed as I exited her room. I needed a shower as well because I smelled a bit ripe.

Mechelle, as usual, took longer than I did to clean up. I ambled downstairs to spend some time with Phyllis. I found her folding clothes. "Want some help?"

Phyllis tossed me a towel. "I'll never turn down an offer for help." She pulled a towel from the dryer and folded it. "It'll be nice when I don't have to try to figure out a way to get Hal out of the house for your meetings. The excuses are draining me."

I selected another towel and lifted my forehead. "How about I treat you to dinner?"

Phyllis put the washcloth she was folding on the pile of towels and gave me a side hug.

"Seriously," I said pulling my credit card from my pocket. "I do have a favor to ask first?" I bit my lip as I waited for her reply.

Phyllis raised one eyebrow and slightly tucked her chin and asked, "What would that be?"

I folded another towel and without turning toward her, I said, "I'm going to fold these towels and put them away while you pretty yourself up. I need you to order some chicken wings and fries for the meeting tonight." I popped my head up at her and put my praying hands up with the towel smashed between them.

"Fine, but I'm choosing the flavors," she said as she enthusiastically snatched my credit card from my hand and exited the laundry room.

I hollered, "Celery too please." An inspection of the dryer revealed we had folded all the towels. Somehow, I knew she was aware there was none left. I couldn't help but laugh.

I rushed to put the towels away and set the table with paper products before Phyllis tried to do it herself. Mechelle caught me off guard when she came into the kitchen while I was stirring up a batch of Tropical Punch Kool-Aid. Without asking Mechelle brought me ice to put in the pitcher.

We had about an hour until the meeting. Mechelle and I poured ourselves a glass of punch and caught up on what had been happening as we sat on the back patio. As we chatted, I wanted to tell her about the building I bought, but she was a Bloom Keeper now and needed to wait to find out with the others. Usually, I confided most things in her and Greg, but I thought they both had come to realize that Bloom Keeper business was different. They would have to find out information when they needed to know.

Fifteen minutes into our conversation, Hal pulled up. He seemed to be hustling to get inside. "Hello, ladies," he said tipping his head in our direction as he passed us.

We both greeted him with a hello.

"Perhaps someone's running late for their date?" Mechelle joked.

"I think you're right," I giggled.

"G'day girls," Greg said in a mock Australian accent as he climbed the stairs with a wry smile. As usual he had my heart pitter pattering. As he moved toward me the breeze blew his cologne in my direction making me feel warm.

Control yourself.

He kissed me before he snuggled up next to me.

Mechelle asked Greg, "Do you want some punch?"

"Sure. Thanks."

Mechelle went inside.

"I've been missing you today," Greg said as he stroked my leg.

"You know that's funny because I've been missing you too."

Greg's eyes were hypnotic as he gazed at me. His gaze locked on my lips as he moved closer. I closed my eyes in anticipation of the gentle touch of his mouth. He certainly did not disappoint me. The tenderness of his kiss withered away as the heat between us increased. I was lost in the pleasure I was experiencing. That was up until the back door flung open.

"Enough of that," Mechelle announced as she handed Greg his drink.

As the two of them talked I was lost thinking about how much Greg, and I desired to be together. Had I thought about becoming more intimate with him? Absolutely. I watched Greg talk to Mechelle about repairing fences with Austin earlier in the day. It boggled my mind when I realized I could have heard the same conversation from someone else and it would have bored me. It confused me why it sounded interesting coming from him. I guess that is what they mean when they say love is blind.

It was nearly time for everyone to arrive. I suggested we move inside. Phyllis was engrossed in her novel when we came in and interrupted her. She placed a bookmark in it and placed it on her lap. Phyllis turned to Greg and asked about his parents.

As Greg was explaining about his mother's complete recovery, Hal trotted down the stairs.

"See sweetheart, I'm still on time," he said to Phyllis.

111

Phyllis stood up. "Thank you again for this Brooke."

I inquired, "Did you remember to bring my card?"

"Yes," Phyllis replied as she kissed me on the top of my head.

Hal shook his head. "Am I to understand Brooke is buying us dinner?"

"Yes, you deserve a nice night out," I replied.

"I'm sorry Brooke, we can't accept. You're not even working right now. You need to save your money for any unexpected business expenses. As a business owner I know they creep up on you when you least expect it," Hal said firmly.

I chuckled.

Such a sweetie.

"Now Hal, I'm not going to argue and you're not going to take away my blessing," I said standing my ground.

"I think she told you dear. Accept her gift graciously," Phyllis replied as she picked up her purse from the desk.

Hal inhaled and exhaled deeply. "Fine, but don't make this a habit," he said. He spun around and followed Phyllis.

The doorbell chimed. Jacob and Juliet came in and joined everyone in the sitting room. He sat and shook his leg. It was bouncing so much Juliet placed her hand on it to try and stop him. I was about to ask what was up when the doorbell chimed again.

The food arrived and Greg and Jacob carried it into the dining room. Juliet and I opened the containers. Mechelle appeared to be texting. I suspected she was trying to find out why Austin was late. When everyone sat, Mechelle darted toward the foyer. She returned with Austin.

We enjoyed our meal before getting to the Bloom Keeper business. I could not help but notice, Jacob gulped down his dinner and did not participate in the conversations going around the table. He was like this the entire meal. As soon as everyone appeared to be done eating, Jacob leapt from his chair and cleared the table.

Greg and I made eye contract. With one brow raised, he nodded his head in Jacob's direction. This was followed by him shrugging his shoulders. I shrugged my shoulder to show my confusion with his behavior.

Jacob returned and plopped himself in his chair and opened his computer. His eyes darted around the room and started tapping his fingers on the table.

Should I let him suffer and delay the start of the meeting? Probably not.

Once everyone had settled back into their chairs, I called the meeting to order. I explained our new mission and we determined who was going to be searching for the homeless man. Juliet would be going with me. Greg and Austin could not come on the assignment.

Jacob spoke up, "I thought for sure April would have contacted the mole following your meeting, but she didn't. I was nearly late getting here because I had to pull over to listen to her. She called someone with a Virginia area code. She told the woman about the mission and about you being at the meeting. She also sent her a jpeg of you." He flipped his computer around exposing a picture of me from the meeting Allison and I had with her.

She had a secret camera. Sneaky little lady.

Jacob continued, "April told her to take care of you. To quote her, 'Brooke has become a problem. Deal with her.' That's all I have right now."

"Wow, thanks Jacob," Greg commented.

We concluded the meeting. Jacob and Juliet rushed out so he could figure out who the mole was. Greg had some things to do at home. I retired to my room to give Austin and Mechelle some quality time alone.

Sixteen

Jacob and Juliet showed up at 7:00 am for breakfast. Hal seemed surprised to see them.

Hal asked, "Where are you three going so early in the morning?"

Jacob spoke up, "Occasionally, we like to get an early start on our training."

Hal nodded and said grace when Phyllis brought in a Cheddar Spinach Frittata with Bacon. The savory custard made my mouth water. Phyllis served it in a cast-iron skillet to keep it warm.

Jacob took a swig of his orange juice. "Phyllis, you should open a restaurant. This is amazing," he said as he shoved another fork full in his mouth.

"There's not enough time in the day for that," she informed him.

Hal rushed through his meal and excused himself as he hurried off to work. As soon as we knew he had left, we went upstairs. We did not wear our Bloom Keepers outfits in case we found a need to talk with April or her men. I teleported us to the tunnel. Once I had my bearings, I sent Jacob toward the exit. We would be meeting him in town later. Juliet and I teleported to the room with the weapons.

Lord, please help him find the homeless man.

Everything was still there. I figured it would be a while before she showed up. Jacob had messaged me in the middle of the night to tell me she was traveling to Plymouth. She would be there early in the morning.

We waited there for hours, and I wondered if Jacob was having any luck. Juliet even dozed off for a while. I found my head bobbing back and forth as my eyelids became like weights. The next thing I knew, my body was shaken. I opened my eyes and saw Juliet above me. She motioned for me to get up. I was up just before the door hurled open. Some men came in and moved the weapons. Using telepathy, I said to Juliet, "April's not here. We need to find out where they are transporting them."

Juliet nodded in agreement.

They picked up the last load. Juliet and I followed the men at a distance. They moved to the exit but not the one Jacob went to. As we excited the tunnel, an unmarked white van waited with the engine idling.

Another stalky man with a ponytail jumped out and opened the back of the van. They started loading the cases.

Suddenly, several cars with dark tinted windows blocked the van and men with guns jumped out taking them by surprise. The driver of the white van got into an altercation with a tall man, but he collapsed to the floor after being struck. The tall man jumped in the van and the other men returned to their vehicles while keeping their guns directed at April's men. They sped away, nearly hitting an oncoming vehicle as they fled.

I grasped Juliet's arm and teleported us to the back of the van. Immediately, we were both flung to the driver's side of the vehicle as it turned. We tried to hold our positions as we bounced around like we were riding a bucking bronco.

It was difficult to keep quiet. Fortunately, we were both determined to remain silent. The van stopped. I slid over to Juliet and laid my hand on her to heal her from any minor injury she may have encountered from the experience.

The driver made a call and told someone to open the door. Suddenly, the van sprang forward. The sunlight entering through the front windshield disappeared. I stuck my head through the wall of the van and discovered we were inside a warehouse.

The vehicle came to a stop. I teleported us just outside the van.

The driver jumped out and opened the back doors of the vehicle. From an office at the far end of the warehouse Mark and Chester came out and were making their way to the van.

Mark said to the driver, "Well done. Perhaps, Ms. Demeanor will think twice about stealing from me." Mark turned to Chester. What kind of a name is that anyway. Ms. Demeanor?

"Don't know but it's clever and I dare say catchy," Chester snickered. "I can't believe she palmed you a load of fake green and folding."

Mark pivoted back to the driver, "Stow those away and dump and torch the van." He and Chester started back to the office. "We are going to need to lay low for a month or so with these. Little Ms. Dodgy should give up searching for them by then."

A month or so.

I placed my hand on Juliet's shoulder and teleported us back to the exit of the cave. April's men were no longer there. We met Jacob at Plymouth's Central Park. We picked the park because of the location and the extensive amount of foliage. We appeared in a heavily wooded area near a path. Once the coast was clear we became visible. We rushed over to the picnic tables for our meet up, but Jacob had not arrived yet.

Juliet scanned the area. She asked, "Shouldn't he be here by now?"

She was right. We had been gone for hours and he had plenty of time to find the homeless man and meet us. I replied, "Perhaps he had to use the restroom."

Come on Jacob.

I scanned the area too hoping for a glimpse of him.

We waited nearly thirty minutes. Juliet now had her arms and legs crossed and was shaking her foot.

"I'm sure he's fine," I said encouragingly.

Lord, please let Jacob be okay.

Another thirty minutes passed. Juliet paced and ranted about the fact we should not have left him by himself.

Perhaps she's right.

I felt a lump in my throat as I thought about the many things that might have gone wrong.

Fifteen minutes later, Juliet plopped down on the bench in tears. She uttered, "I know something bad has happened." Tears streamed down her face.

I moved next to her and wrapped my arm around her. "It's going to be okay," I said not knowing if I was being truthful.

"What's going to be, okay?"

I flung myself around as I heard his voice. The sight of Jacob standing in front of me alive released tears of joy from my eyes. Juliet jumped up and flung her arms around him. After a moment, she stepped back and demanded an answer to where he had been.

"I wandered around the area trying to find homeless people. There were a few that lead me to the man I needed. I explained to him his life was in danger. We pulled some clothes off a close line for him, and I snagged a hat from someone that left it on a picnic table. This should help him from being discovered so easily."

Juliet interrupted, "Where is he?"

"He's hiding back there," Jacob nodded his head toward the wooded area.

I asked, "He's here?"

"Yah. I couldn't leave him there. I figured we could come up with a safe place for him to hide," Jacob answered as he sat on the top of the picnic table with his legs dangling off. "Oh, I saw April."

He motioned for Juliet to come to him. Juliet didn't hesitate and stood in front of him with her arms wrapped around his waist.

I rolled my eyes. I hollered, "Jacob! Tell us about April."

Jacob threw his head back. "Oh, yah. Well, she was watching me as I talked to the homeless people. She was in a nearby car. I darted off between some buildings. Eventually, I lost her. While I was hiding, I came across Kyle."

Juliet asked, "Kyle's the homeless guy?"

"Yah, he's been hiding out since he came across the weapons. To quote Kyle, 'Several dodgy looking geezers' have been questioning people to try and find his whereabouts."

I said sarcastically, "Where do you suggest we take him?"

"I don't know but your cousin needs his testimony. Perhaps she can suggest a place," he snapped.

I bit my lip and lowered my head before making eye contact with Jacob. "That's a great idea." I searched for somewhere to teleport from. The only area was the area Kyle was in. I asked Jacob and Juliet to keep him distracted. I would go behind him and teleport to Allison's office.

As we approached Kyle, I noticed he was a tad husky. His long beard had a bit of gray going down both sides of his mouth. He was wearing a ball cap, jeans, and a T-shirt. Jacob talked to him. I nodded as I moved past them and teleported before he had time to turn around.

Allison was eating a salad when I arrived. As a joke, I quietly snatched a few paper clips and let them cascade back into the container.

This sent her back in her chair. Her eyes darted around the room. "Brooke?"

I laughed. "Sorry, I couldn't resist." I explained the situation to her.

"It's not safe to leave him in the UK. April is aware of all the safehouses there. Take him to Leonardo. He'll take care of him until

I can find out who the mole is here," Allison said. She tapped on her glass before she drank it. "I'll call him and let him know you are on your way. He can bill the room to us once this is settled."

Before returning to Plymouth, I stopped by the house for a dark pillowcase. I snuck up behind Kyle to make sure he did not see me appear.

After introducing myself to him, I said, "Kyle today is your lucky day. You're going on a trip," I exclaimed. Using telepathy, I told Jacob and Juliet we would be taking him to the villa, which was about nine hours of traveling. I attempted to place the pillowcase on his head, and he backed away from me.

Kyle nervously said, "What's that for?"

We're going to take you to a safe place to protect you. It's for your own protection we can't disclose the location.

"That sounds fishy," Kyle said stepping back more.

Jacob raised his hands up and said, "Jacob, I assure you we are going to protect you. You'll have a nice room and free food, and housekeeping."

This is ridiculous.

I concentrated on convincing Kyle to allow me to blindfold him. I placed the bag on his head and teleported him to the area near the cabin Kevin had shown me. We walked him around for a while to tire him out. When he asked us to stop, I teleported us to the villa and motioned for Jacob to provide him with the desk chair so he could sit. Using telepathy, I told them I would be back. I arrived at Isabella's room, but it was empty. I found her talking with a guest at the entrance.

After a quick explanation of the situation, she told me she would have Leonardo meet me in their room.

He showed up a few minutes later. Leonardo darted into his bedroom and returned. He clutched my arm and nodded.

I teleported us to my room.

"Kyle, my name is Leonardo. You'll be coming with me to a secure location with a shower and splendid food. When you wake, you'll need to shower. There will be clean clothes for you. Dial zero when you are dressed. To protect you we'll need to get you a shave and a haircut. Do you understand?"

Kyle nodded.

Leonardo pulled a cloth and a vial from his pocket. He dabbed the cloth with the liquid from the vial and shoved it under the pillowcase. Almost instantly, Kyle fell over, but Leonardo caught him and asked us to help move him to the bed. "He'll sleep for hours," Leonardo assured us as he pulled the pillowcase off Kyle's head.

I returned Leonardo back to his room before arriving in the pantry with Juliet and Jacob because we were all starving. I called out to Phyllis when I opened the pantry door. There was no answer.

Jacob had moved to the back door. "Her car's gone."

I pulled out a bowl of grapes from the fridge and snagged a few before placing the bowl on the counter. There seemed to be a small battle for each of us to grab a few to devour. I made us a couple of peanut butter and jelly sandwiches to split. Once our stomachs settled down, we filled Jacob in on what had happened with the weapons.

Everyone suspected April was angry. We just could not figure out how Mark found out where they were stored. Jacob had some side work to do, so he and Juliet left a short while later.

Wanting to read Phyllis's new book, I picked it up along with my glass of fruit punch and meandered to the patio. I curled up on the sofa. I glanced at the cover.

Okay, Audrey Rich, what's Trina Weber up to now.

I was several chapters into 'Thinking About Love' when Phyllis's car caught my attention. I tried to finish the last few paragraphs on the page while I waited for her.

I was surprised when I was greeted by Mechelle. "I didn't know you were with Phyllis," I commented. Honestly, I was so self-absorbed, I had not noticed she was gone.

Shame on you, Brooke.

Phyllis asked me to run a few errands and have lunch with her," she said with a smile and then winked at Phyllis.

Odd.

I narrowed my eyes and tilted my head. "Is there something I should know?"

They both laughed. When they had settled down Phyllis explained she had been approved to purchase the house. She and Mechelle went down to tell Hal and to celebrate with him.

Seventeen

The next week and a half, I was busy with getting the final touches on my contracts and forms done for Davis International Investigative Service.

Boy, I love the sound of that.

Phyllis was going to keep Mechelle busy while I picked up the documents from the printer. Angela had asked me to come by the office because she wanted to run an idea by me.

My car was packed with the forms and the office essentials we needed. I pulled up to the Davis International Investigative Service and was shocked at the exterior. The paint had been refreshed and the yard had a wide walkway leading to the front entrance. The landscaping was done beautifully and did not appear it would require a great deal of maintenance.

Once parked, I texted her to let her know I had arrived. She and Juan greeted me on the walkway.

"Brooke. I must be honest, the only remaining thing we need to do is show you your new office," Angela said grinning.

"Really?"

She and Juan led me to the front patio. As they opened the door, they looked at me.

I jumped up and down enthusiastically. "This is perfect!" My eyes darted around the room as I entered. I did not know where to begin the tour. My eyes darted around to try and take everything in. Everything was so tastefully done. She had captured the modern farmhouse style I liked. The mixtures of wood and iron worked perfectly together with the soft grays and off whites. The kitchen opened onto the living room. Beams of exposed wood along the ceiling added to its charm.

I turned to them. "This is magnificent! The reception area doesn't take away from the charm of the rest of the area," I said as I ran my hand against the fabric on the chair. I stood there taking in everything from the painting of the horse above the fireplace to the hint of green plants in the room. She opened the kitchen cabinets and drawers revealing the off-white China and silverware she had provided.

Angela guided me to the first office, which was the larger of the two guest bedrooms. Along one wall was a single desk. It matched the two desks that ran along the wall with a window.

Juan motioned to the single desk. "That one is for you," he announced.

Three walls were covered in an off-white painted shiplap. The wall behind my desk was painted with large horizontal black and off-white stripes. There was a painting of a lamb directly behind my desk. Perched in the corner of the desk was a picture of my grandmother and me. "Where did you get this?"

Angela smiled. "Mr. Thomas came by a few times to make sure things were moving along smoothly. On one of his trips, he provided me the photograph," she replied. She pointed to a table along the opposite wall of the windows. "Your printer and copy machine can go over there."

I nodded and moved into the other office. It had bulkier wood furniture. I had to chuckle when I saw a picture of a bull behind one of the desks and a cow behind the other. The two desks faced one another. Each side of the room was almost a mirror image of the other, other than the paintings. The walls behind the desks had small wood pieces creating a feature wall, which was a dark forest green.

The guest bathroom did not disappoint. Off white cabinets that ran along the wall, black framed mirrors adorned a ship lap wall. The other walls were a soft beige.

Angela commented, "We removed the shower out of this room because we needed more room for the offices and storage."

"I suppose it would be a little odd having a shower in an office bathroom," I replied.

"We still have the shower in the master bedroom," Juan said motioning me out of the bathroom.

I entered and the first thing that came to mind was that Jacob was going to love it. The back wall had a feature wall like the one in Jacob's office. There was a metal chandelier in the center of the room. A small sitting area with two chairs and a small table between them was on the opposite wall to the bed. The large walk-in closet came equipped with drawers for socks and things leaving no need for a dresser. The master bath was designed the same as the other bathroom, only it had a walk-in shower and double sinks.

Words escaped me for a moment. "This is far more than I expected. Thank you," I said as I pulled Angela in for a hug. When I let go, Juan approached for his much-needed embrace.

Juan said, "The electrical work was done by Simon and his assistant. He'll be back to set up anything else you need done once your equipment is in. He's quite good with computers too if you need them set up."

"We have a computer specialist. Thanks, I'll have Jacob contact him," I said as I reached out for Simon's business card from Juan.

They handed me the key and explained the sign would not be ready for a few more days. They said their goodbyes before leaving.

Perfect!

I texted the Bloom Keepers and told them there was an emergency. I provided my new business address with a brief blurb about dinner being provided. Thankfully they had no idea about the building. Sadly, I could not invite Phyllis because we would be discussing the Bloom Keeper business. She would need to wait until the official opening.

I placed an order for dinner to be delivered thirty minutes after their expected arrival time. I teleported home to get dressed in one of my professional business suits. I tried to be discreet when Mechelle came by my room.

She asked, "What time are we leaving?"

"Oh, I'm sorry but I've some things to take care of. I'll need to meet you there," I said.

"No worries," she said before closing my door.

When it was nearly time. I teleported over and set the table for six. I shut the lights off and waited for everyone to arrive.

The doorbell chimed. I teleported invisibly outside to see who was there. Austin and Greg were patiently waiting for me to answer. They rang the bell again.

"Brooke's car is here but it doesn't look like she or anyone else is here," Austin said.

They both sat on a bench and talked about their day. Jacob and Juliet pulled up with Mechelle right behind them. I teleported myself back into the building and started turning on the lights. Suddenly, the doorbell chimed again. Once all the lights were on, I opened the door and let them in.

Mechelle commented, "This place is gorgeous."

Juliet agreed and asked, "What are we doing here?"

I asked them to have a seat before I explained what I had been keeping from them.

Austin asked, "So you really are going to hire us?"

"Absolutely. I have drawn up contracts for each of you. I do ask that you keep the details of your salary, and any details of this business, a secret, as you would with any position. The letters are in an envelope on your desks," I said.

Mechelle asked, "Our desks?"

"Yes, but your desk is a little far, so I placed yours on the reception desk," I said pointing to the envelope. Everyone went searching for the first office with the three desks.

"There's not an envelope on that desk," Jacob commented.

I smiled. "That's mine. You and Juliet's are in the next room."

I followed them, leaving Austin and Greg spinning around in their new office chairs with their contracts clinched in their hands.

"Brooke, this is stunning," Juliet said as her eyes danced around the room.

Greg and Austin peeked in before strolling toward the back of the house.

Greg hollered, "Brooke are you moving in here?"

Everyone made their way to the master bedroom.

Greg repeated his question.

I shook my head. "No," I said pivoting toward Jacob. "Jacob, with all the snooping and things you do, I thought it best you are not living in your parents' home. Your salary includes living here."

His eyes widened and his mouth dropped open. Immediately he put his hands over his mouth and stepped back. He asked, "Are you serious?"

I replied, "I am. However, you must keep this place clean. I don't want to be coming in here to work and have dishes and things all over the place."

"Deal," he exclaimed.

"Phyllis and Hal will be moving out in a few weeks. She'll still be working for me, but Hal won't be underfoot any longer. Mechelle's moving to Italy soon. Juliet, you could move in with me. That would make things easier when we go on a mission and I will have another girl to hang out with," I suggested.

"You know Austin with your new salary you should be able to move closer to the office. The thirty minutes it takes can mean a world of difference when we must rush off somewhere," I suggested.

"I don't know the city is pretty expensive," Austin commented.

I watched them.

No one has opened their letters.

I asked, "Why have none of you read the contracts?"

Everyone's eyes darted from one person to another. It was as if they didn't know how to respond.

"Go on, open them," I demanded.

The shock on their faces was priceless. Austin even raised his palm and smacked it against his forehead.

"Are you crazy? We can't commit to this amount," Juliet said waving her paper in the air.

"We can. I assure you there have been many people working on this to assure you are taken care of. You'll even have health insurance and a retirement plan," I assured them.

Juliet continued reading her letter. She blurted out, "I'm the CFO!" She was grinning ear to ear.

Greg kissed me. "This is insane I'm the Office Manager as well as an Investigator." he said and kissed me again.

Austin strutted over and said, "That's cool. I'm an Investigator too. Sorry Brooke no kiss from me, but..." He snatched me from Greg and gave me a big bear hug.

Juliet asked, "Jacob, what is your title?"

Jacob tried to hold back his excitement when he replied, "Computer Forensic Scientist."

Mechelle whispered in my ear, "This plus what I'm making at the villa is way too much."

I pulled her away from the others. "Mechelle, your job is just as risky as ours if you get caught. It should be more, but that's all I can offer at this time," I whispered.

"I want you to know when we start making more money and pay back what I borrowed from my account, you'll get a raise but until then I can only guarantee this amount."

Juliet asked, "I guess that makes you the CEO Brooke."

I bowed my head and smiled. "It does."

We were interrupted by the food delivery. Everyone leant a helping hand to get the food from the driver.

I said, "I ordered a bit of everything, I figure we can all get a little of whatever we want. There's..."

"Calamari and mozzarella sticks," Jacob shouted.

"I've lasagna and chicken parmesan in these," Austin added.

Juliet chimed in, "Here's the salad."

"There should be Fettuccine Alfredo and lots of Cheesecake," I commented.

Once everyone had settled in with their plate of food, I continued our conversation about their positions. "Everyone's salary will be effective Monday. I have placed some paperwork that each of you needs to complete in your top desk drawer. Mechelle, I know you have already completed your paperwork for the villa, but you'll need to fill it out for us as well. You'll be on the books as a consultant. If anyone is available to volunteer their time to help me get everything ready for Monday, I would appreciate it."

"Austin and I are going to need to give Bill two weeks' notice," Greg announced.

"I expected that. Just let me know when your start date will be."

"Brooke, I'm amazed you did all of this without us knowing. Well done," Mechelle said.

"I assure you it wasn't easy. Phyllis, Hal, Leonardo, and Mr. Thomas are the only ones that I confided in. I wanted it to be a surprise. Oh, and the decorators," I said as I swirled my pasta on my fork. "I nearly forgot; we have a client already. I texted them earlier to see if they can meet Monday afternoon."

Juliet asked, "What kind of case?"

"I honestly don't know," I said shrugging my shoulders.

"The letter head says Davis International Investigative Service. Lillie would've liked that," Mechelle commented.

We spent the remainder of the evening working out details of who would be able to help and when. Jacob and I had a brief discussion about the electrician, and he would be contacting him.

Everyone helped me unload the office supplies and forms from my car before they left.

Greg followed me home and came over to hang out for a bit on the back patio. We snuggled. I asked, "Are you mad I didn't tell you about what I was doing?"

He chuckled, "No, I think it was a fantastic surprise. I'm very impressed. The place is incredible." Greg started playing with my fingers. "Brooke, I'm very proud of you. Lillie would be too."

The thought of what she would say choked me up a bit. I wished she was still here. I fought letting a yawn out but was unsuccessful.

Greg asked, "You're exhausted, aren't you?"

I flipped my eyes up at him. "Maybe." I bit my lip.

Greg gently turned my lips toward his and kissed me. "Sweetie, you need to go to bed." He helped me up and kissed me on the forehead. "I love you. Now go to bed." He moved me toward the back door.

"Goodnight," I said as I moved through the doorway.

Greg flipped his hand toward me. "Go on."

Once the door was shut, Greg waved before leaving.

Hal and Phyllis were in the sitting room. Phyllis asked, "Where's Mechelle?"

I explained Austin and her were hanging out. I briefly told them how the evening went before ambling up to my room. It had been a long day. I was exhausted and went straight to bed.

Eighteen

Over the next few days Mechelle, Juliet, Jacob, and I set up the office. Everyone completed their paperwork and I processed everything. Greg would be taking over these types of responsibilities when he started. The electricians will be returning to install our security cameras and the lights for the sign.

The last few days Mechelle, Juliet, Jacob, and I had been working out before making our way to the office. Phyllis had been a peach and provided us breakfast afterwards.

Everyone beat me to the office because I had promised to help Phyllis move some boxes. She was very excited about her new home. I arrived when the electricians were working on the security cameras.

Simon and Julian, his assistant, had become regulars around the office. I was grateful Angela and Juan recommended them. Jacob had been picking their brains about various types of recording equipment. There was a fear he had a long list of things for Leonardo to purchase for us.

Everyone was in my office helping Jacob set up the new laptops for each desk.

It's really happening.

Everything was coming together. Tonight, was going to be a small gathering to thank everyone who helped me. Unfortunately, Leonardo and Isabella could not come. We didn't want there to be a connection between us.

Simon and Julian joined us for lunch. It was the least we could do. Most of the meal consisted of Jacob, Simon, and Julian discussing the latest spy gear available. Jacob seemed impressed with their knowledge. Everyone rushed back to finish their jobs when lunch concluded.

Once my computer was set up, I installed all the files I had created on my personal computer and organized my desk. I was filling my new stapler when Simon came in.

"Ms. Brooke, would you mind coming outside," Simon requested.

I exited the office and immediately saw the sign near the road. "Wow! So cool," I exclaimed.

Everyone must have heard me because they came out and nearly had the same reaction.

"The cameras are set up in the second office. Follow me," Julian instructed as he approached Juliet and Jacob's office.

I entered Jacob and Juliet's office. Centered on one wall was a screen showing eight cameras around the property. We had them set up in the common area as well as the two offices. Jacob's room and the bathrooms were the only areas without cameras.

Everyone helped clean up the office and went home to change. I asked them to be in business casual for the grand opening. I teleported Mechelle and I home. We quickly cleaned up and rushed back to prepare the table before the food was delivered. The Bloom Keepers were asked to arrive early, which they did. We sat around complimenting each other on our positions and the work we accomplished to make sure the office opened on time. Mr. Thomas was one of the first to arrive.

A few minutes later Phyllis poked her head through the door. She asked, "May we come in?" She opened the door, and my mom was behind her.

My mouth flung open. I screamed, "Mom!"

She leaped into my arms. "Surprise," she laughed.

It felt amazing to be able to hug her and holding her comforted me.

Suddenly, she gently pushed past me. "This place is fantastic." She spun around with wide eyes. "I hope you're not putting yourself in debt."

I assured her everything was fine. Mr. Thomas confirmed my statement.

Mechelle led Mom on a tour while the others and I greeted the guests. Hal had come in with Phyllis and was already snacking on the hors d'oeuvres. Andrew, Joann, and Karen joined us. They were like family.

They will be someday.

Tonya Greenwood, our realtor, came in with flowers. Angela, Juan, Simon, and Julian ambled in together.

Everyone complemented Angela and Juan on how stunning the place was. There were lots of questions about our clients, but that information was confidential.

As the party came to an end, I thought about inviting everyone back to my house. I changed my mind because I wanted to spend time with Mom. It was weird, having Jacob say goodbye to us as we left the office.

Mom and I walked out. She asked, "Where's your car?"

Think quick, Brooke.

I had teleported Mechelle and I there. I responded, "I rode over with Greg."

Mechelle waved as she leapt into Austin's truck.

Hal drove us the few blocks home. Phyllis asked Mom questions about her friends in Palm Beach County. The conversation continued as we entered the house. It was obvious, Mom was glad she was there. Everyone was doing well, and she has made new friends.

When Hal and Phyllis turned in for the night, Mom and I were able to catch up on the things going on in my life. She was mainly interested in Greg and me. She confided in me she had been on several dates, but they were not worth talking about.

Mom was disappointed when I told her I would not be down in the summer. Luckily, she understood I needed to concentrate on getting my business running. It broke my heart, but this was too important. She and a friend planned on going on a cruise. They had not agreed on the destination yet.

I spent the rest of the weekend with Mom shopping and dining out. We had an outstanding time.

After church, I drove her to the airport. It was sad to see her go. I knew my life was about to change. My intent was to go to bed early, but my mind would not stop racing with thoughts about my business.

I woke up early filled with excitement, I called Greg to pray with him. He was still sleeping, which was odd since he started work at the farm at sunrise. As soon as we finished praying, he rushed off the phone.

I thought about what it would be like working with him five days a week.

Please Lord let it strengthen our relationship.

Phyllis had sweat on her brow when I entered the kitchen. It appeared as though we had been invaded by the muffin man. I asked, "What's with all the muffins?"

Phyllis wiped the sweat from her forehead with a towel. "I wanted your first day to be special. These are for your office," she said as she rinsed a bowl.

I wrapped my arms around her and kissed her on the cheek.

She splashed a small amount of water at me and laughed. She dried her hands and handed me a Tupperware container. "Please box these up for me." She picked up her hot tea and leaned against the counter. "Please leave a chocolate and a lemon blueberry for Hal and I."

My eyes widened. "No not one of my lemon blueberry ones," I said as I set one aside for her.

"It's your own fault for introducing me to them," she giggled.

I pulled out my mirror to teleport to the office.

Phyllis placed her hand over the mirror. "Too many people around here know your business is opening today. They're not expecting you to walk to work every day," she advised.

She was right. "Let Mechelle know she's welcome to join us for lunch. I'm ordering pizza for everyone. You're welcome also," I said.

"I'm too busy. I'll let Mechelle know when she wakes."

I pulled my keys from my pocket as I meandered toward my car. As I was about to get in, Joann hollered, "Nice suit. Good luck today."

I glanced down at my light gray pants suit and my black loafers. "Thank you," I bellowed back.

As I pulled into the drive. I realized we needed to do something about the parking situation. Five vehicles plus our customers would not fit. We didn't need everyone parking on the street. Before exiting the car, I texted Greg to let him know that was the first thing he needed to take care of when he started in a week.

With muffins in hand, I set off for my first day of work. My eyes shifted back and forth.

This is my first day ever working.

Sure, I had volunteered at church many times but never have I had a real job.

Crazy.

The aroma of coffee hit me when I opened the office door. Jacob was standing behind the kitchen counter and Juliet was sitting on the bar stool across from him.

Jacob asked, "How do you like your coffee?"

I froze in place and stared with wide eyes. Juliet, I expected her to do something like that, but this was a little out of character for Jacob. I answered, "Cream and two sugars, please."

I placed the muffins on the counter.

Juliet asked, "What's that?"

I popped the lid off and was hit with a whiff of chocolate and lemon.

"Yum," Juliet said taking a lemon blueberry muffin. "Phyllis knows how to please."

Jacob swung around with my coffee. His eyes opened wide at the sight of the muffins. That boy can eat. He snagged a chocolate one. I selected a lemon blueberry and sat on the stool next to Juliet. Jacob led us in saying grace.

Juliet was right. Phyllis did not disappoint. The lemon was not too strong and there were blueberries in every bite. The muffin left a delicate sweet aftertaste.

Juliet cleaned up. "What should I work on today?"

"I sent you an email about Allison requesting a detailed expense report from us. She explained that you need to get the rates from a local airline to get pricing and flight information. Try to give an estimate for our expenses for the time we're there. Leonardo can help you with proof of flights, rental cars, food, and hotels," I said.

"It seems deceitful to charge for things we didn't use."

"I agree but telling them the truth would either put us on the funny farm or alert others about the power we possessed. I ask God for forgiveness," I informed her.

"I suppose you're right," she said placing the last cup in the dishwasher. With her head down, she lifted her eyes to me. "We're going to need a lot of forgiveness."

I nodded and went to my office. The two empty desks across from me would soon be occupied by Greg and Austin.

One more week.

I opened my computer and stared at the screen.

What am I supposed to work on?

132

I checked my company email box. There was nothing. Jacob had set up a website for us. I reviewed it for about the fifth time.

Nothing to do there.

I set up a LinkedIn account for the company and myself.

This can't be what office life is like? I'm going to go crazy.

I meandered into Juliet and Jacob's office. They were both focused and working hard.

Juliet's eyes shot over to her screen and asked, "Do you need something?"

"No, sorry," I whispered as I backed out of their office.

About an hour later, my head was on my desk from boredom. The chime went off and I heard the front door open. I leapt from my chair and darted toward the front door. Immediately, upon seeing Mechelle, I stopped in my tracks with a frown of disappointment smashed across my face.

"Well, it's nice to see you too," she said putting her purse on the reception desk.

"I apologized and explained how dull my day had been."

"Well, I'm here now. So, it must change," she said sauntered toward the kitchen. "Are these the muffins Phyllis mentioned?"

I nodded and followed her. "The muffins are the real reason you came. Aren't they?"

"You know it," she said taking a bite. "Oh, coffee too. You really know how to spoil your employees." She proceeded to make herself a cup once she found a mug.

She and I chatted about old times until lunch.

Thank God Mechelle's here.

The day dragged on but not as badly as it had been before she had returned.

Jacob and Juliet came out to fill their bellies before burying their heads back in their work. It amazed me how quiet they were.

I watched the clock as it got closer to 2:00 pm. I was excited about our first real client. Technically we were working for Allison but she's family and part of the Bloom Keepers.

In a hushed voice, Mechelle said, "They just pulled in. Go to your office and I'll come get you."

I did as she instructed. The monitor just seemed to be tormenting me as I tried to decide what to do. I logged into my personal email. There were 365 unread emails. I rolled my eyes at the thought of dealing with them. I scrolled in the hopes I might find one of value among all the spam.

Mechelle greeted them and asked them to have a seat. A moment later, her head popped through the doorway.

"Your 2:00 appointment is here," she announced. She spun around and disappeared. I called Jacob's desk and asked them to join us in the waiting room. I giggled because it was more of a living room.

Ms. Kate, as I called her, was sporting a lovely yellow dress and was adorned with several bracelets and necklaces. She appeared to be in her early sixties. Mr. Jerry sat to her left with his hand wrapped around hers.

"Good afternoon," I said, as I went to shake their hands.

Ms. Kate tilted her head and said, "Child, we're family. Now, give me some sugar." She stood up and gave me a hug. Mr. Jerry did the same.

I introduced them to our team before asking what they needed help with.

Ms. Kate's eyes moved to Jerry, and he shrugged. "Well...," she said. She inhaled deeply. "Jerry suspects our accountant... Well, has had his hand in the cookie jar."

Jerry barked, "I don't suspect. I know!"

Ms. Kate shook her head. She turned to Mr. Jerry in a calm voice she said, "Hush your mouth." Her attention returned to us, "Forgive him. He's madder than a wet hen. Cletus has only been working for us for a few months." She lowered her head and shook it.

With eyes narrow, Mr. Jerry announced, "I tell ya, he's been skimming off the top." He exhaled deeply before crossing his arms.

"I see," I said glancing over at Jacob and Juliet. "Jacob and Juliet are the team to handle this. Juliet's a whiz at accounting and Jacob's our Computer Forensic Specialist."

Jacob rubbed his hands together. "Absolutely. I don't suspect it will take long to figure out how long and how much he has been taking."

"First, we need to verify it's not just an accounting problem before we accuse him. We'll provide a detailed report for the police if he has been stealing," Juliet informed them.

Jacob and Juliet took turns explaining what they needed to begin the investigation and assured them they would make it a priority.

Ms. Kate turned to me and lowered her head. "Brooke, how much is this going to cost?"

Juliet and I made eye contract. She tilted her head and lifted one eyebrow. I turned back to Ms. Kate. I knew they were hard working people that gave back to the community. "You're our first client and this really should be easy to solve. Really, you're helping us to work out the kinks of starting a new business," I pulled out my phone and pretended to be calculating a number. I lifted my eyes. They were both sitting on the edge of the sofa. My eyes returned to the calculator on my phone. "Let me consult with my accountant," I said as I shuffled over to Juliet to show her the number on the phone. Using telepathy, I told her what to say. Juliet nodded.

Juliet eyes darted to them and back to me. "Yes, that will work."

"Very well." I turned to them. Ms. Kate was biting her lip and Mr. Jerry was fidgeting with his ring. "I don't want this to be a hard ship. You realize we're a new business trying to make a name for ourselves." I paused and darted my eyes between them. Mr. Jerry clutched Ms. Kate's hand. I flipped my phone around revealing the number one on the screen.

"Now darlin' you must have hit something. It's only showing a dollar," Ms. Kate announced.

I flipped the screen back to view it. I announced, "No, that's correct." They both leaped from the sofa and nearly knocked me over to thank me. Once things settled down, I said, "If possible, could we have a new dollar bill. I want to frame it."

They were both elated. Ms. Kate clinched my hand in hers. "Now don't you fret none. We'll bring a framed dollar for you. One that will match the decor."

Jacob and Juliet arranged to stop by after Cletus left for the day. They said their goodbyes and told us they would meet us at church.

Jacob and Juliet seemed excited about taking on this case. They headed off toward their office to compile a list of things they needed to check. Mechelle announced she was leaving because she and Phyllis would be making dinner together.

Standing in the entry to my business alone I knew I would not let this day end sitting staring at my computer screen, but what should I do?

Parkour or check to see if the weapons are still in the warehouse.

Suddenly, Jacob darted out of his office. He blurted, "April's mad. She has been calling all over trying to find out who has the

135

weapons. She told someone named Chelly to keep searching for the homeless man and to notify her if anyone else was searching for him. To quote her, 'deal with them.' She's on her way back to her hotel."

A grin appeared across my face. "Thanks Jacob. I'll be in Plymouth. I rushed to the bathroom and teleported invisibly to the ladies room of April's hotel.

I strolled to the reception area and asked them to ring her room. There was no answer. I made my way to a bench at the front of the hotel and waited for her to arrive. About fifteen minutes later, the sound of tires squealing was heard from down the road. Moments later, April came zooming in, nearly running over an older lady in the parking lot as she flew down the drive.

Her ranting could be heard as she approached the building. "I don't care! You need to find them, or you'll be done in this town," she barked.

For such a small lady she has a big bark.

She did not seem to notice me as she marched toward the entrance. I called out, "April!"

She swung her body in my direction, but her gaze went past me. I waved at her.

April's eyes scrunched up. She snapped, "What are you doing here? You should be out there trying to find that homeless man."

"Well, it's nice to see you too," I said in a sweet yet annoying voice.

She rolled her eyes and started moving toward the door. "What do you want?"

I caught up with her. "My team is having some difficulty with the homeless man," I said trying to have her believe me.

She stopped and turned toward me. After what seemed like a short sparing match, she blurted, "I don't know why Allison thinks so highly of you. Are you even qualified for this work? I mean you didn't show up for the sale and now you can't even find a homeless man. How hard can that really be?"

It must be hard since you're still looking.

I snapped back, "I've been all over town."

Not lying, just not searching for him.

"He's nowhere to be found. I think he may have skipped town."

I read her mind and she said, "I think so too. Something in my gut tells me you're in trouble."

April took a deep breath, "Okay, it is what it is. I'll have my men take care of finding him. Why don't you return to the states."

In her head she said, "Or you might be the next one to go missing."

You would like that wouldn't you?

I asked, "Do you have any leads on the missing weapons?"

"We are trying to find the vehicle used. Other than that, we only know we are searching for someone named Ms. Demeanor," she snapped.

"Seriously Ms. Demeanor? Couldn't she have come up with a cleverer name. I mean really Ms. Remington or Ms. Beretta. I think those would have been more appropriate," I said with a giggle.

April pressed her lips together before trying to compose herself. "Oh, you're clever," she said with a smile.

And you're annoyed.

I smiled back.

"I'll tell Allison you tried your best and I sent you home. My team and I will take care of this," she said firmly. She turned and with her head held high she stomped off into her hotel.

I returned to the office and gave them a report of what had occurred. Allison seemed the type to just want the major details, which I had nothing of significance to report.

Nineteen

Over the next week, Jacob and Juliet were able to prove Cletus was stealing from Mr. Jerry and Ms. Kate. They provided all the evidence to the authorities which included the account the money was moved to.

Since opening we had several minor cases, lost dog, stolen bicycle, and a stolen car. We even signed a new customer on, but the team is needed to keep an eye on the weapons because Mark was preparing to move them. We were trying to figure out a schedule to have them covered around the clock, but there were not enough of us. Fortunately, Juliet came up with a brilliant idea. She and I would attempt to recruit criminal acquaintances and offer them an honest job.

When we arrived at Eddie and Nadine's home, they were sitting on the sofa arguing over what to watch. I decided they needed to see us, but we wore our Bloom Keeper's uniforms. When I made us visible, Nadine slowly slid herself up the back of the couch to the standing position and pinned herself up against the wall. Eddie froze in place.

I asked, "Hello, have you missed me?"

"Missed you? I don't know who ya are," Eddie said with a quivering voice.

Juliet commented, "Perhaps I'm Casper."

I giggled, "Oh, I know and I'm Beetlejuice." We both laughed. Sadly, they didn't. "Seriously, we have a paying job for you and if you do well with this, we might send more work your way."

Juliet handed them an envelope with detailed instructions on who they were to observe to see if they were cheating on their spouse. "We need photos," she informed them as she stepped back.

"If you want to be reimbursed for your expenses, we'll need receipts. There's a PO Box listed in the paperwork. Send everything there. You'll receive a reasonable payment," I said.

"We need a decision before we leave here," Juliet added.

Nadine asked, "What do you think Eddie?"

"Seriously Nay! These people…" Eddie said shaking his head. "If they are people, just appeared in front of us like aliens or something. They know who we are." He turned and glared up at her. "Nay, they know who we are. Do you want to anger them? I don't wanna. I don't know what else they are capable of. Are you listening to me?"

Nadine was still frozen in place. She muttered, "Are you aliens?"

"No, we're not aliens, and Eddie, we are capable of much more," I announced.

With his voice quivering, Eddie said, "Nay, I say we help them."

With her eyes nearly popping out of her head, Nadine nodded several times.

Without another word I placed my hand on Juliet and using telepathy I told her not to say a word. I brought us back invisible.

Nadine uttered, "Are you sure they're gone?"

"Eddie sarcastically said, "Do you see them?" He widened his eyes and glanced around. "No not here." Jumping from his seat, he danced around where we were standing and flailed his arms around. "Nope, not here either."

I must admit, I was having a hard time keeping quiet, but what a show.

Nadine eased herself off the wall and slid back to her seat on the sofa. "I'm freaking out. Two people in black just appeared in our living room and offered us a job." Nadine started pacing the floor. "I've lost my mind. There it is. Lifetime criminal leaves the life of crime because of a ghost. I've officially lost it," she spouted waving her hands in the air like it was the headline of a movie.

Eddie joined in by jumping around the room and waved his hands like hers. "She brings her husband to crazy land with her."

Nadine slapped his arm.

"Seriously Nay, we need the money."

"I know," she said bringing her knees to her chest.

"They've got to be from the future," Eddie said joining her.

Nadine picked up the envelope and read the documents.

We teleported back to the office.

Jacob was at his desk with his feet propped up and his laptop in his lap. He asked, "How did it go?"

Juliet and I could barely get the story out because of our laughter. We would calm down and try telling it, but before we knew it, we were rolling in laughter again.

Jacob shot his eyes between us before he gave up and returned to his computer.

After we finally calmed down, he asked, "Are they going to do it?"

Still giggling, Juliet said, "Yes."

Greg entered and said, "I've nearly worked out the schedule. Brooke, are you sure you want someone else using the stone?"

"I certainly don't want to be in the room until they return. I still need to show my face around the house until Hal moves out," I explained.

Greg asked, "Okay, I'm grabbing a bottle of water. Does anyone one need anything while I'm up?"

I followed Greg to the kitchen filling him in on what had happened with Nadine and Eddie. He got a kick out of it too.

"I nearly forgot. Kate came by. The framed dollar is sitting on the reception desk. I didn't know where you wanted to hang it," Greg said as he snagged a bottle of water.

I lifted it from the desk and noticed the lovely frame that complemented the décor. I decided to place it on my desk as a reminder to always stay humble and who was our first official client.

Austin strolled in from his office. "Guys why don't we just set up surveillance cameras and watch them from here rather than us all go there. Jacob could easily set it up. That way we could easily let Allison know when it's going down," Austin suggested.

"That's a great idea," I complimented.

"I'm on it," Jacob hollered from his office.

"Ya know he acts like he's not paying attention, but that boy must have eagle ears," Greg commented.

"Give me an hour or so to determine where they need to be installed and to get the equipment together," Jacob hollered.

With Greg caught up with his new responsibilities, Jacob trying to set up surveillance, and Juliet working on our billing, Austin and I decided to check up on April.

We first teleported to her hotel room first, but she was not there. Then, we checked her vehicle. We stepped out of the compact car and noticed it was parked outside of an office building. We had no choice but to wait for her to return to her vehicle.

We had been waiting about thirty minutes, when Austin asked, "Jacob could track her phone, right?"

Brilliant!

"Yes," I said.

We returned to the office and found Jacob putting equipment in a bag. "I'm nearly ready," he said brushing his hair out of his eyes.

Austin said, "We were hoping you could tell us where April is."

"The cameras are more important. We can find out what she's up to later," I informed Austin.

We waited for Jacob to finish collecting his equipment before teleporting over to the storage facility. I stood outside while Austin helped Jacob install the camera in the building. Periodically, we needed to stop because people randomly came in with things, but they left relatively quickly. The interruptions caused us to take longer than expected. I waited patiently for Jacob to tell me he was done.

I found myself pacing back and forth from boredom. Finally, Jacob called out to say he had finished. We returned to the office.

Jacob described how difficult it was to find locations for the cameras to keep them from being detected. The warehouse was bare, and he hoped they would not be detected.

Before putting his tools away Jacob told us April was still at the same location. He assured me he would know if the cameras were working by the time we returned.

Austin and I returned to April's vehicle and waited. It was too hot to be in the vehicle, so we sat on her trunk to make sure we were not in any pedestrian's way.

Austin and I used the time to discuss a variety of topics telepathically allowing us to get to know one another better.

Austin said, "Everyone is grateful ya came into our lives. Not just because it's like working with a superhero but because of the friendships." He gazed at the building we had presumed April was in.

"Cause Greg and ya are together, Mechelle was brought into my life."
He shook his head. "I can't believe I'm telling a gal this. I love her. I
don't want to be without her. Mechelle told me what ya said about
making sure we see each other. I appreciate it."

I refrained from commenting because it seemed he was having a
difficult time opening up to me.

"I need to be honest with you, you deserve that," Austin said as
he lowered his head toward his feet and banged them together.
"Mechelle and I both feel we are doing God's work." His eyes darted
back and forth between his feet and the entrance to the building.

Please don't tell me you're quitting.

"If us being apart so much becomes a problem, I might move to
Italy and work with her. Obviously when we get married that is my
plan. At least that way I'll still be helping," he concluded.

Aww, he wants to marry her.

"Austin, I can assure you I have already run multiple scenarios
through my head of what could be done to keep the team together
and still allow us to have lives. I had already considered having you
over there with her if Leonardo was to die," I informed him.

"He's not though, right?"

I chuckled, "No, he let me heal him, but he and Isabella have
been doing this a long time. They need time to enjoy life. Once
Mechelle has mastered everything at the villa and she has proven to
Leonardo's connections she is trustworthy, I'll ask them if they want
to step down."

Austin put his feet on the bumper and turned to me with a smile
as he shook his head up and down.

"Besides, I have a vineyard there that could use the skills of a
good farmer to maintain," I joked.

Unexpectedly, Austin tapped my leg with the back side of his
hand and pointed to the building. April was on the move. I
teleported us to the back seat of her car. Austin had to move
sideways to adjust his position because of his size in such a small
space. It was small even for me.

April slammed the door and immediately started fiddling in her
purse. She pulled out the small phone she had in her room. She made
a call and turned the speaker phone on. A voice on the other end
said, "Sweetheart, I've been worried about you. Why haven't you
called sooner."

Austin reached into his pocket and pulled out a small recorder.

Where did he get that?

"Someone snatched everything. I've been trying to hunt down who it could be…,"

The man interrupted, "You need to find them soon or we'll be in prison rather than a tropical beach."

"You say that like I don't know," April snapped. She dug through her purse and pulled out a piece of gum from her purse and chomped on it. "I've been in a meeting with Chelly. Her connections are leading her to believe it was Mark Cooper."

"Mark? How did he find them?"

"I suspect he had a tracker on them. Surely, he knows by now the money is fake. Something tells me that man was going to steal them back after the buy anyway," she said as she gazed at herself and appeared to be inspecting her makeup in the rear-view mirror. "Don't worry, I'll find him and the weapons. I may need your help with locating them though."

"Darling, you know I would do anything for you. I miss you immensely," he said in a loving voice.

April lowered her head. "Oh Levi, I miss you too. I'm going to get these guns so we can both leave this business and start new lives as ordinary people." She paused for a moment. "Any word on Allison?"

Levi, huh.

"No, I think her stupid secretary may have figured out I have been flirting with her to obtain information. I'm trying to not talk work to throw her off. I promised to take her out for dinner tomorrow night," Levi stated.

Sounding annoyed, April commented, "Must you."

"Darling, you're the woman I love. Brenda means nothing to me. I'm doing this for us, just like you're doing what you do. One day soon we will be together."

"Yah … That better be all it is," April snapped before hanging up the phone. She pulled away from the curb as though she had someone trying to catch her.

I braced myself for the ride. I neglected to tell Austin about the carnival ride he was about to endure. Austin was already squished into the back seat, but as we came around corners, he was flung around like the ball in a pinball machine with his eyes bulging out.

When the vehicle stopped, I noticed we were at Plymouth Central Library. I teleported Austin and I to the section she had met the man the last time. Austin scrunched his eyebrows as though he was confused. April strolled to the back of the building and pulled a book from the shelf. She pretended to be reading it as she scanned the area.

A few minutes later, Devon came up to her and placed a book on the shelf. He whispered, "The boss is mad. He wants his delivery."

April pressed her lips together and rolled her eyes. "I'm going to get it back. I am certain I know who took them. I just need to find out where the delivery is," she assured him.

Devon glanced around the library, "My boss doesn't like to be made to look like a fool. Ms. Demeanor, there isn't much time for you to rectify this situation. My boss, he knows who you really are."

April's eyes widened as she had a blank stare.

He placed the book back on the shelf. "So, April Duncan, tick tock." He motioned at his watch and Devon walked away.

April slammed the book back on the shelf. She mumbled, "Crap." With her head lowered, she rubbed the nape of her neck.

I was torn. Do I stay with April and find out what her plan is or follow Devon and find out who wants the weapons?

Follow Devon. Allison wants the big fish.

I tugged on Austin's arm and motioned with my head for him to follow me. I picked up my pace to catch up with Devon. He turned in the direction April was in, but she was not in sight. He darted into the back offices of the library. We followed. He entered an office and closed the door. The office had a window to view the library, but it appeared to be a two-way mirror. April could be seen moving toward the exit. Devon watched her until she was out of view.

Does he work here?

Devon picked up his cell phone and made a call. I glanced at the number. A muffled voice could be heard.

Put on the speaker phone.

"Yah, she's freaking out. I told her she didn't have much time," Devon informed the person.

I only caught the person say, she was a pawn.

"A gorgeous pawn. How do you do it man? You've always been good with the ladies. Hey, do you remember that one woman you swindled all her jewels from?"

I leaned in closer to see if I could hear better.

"That was a shame I really liked her, but money and power is what I want. Chicks are a dime a dozen," the man said.

I know that voice.

I count remember from where, but I was familiar. I leaned back trying not to breathe on Devon.

They chatted for another few seconds before Devon hung up. He started going through the computer email.

I grasped Austin's shoulder and teleported us back to the office. As soon as Jacob realized we were back, he started rattling off what he had discovered.

"April made a call…"

I interrupted, "Let me guess to Levi."

Jacob scrunched his eye up. "How did you know?"

Austin commented, "We were there when she made the call."

Jacob's excitement faded like a balloon losing air. "Well let me show you anyway. April called Levi and this is where it gets interesting. The number she called was to a burner phone that was in Allison's office building." Jacob pointed at the phone number on the screen.

"No way!" I said as I inspected the number.

Austin asked, "What?"

I leaned back biting my lip and half smiling. "I can't believe I didn't see it. Levi, you're a clever man," I backed up with my hands on my mouth.

Juliet, who had been buried in her computer screen chimed in. "Spit it out Brooke!"

I was still in disbelief. "Levi claims to be in love with April, while he is dating Brenda…"

Juliet interrupted, "Who's Brenda?" She stood and joined the group at Jacob's desk.

Jacob answered, "Allison's secretary."

"Yes, Brenda is Allison's secretary. Levi's using her for information about the case." I raised my eyes up and shook my head, "Oh, he's good. He's the arms dealer trying to buy the weapons, and he has convinced April to do the dirty work using their future together to lure her. I suspect he will dump her once he has the funds from the sale."

Everyone leaned back and commented about how much of a mastermind Levi was.

145

I pulled Austin aside and asked him about the recorder he was using with April.

Austin replied, "Jacob told me we might need it and he tossed it to me before we left. Should I have not used it?"

"No, it's fantastic you did use it. We should be able to use it against April.

I excused myself when Austin began telling them about our adventure.

I teleported to Allison's office to fill her in, but she was not there. I peeked through the door to see if Brenda was at her desk. She was gone also. I meandered through the office searching for either of them. I came across two men chatting about an agent. Using the power of persuasion, I asked them to tell me where they were.

One of the men spurted, "In the conference room."

The second man asked, "What about it?"

I asked him where the conference room was.

The man pointed toward a door and said, "It's right there."

The second man scrunched his eyes, "I know where the conference room is. Why are you acting so weird?"

"Didn't you just ask me where Allison Dunara was?"

"No."

I left them and went to the conference room. I went through the door and Allison and Brenda were in a meeting with several other people. The room smelled of coffee. Using telepathy, I told her I needed to talk to her.

Allison's eyes bounced around the room but did not move. A man at the end of the table seemed to be in charge. Everyone listened as he discussed agency policies with them. A few minutes later he dismissed them. Allison was at the far end of the room. As people exited, I had to sink into the wall to avoid being run into. As two men strolled by, I heard the familiar male voice.

So, you're Levi.

He was wearing a nice suit and had a short well-trimmed beard.

A woman asked Allison if she wanted to grab lunch, but Allison told her she had a call to make. Once everyone was out of the room, I followed Levi to his office. He snatched his car keys and phone from his desk drawer and rushed to the elevator. He pulled a second phone out of his pocket and started texting someone.

LEVI: The shipment has been delayed.

146

As others piled in the elevator he moved to the back of the elevator and waited for a response. I followed him to his vehicle. Levi climbed in and stared at the phone. I teleported to the back seat and listened to his thoughts.

Levi's mind was all over the place. "I'm going to kill that girl if she doesn't get me those weapons. Heck, they're going to kill me if I don't deliver them. I can't believe I've spent the last year programming April's mind to have my whole plan fall apart. He chuckled.

Program her mind?

I was lost in thought about how I had heard about cults and things programming people.

It must have been difficult to program someone with her skills.

He read a new text. I peeked over his shoulder to read.

555-555-0691:	I noticed Matti is excelling in school. You should be proud of your daughter. It's difficult to get straight A's.

The photo was of a teenager wearing a navy blue and green plaid skirt, navy blue sweater with high white socks, and a collared white shirt. She was standing in front of a trophy case and to her left was a sign that read 'Rathdown School'.

Levi's eyes widened. He began rocking and running his fingers through his hair. He mumbled out loud. "Oh, Matti." His rocking got worse, and his face contorted more as a vein throbbed in his neck. This was followed by him slamming his fist down on the steering wheel. A few minutes later, he texted the person back.

LEVI:	It's just delayed. You will have it.

555-555-0691:	That's a good thing. We certainly don't want her having an accident like your wife.

Levi heaved the phone into the passenger's seat and started his car. I teleported to Allison's office and waited for her. A moment later the door opened. Allison rushed in and was followed by Brenda. Allison told her, "Yes, I need that file, but it can wait till you get back from lunch." Allison picked up a pile of files and handed them to Brenda. "These need to be filed. Thanks."

Brenda started to leave, but turned around abruptly and asked, "Do you want me to grab you something?"

"That would be great. I think it's going to be a long night for me," Allison said as she fiddled with her wallet. "Here." She handed her a credit card. "You know what I like. Surprise me and your lunch is on me."

"Thanks," Brenda said with a smile before turning and leaving.

As soon as the door was closed, Allison whispered, "Brooke?"

I immediately informed her in on everything we knew about Levi, Brenda, Mark, and April.

Allison leaned up against her desk. "I don't know why I didn't see it. Knowing about Levi explains a lot about some odd things I've seen going on around here. Poor Brenda, that girl just wants to be loved. She's a bit naive. When this is over, she and I are going to need to have a chat. She'll also need to be written up and put on probation." Allison shook her head and moved to her desk chair.

"At least you now know who you can trust," I commented.

"True. Tell Jacob I'll be contacting him again."

"Jacob?"

"Yes. Oh, he didn't tell you." Allison chuckled. "I contacted him and asked him to monitor Brenda. I suspected she might be involved somehow or that someone might try and get information from her. He's fantastic by the way. If he wasn't working for you, I'd snag him from you. Not even telling you tells me he can certainly be trusted."

"Well, he knows you have been protecting the stone much longer than me. I'm sure he knows you are trustworthy. He certainly knows you are part of the team," I commented. Allison and I tossed around some ideas about how to deal with the situation before I returned to my office.

Greg was out running errands, I figured one of us would bring him up to speed when he returned. Meanwhile, I filled everyone else in on what had occurred, and we discussed what to do next. Jacob would continue to monitor the warehouse and I would keep an eye on April and Mark. Greg and Austin would likely help me. Austin seemed pleased with that. It had been a long day already; I had made a management decision to leave early.

As I was about to leave Greg flew in the front door. He shouted, "I have good news!"

148

Everyone came out of the offices to see what was going on.

Greg had a few envelopes clutched in his hand. He placed all but one on the counter. He said, humbly, "I thought it was a long shot but Juliet you are brilliant?"

Juliet lowered her head and raised her eyes to him. She asked hesitantly, "Why?"

Greg glanced around the room locking eyes with each of us. He asked, "Do you know what I have in this envelope?"

Jacob snapped, "Enough with the games. What is it, Greg?"

"Eddie and Nadine came through. They sent us pictures that prove an affair was going on. Juliet, we are going to need to cut them a check," Greg said proudly.

I asked, "Juliet, do you want to go pay them a visit?"

"You know I do but I have a lot to do, and Jacob is taking me on a date after work. Sadly, I need to pass," Juliet replied.

"Austin, you are welcome to join me," I said putting my mask on."

Austin did the same in record speed.

I love his enthusiasm.

I expected them to be in the living room watching television, but they weren't. Clanking could be heard from the kitchen. Eddie was oblivious to our arrival because he appeared to be knee deep in pots and pans.

I asked, "What's for dinner, Eddie?"

Eddie nearly fell over. Thankfully nothing was in his hands. In a trembling voice he said, "We did what you asked. Nay already mailed everything I promise."

"That's why I'm here. My friends were very pleased with the work you did. You will be getting a check sent to you soon. I think you'll be surprised who you've been working for."

I stopped because Austin lunged toward the stove to keep a pot from boiling over. "Ya need to keep this on a lower temperature man," Austin informed Eddie.

I continued, "See your new employer is a friend. If you upset her, you upset us."

Eddie raised an eyebrow. "Who is it?"

"Davis International Investigation Service," I informed him.

Eddie lowered his head and seemed to be trying to figure out who that could be. He asked, "Davis as in Lillie Davis?"

"Eddie, Lillie's dead"

149

"I know that, but I thought maybe you were too," Eddie said with complete sincerity.

"You're working with her granddaughter Brooke. I'm sure you remember her. It's time you be on the right side of things," I said as I moved next to Austin.

Eddie crossed his arms and leaned against the counter. He mumbled, "Brooke Garrison, really?"

"Yes, and I recommend you don't cross her," I said sternly.

Austin stepped forward, "If you add a touch of red wine to the sauce it'll bring it to the next level."

I gazed at Austin with a raised eyebrow.

Who is this man?

We returned to our office and called it a day.

Twenty

The last few days had been slow. I worked on social media ads with Greg all morning to try and stir up some business.

Greg and I were tweaking some final touches on the ad, when Jacob hollered from his office, "They found the cameras!"

Everyone ran into his office to see what he was watching.

Jacob pointed to the monitor, and said, "Look, this guy tore this one down." He pointed to the black box on his screen.

It was apparent they were searching for more cameras. One man was on the phone and seemed to be ranting.

"Yah, well they found another one," Juliet commented. The screen went black.

"There are still two," Jacob announced. "Scratch that. Only one now." We watched for another ten minutes. Before Jacob said, "I don't think they can find it."

Austin and Jacob knuckle punched each other.

I agreed. Everyone on the video screen seemed to be calming down. "At least we still have a good view of the area," I said.

Everyone returned to their desks and continued working until Jacob hollered at us again. "The weapons are being moved again."

We were all trying to see what was going on. Jacob enlarged the screen and leaned forward toward it. He pointed at an elderly man. "This is odd. The same few men have been at this warehouse. No one new has even been allowed near this warehouse, yet this man here I have never seen," he said with one eyebrow raised.

Austin asked, "Why would they rely on some old man to move the weapons?"

"That's odd," Greg said. He pointed at another old man walking toward the vehicle. "Who's he?"

Jacob narrowed his eyes as he watched the person. "I've never seen him either."

"Greg said, "We need to get over there."

I agreed. "We can't all go. There will be limited space in the back of the van. Everybody get dressed in case I come back for you. Jacob, let Allison know what's going on. I may need to get her for the arrests. For now, Greg and I are going," I instructed.

Greg and I both changed into our uniforms and nearly collided as he exited Jacob's room and me as I exited the restroom.

Jacob had been waiting in the hall for us. "Brooke, take this."

It was a small folded up piece of aluminum foil. I tilted my head as I snatched it from his hand.

Should I even ask what this is?

"It's a tracker. Don't remove the aluminum foil until you are visible. Allison or her team may need to locate you to find the weapons. It won't work with the aluminum foil on it," Jacob said.

I nodded and teleported Greg and I to the back of the van invisible. The two men said nothing during the ride.

When the back door of the van opened, I realized we were at Victoria Wharf. The two men easily moved the weapons to the boat. Using telepathy, I told Greg, "Those old men are strong."

He replied, "I know my grandpa couldn't move them that easily and he's in good shape."

Using telepathy, I told Greg, "Allison is going to need to know who they're selling them to."

Greg nodded.

The taller of the two men said in a British accent to the other man, "It should take you ten days to get there. I'll be over as soon as I can. Sit tight until then."

The shorter man rolled his eyes, "I know the plan. You better show up. They don't know me, and I'll be dead before I even have a chance to tell them. Now come help me organize these supplies before I leave. I want to make sure I didn't forget anything."

The taller man joked, "You mean like the time you were traveling to Iran and forgot the loo roll."

The smaller man rolled his eyes and let out an exasperated sigh as he shut the van doors.

I teleported Greg and I to a nearby roof. "Keep an eye on them. I'm going back to see what Allison had to say. You'll be visible so stay low," I instructed. I handed him the GPS. "When I leave, unwrap the device," I instructed before returning to Jacob's office.

Jacob was so focused on his computer he did not flinch when I arrived.

I asked, "What did Allison say?"

Jacob gasped. "She's deploying April's team and wants you to pick her up. She's been in the UK since yesterday.

I asked, "Why's she there?"

Jacob replied, "I'm not getting into her business. She said she'll meet you in April's room."

I nodded and arrived invisible. She and another woman were searching April's room.

Okay now what?

Using telepathy, I told her I was there. She told me to knock on the door and I did as she requested.

Allison opened the door and held her hand up as if to tell me not to enter. She told her partner, "I'm going after the weapons. Find everything you can here."

She pulled me in the doorway and motioned for me to be quiet before wrapping her arm in mine. Allison glanced to see if she could see the agent, but they were not within eyesight. She nodded. I

153

teleported us to Greg. We quietly told her what was going on. Her lips tightened as we told her what we knew.

Allison asked, "Ten days? Where could he be going?" Her eyes shifted down for a moment. "Something's not right. I say our best chance of getting the weapons is to take them from these two old fogeys." She pulled out her phone. "You guys go apprehend them. I'm going to see what April's up to and get my men over here to officially charge them and to confiscate the weapons."

I grabbed Greg's arm to teleport him, and he pulled it away.

He said, "We have GPS and there are cameras here. They'll see us."

He was right. We scaled down the building and slowly made our way to the stern. Greg stepped on and was immediately confronted by the smaller of the two men. He immediately struck him with a forward kick. "Go on. I'll take care of gramps," Greg instructed.

The taller man was in the kitchen stowing some food in a cabinet. I jumped down to the lower level and charged toward him.

With stealth-like moves he picked up a bottle of wine and broke it on the counter spewing wine all over the area and lunged toward me with the broken bottle.

I flipped myself backwards to the sofa narrowly missing the razor-sharp bottle.

The man dropped the bottle and flung himself over the counter onto the sofa.

What old man can move like this?

I found myself backing up to the doorway. In a swift movement I yanked the fire extinguisher from the wall and hit him on the head with it. He collapsed.

I rushed to the kitchen to see if there was something to tie him with.

Come on, a charger, small appliance cord.

I opened drawers searching for those things.

I was focused on finding something and did not see him approaching. He pulled the necklace causing me to fall toward him.

Breath, I need a breath.

I put my legs up on the counter and pushed back flinging him into the other counter. He would not let go of my necklace.

Can't breathe.

I concentrated on moving through the necklace and released myself.

154

The man stood there holding the Bloom of Dreams as I coughed. He tossed it into the sink. We both assumed a stance and threw punches at one another. There was little room in the small galley. The man slipped on the wine and fell backward into the stove. I placed a hand on both counters and jumped up pushing both feet into his chest. He hit the stove so hard his wig fell off.

What in the world?

I commented, "Oh, are we letting our hair down?"

He grabbed a knife from the block. Pieces of flesh colored plastic feel from his face.

Who are you?

I was able to dodge the strikes, but I was hurting from the strikes I had received. I managed to kick the knife out of his hand causing it to fly into the wall. I kept trying to reach the stone but was unsuccessful. I leapt over the counter to the sofa. The man followed. I was able to hit him with a spin kick to the face. This tore the mask a bit. Covering one of his eyes. I rushed past him and recovered the Bloom of Dreams from the sink.

The light coming from the doorway was blocked by someone. It had the man's attention long enough for me to put the necklace back on. Immediately, it began healing me.

Greg!

He appeared to be barely hanging on. It was apparent he barely survived his fight with the shorter man, but he was the perfect distraction. While he and our mystery man fought, I leapt on the man's back and put him in a choke hold. He slumped down and collapsed to the floor.

I yanked the mask off him.

Mark Cooper.

He truly was a master of disguise.

Greg mumbled, "Wait what? That guy out there must be Chester."

Allison suddenly appeared. "That would be correct. Your team did an amazing job" A man came in and handcuffed Mark as he was beginning to stir.

"You should bind his feet that one has skills," I suggested.

The man glared at Allison.

She nodded. "Sounds good." Allison turned to Greg and me. "I appreciated all you've done. April's suddenly missing but I know we'll catch her." She chuckled. "She should have been better about not storing her things in her room. We've uncovered a treasure-trove of evidence on her."

I said, "That's great!"

Greg leaned up against a wall with his head down, holding his side.

"You're not looking so good," Allison said to Greg. She turned to me. "You two should get out of here. Send me a report on what happened."

Two men hauled Mark out.

"Everyone's busy collecting evidence. Get out before anyone else returns," Allison ordered as she strutted to the door spouted orders to her staff.

I wrapped my arm around Greg's waist and teleported us to Jacobs room. I helped Greg get on his bed. I pulled Greg's mask off. He curled up in a ball and groaned. I lifted his shirt which revealed several large dark purple bruises.

Oh Greg.

"Lord, please heal him," I said as tears streamed down my face.

Jacob suddenly appeared in the doorway. "What happened!" He ran over to assist Greg. "Brooke, that looks like internal bleeding."

I placed my hand on him and immediately the stone heated.

Jacob commented, "Do you think the stone can heal him? He's in bad shape."

"I have faith. God's going to heal him," I said as I wiped a tear from my face. Jacob and I watched as the purple bruises slowly disappeared. Greg sluggishly uncoiled himself. He closed his eyes and dosed off.

"I think he's going to be alright," Jacob said as he rubbed my back. He turned and left the room.

I gently ran my fingers through his hair and continued praying for him.

Jacob returned with two bottles of water and placed them on the nightstand. He, like me, just stared at Greg waiting for him to show signs he was doing better.

The stone began to cool.

Why isn't he moving?

I gently shook him. "Greg," I said softly.

Suddenly, Greg rolled over and with one eye closed and his tongue sticking out of the left side of his mouth before bursting into laughter.

I closed my eyes.

Thank you, Lord.

Greg grabbed me and pulled me toward him as he rolled toward the opposite side of the bed.

"Yah, that's my queue to leave," Jacob announced.

I fought back tears.

"Sweetie why are you crying? I'm fine," Greg assured me.

"That was close. What if I hadn't gotten the stone back? You could have died," I said wiping away another tear.

"But I didn't. God is going to take care of us," Greg said as he collected another tear from my cheek with his finger. He kissed me on the nose. "Come on. We need to get out of Jacob's bed."

"Good idea," I agreed.

Twenty-One

Over the next two weeks, we turned in the invoice and evidence we had against Mark and April to Allison. She assured me she would contact us if she needed further assistance with locating April. Mr. Thomas hired a company to help Phyllis and Hal move. She had asked me to wait to come over until her housewarming party. She wanted it to be perfect.

Only Greg and I would be working out that day. Austin was needed on the farm, and Jacob would be helping Juliet move in. She was moving into Phyllis's old room. Mechelle was visiting friends and family in Florida before her big move to Italy.

As I meandered to the kitchen, I noticed how eerily quiet it was without anyone here. It was the first day without Phyllis because she generally only worked on weekdays. I found myself staring at the coffee pot.

When was the last time I made coffee for myself? Forever.

Thankfully, after a search of the pantry, I found the coffee filters and coffee. I waited impatiently as it brewed. I brought my coffee and a yogurt to the patio table and read the Bible as I enjoyed my breakfast. As I read 1 Thessalonians 4:3-4, 'It is God's will that you should be sanctified: that you should avoid sexual immorality; that each of you should learn to control your own body in a way that is holy and honorable', I felt proud that Greg and I were still honoring God, but it was not easy.

I was washing my dishes when I was startled by a tapping on the kitchen door. It was Greg.

"Good morning beautiful," he said shutting the door for me. He pulled me in for a kiss.

"Good morning handsome."

"Man, it's quiet here and something else is missing…Oh, I know the amazing aromas from Phyllis's cooking. I was hoping to get some scraps," Greg joked.

"I can make you something if you're hungry," I offered.

"No, I'm good."

As we went for our morning run, I was reminded of the first time he had me run with him. I had been a disaster. On occasion Greg or I would just take off in a full sprint to see if the other would keep up. My mind was focused on how well the Bloom Keepers worked together. When things were slow, we spent most of our days developing our skills. Until we built more clients, it would be a common occurrence.

After six miles, we returned home. Juliet and Jacob were sitting on the front porch. As I opened the iron gate, I asked, "Hey, are you all moved in?"

"Juliet forgot the key," Jacob announced.

Juliet commented, "It should be on the desk in the library."

I chuckled as I unlocked the door for them. Greg and I helped them bring her things up. While she unpacked, Greg and I sparred in the attic for about thirty minutes before we continued my training by throwing stars. My skills had improved enough that I could practice indoors. I initially started training in Greg's backyard. I had nearly hit the shed a few times.

As I was throwing, the door flew open. Jacob blurted, "Allison called. Her team received a lead, and she doesn't have the manpower to surveil the area. She asked us to do it."

Greg asked, "That's great. Where's she at?"

Juliet and Jacob immediately turned to one another and grinned.

Juliet announced, "She's here."

Is she crazy?

I asked, "Really? Why would she return to the States?"

"Brooke, she's in Louisville," Juliet clarified.

"Allison believes she's here to find out more about you," Jacob added.

"What makes them think she's here?"

Jacob replied, "Allison had a team locate her, but they were unsuccessful in bringing her in. They lost her soon after locating her."

We spent the next hour trying to figure out what she may have discovered and attempting to figure out where she might be. Only to admit that we knew nothing more than when we started.

Greg headed home to shower and get some work done for his parents. While we went to Juliet's room to hangout for a bit while she unpacked. While we chatted, Jacob asked me about Kyle.

"Who's Kyle?" I asked.

He clarified, "The homeless guy...We dropped him off at the villa."

"I forgot about him. I don't think I even mentioned him to Allison. She's going to need his testimony," I replied.

"Allison will get back to you when she's ready to talk to him," Jacob informed me.

"I'm going to clean up and check on him. I'll be back shortly," I said as I exited.

I wasn't sure if Kyle was still using my room, so I teleported to Isabella's room. Fortunately, they weren't there. I exited. She was talking to a guest about the local tourist spots they should see at the front desk. When their conversation concluded, I asked about Kyle.

"I can't thank you enough for him. He's fantastic. He's been assisting in the orchard. Apparently, his grandfather had a small orchard and taught him a lot."

"That's great. Where can I find him?"

She turned and picked up the phone. "I'll let him know you're here."

Leonardo approached and gave me a hug. "Thank you again," he said with a smile. "Lord knows why I wanted to suffer so long. I should've listened to you sooner," he said.

"Brooke, Kyle's going to meet you at a table outside," Isabella informed me.

"Is he still in my room?"

"Oh no, we moved him as soon as he was cleaned up," Isabella assured me.

Leonardo smiled and said, "Love that man. Enjoy your time with him." Leonardo rushed off in the direction of the kitchen.

I strolled out to the side and found a couple sitting at a table. Both reading what I suspected were good books because neither of them lifted their noses from them. I made myself comfortable at a table with a view of the orchard.

A handsome gentleman in a green shirt came out of the building and seemed to be scanning the area. When he made eye contact with me. I nodded to say hello. I peered past the man to see if Kyle was behind him. He wasn't.

The man in the green shirt approached me.

Please don't flirt with me.

He said, "Brooke, it's nice to see you again."

With a furrowed brow, I asked, "Do I know you?"

"I'm Kyle."

I inspected him. The beard was gone along with the filthy clothes. I leaned back with my mouth wide and said, "Gorgeous! I didn't recognize you without your beard."

"Thanks. I must admit the ladies seem to like the new me, but I miss my beard," Kyle said with a chuckle. Once the small talk was over Kyle explained he was an informant for Mark in exchange for food and an occasional night in a hotel. "It was by chance I found the weapons. Mark told me to let him know if I heard anything. I just stumbled across them. I sleep in the tunnel occasionally," he said.

I filled him in on what Allison needed from him.

"Am I going home after that?"

"I know this must be difficult for you, but I'll get you back home as soon as I can," I assured him.

"You miss understand. I have been praying for God to get me off the street and he has. I don't want to leave. The entire staff are fantastic," he said. Suddenly he lowered his head. "Well, all but two of them. They're lazy."

I think I know who they are.

"Well, we'll see what we can do. I need to get out of here. It was nice meeting you," I said before making my way to my room.

I teleported to the pantry because Greg was going to pick me up soon. Everyone was on their way to Austin's for a BBQ. I heard muffled voices when I opened the door. I strolled toward them. Greg, Jacob, and Juliet were sitting in the living room with an attractive ginger man with a medium length beard. He was wearing cargo shorts and a royal blue T-shirt. His hair was long on top. When he flipped his head around to see me, his hair flopped forward into his eyes. He brushed it back.

"Brooke, this is Jared," Greg announced.

"Hello," I said.

Who is he and why is he here?

I sat and noticed the video camera next to him on the floor and his shamrock tattoos going down his arm. "Are you here to film something?"

"Nah, I was filming the street, when I ran into my old buddy here," Jared said motioning toward Greg. "I'm trying to get my name out there so I'm making a variety of videos for my website. The historical homes around here are fantastic. Never thought I would be in one."

"Jared and I went to high school together. I invited him to join us at Austin's tonight." Greg said glancing at his phone. "We should get going. Bill hates it when people are late.

We heard country music as soon as we exited the truck. Jared drove his own car. Suzanne and Lisa exited the house with side dishes. I hollered over to Bill who was at the grill, "Hi." He nodded. I made my way to the table and offered my help to the ladies.

As I followed them back into the house, I noticed Austin greeting Jared with a fist bump. The three of them started talking about what they had been up to since high school. Juliet excused herself and followed me inside.

To my surprise, Mechelle was standing at the sink washing a mixing bowl. I asked, "When did you get back?"

"Austin really wanted me here, so my flight landed two hours ago. We came straight here to help Suzanne and Bill out," she said as she dried her hands. After a hug she returned to drying dishes. "I tried to call you earlier to tell you, but you didn't answer."

"Sorry, it's been busy. I even forgot to bring the phone with me tonight," I apologized.

Suzanne had us bring a few more bowls out. More people had arrived. I asked Lisa, "Who are all these people?"

"A few are neighbors, and that man over there works for Dad. Isn't his daughter the cutest," She placed the pasta salad down. "Oh look, Karen and Ty are here." Karen rushed over to them.

Mechelle and I placed our bowls on the table and watched Greg, Jacob, and Austin put out more folding chairs. Jared meandered around with his video camera filming.

Suzanne thanked us for our help and told us to get a drink and relax. We found an open picnic table and sat. Mechelle and I got caught up on what she did in Florida, when Karen and Ty joined us.

Karen told us she now had three clients for her cleaning business. One was a wealthy lady from church. Karen said, "She wants me to work full-time for her. Cooking and things. My cooking skills are okay, but I suspect she will fire me after a week or so when she gets tired of eating pasta."

Mechelle commented, "You should see if Phyllis can teach you. She and I have been having a blast cooking together."

Karen leaned forward. "Do you think she would? It would be great to have a job like that."

I replied, "The worst she'll say is no, but I doubt she will. She loves teaching people. She could teach you a lot about running a house."

The guys came over and joined us. Jared didn't sit down. He filmed us. Something in my spirit was bothered by this. I asked him, "Don't you need releases from people you film to use them in your work?"

Jared lowered his camera. "Of course, this is more of me developing a style." He placed the camera on the table and pulled out his phone.

As we watched several videos showing brand awareness, drone footage, a testimonial about his company, and a wedding. Jared explained to us the techniques he was using.

Jared commented, "I still need a documentary, and an employee training video. I'm working on a couple of product videos, but they still need some tweaking."

"That is fascinating, but I know I don't want my face plastered out there. Brooke, I don't think anyone at the company should give permission for this," Jacob suggested. He turned to Jared. "No offense, but in our line of work it can be dangerous."

"No, it's cool. I'll delete this. Sorry, I'm just trying to develop my craft," Jared replied. He picked up his camera. "Is it cool if I video the food and the bonfire?"

"That should be fine. Just don't record anymore people," Jacob responded.

Jared rushed off to record the food.

"Good call on that man," Austin said to Jacob.

Everyone chimed in on recognizing the possible consequences of it.

Jacob added, "Honestly, it would be best if everyone was off social media."

"You might be right," I said just before Bill announced for everyone to bow their heads.

"Dear Heavenly Father, we thank you for this food and those that prepared it. We ask that it nourishes our bodies. Thank you for bringing our friends and family here with us today. We ask for safe travel for them when they depart this evening. In Jesus name I pray. Amen."

We let the friends and family of Austin's family get their food before us. Once settled into my seat, I found my mouth salivating over the thought of eating Bill's Western Kentucky BBQ Sauce again. I bit into a piece dripping with sauce. The spiciness was still there but it was sweeter than I remembered. I asked, "Austin, is this the same sauce your dad normally makes?"

"He's been making this for years, but this is his sweet version. It's my favorite."

"I agree, this takes the other one to a new level," I complimented. After our meal we played horseshoes and enjoyed a bonfire. As I watched the flames flicker back and forth, I couldn't help but remember the first BBQ I attended at Austin's house was the night I revealed to Greg the power of the Bloom of Dreams. Greg helped Austin with moving some of the tables back to their normal locations. As he rose, I noticed Jared was watching me. His eyes darted away.

Get out of your head. He's Greg's friend.

I sighed and toasted another marshmallow. Toasted really was not the word I should have used. I blackened it. As I pulled it off the stick, I caught Jared watching me again. That time I didn't break eye contact.

He commented, "That's an interesting way to eat them." He raised his eyebrows and shook his head.

Something was really bothering me about him. Using telepathy, I asked Mechelle, "I need a favor, but you can't tell anyone. Please take a picture of Jared."

She nodded.

About thirty minutes later we went home. Mechelle rode home with us. After I showered, I checked my phone before turning in for the night. I had missed a call from my mother and Mechelle's call she had mentioned earlier. Mechelle also texted the photo of Jared when he was in the house talking to Austin. I printed the photo and changed into my Bloom Keeper's uniform. Time to visit Nadine and Eddie.

They were sound asleep. I turned the lights on and announced myself, "It's your favorite time traveler."

Nadine woke up. She tried waking Eddie, but he was sleeping like a bear. Nadine just stared at me.

I tossed her the photograph. "Jared is the ginger in the photo. He's a videographer. I suspect he's spying on your current employers. His focus was on Brooke Garrison. Find out what he's up to and if he's working with anyone. Let Brooke know your findings." I tossed my business card at her. This is her card.

Nadine nodded as she snatched the business card into her hand.

Without another word, I flicked the light off and returned home.

Twenty-Two

I was excited about our trip. Before even getting dressed, I had begun packing for our trip to Italy. To not raise suspicion, Mechelle and Austin were flying as she needed to have her passport stamped since she would be working in the country and Austin did not want her flying alone. They would arrive there the next morning. We'll meet them at the villa around 1:00 pm. Everyone was coming over here for breakfast before we popped over there. I could easily fill my closet there by teleporting the things I wanted to use or just come back for them, but the cleaning staff might become suspicious if I did not have a suitcase or if I wore clothes they had not seen in my closet.

As I was about to change, I noticed a drone flying outside my window.

What the heck?

I rushed to see if I could find the person with the controls, but no one was in view. The drone flew off.

I teleported to the street invisible and searched for the owner of the drone. I was surprised to discover Eddie and Nadine in a vehicle a few houses down. I teleported to the back seat of their car and remained invisible.

I said, "Don't be alarmed. It's just Beetlejuice." I was surprised they were so calm about my arrival. Well, after their initial shock.

"We're doing what ya asked," Eddie said. He pointed out the windshield. "That guy up there in the red car. He's flying a drone and it was headed toward Brook's house."

I asked, "Have you discovered anything else?"

Nadine pulled out a sticky-note. "According to his computer, he's got a meeting with someone named Ms. Demeaner," Nadine said as she read the note.

I snagged the note with the meeting information from Nadine's hand. "Keep up the good work." I teleported to his vehicle to get a memory to return to before returning to my room.

I changed out of my pajamas and brushed my teeth. It was nice having a day off from work and our daily workout. I did not need to worry about the office because Jacob was there to field any calls that might come.

As I stared at myself in the mirror, I thought about April. I spit the paste from my mouth and rinsed. I wiped my mouth. If only I could pass for April. I turned away from the mirror and hung my towel up.

Too bad I can't snap my fingers and be her.

I chuckled. I snapped my fingers and said, "Make me look like April." I wandered out to the full-length mirror to get a view of my outfit.

What in the world?

I touched the mirror.

How's this possible?

The image in the mirror was not mine.

I'm April.

I fell back on to my bed in astonishment.

I thought about what I could do with such a skill. It also occurred to me that if the Bloom Keepers knew this, it might cause them to wonder who they were really talking to because I could become any of them.

That's not good.

I needed to have them trust one another. I bit my lip.

It's decided. This would be a secret only the journal and I would be aware of.

I changed into something I felt was like April's style and teleported to a bush near the red vehicle. When the coast was clear I approached him and tapped on the window of the passenger side of the car.

He unlocked the door and asked, "What are you doing here?"

Jared.

I said, "Explain to me our arrangement."

Jared tilted his head, narrowed his eyes, and shrugged. "You asked me to show you videos of anything unusual with Brooke Garrison."

"Have you found anything?"

Please say no.

"Yes, but I don't have anything on a flash drive yet," Jared answered.

"Show me," I demanded.

"I thought you and I were going to meet. I had this whole presentation planned."

I snapped, "Show me now."

Jared picked up his laptop from the backseat and appeared to be searching for a file. He flipped the computer screen around and said, "Watch this. See, she's in her room. She walks into her bathroom. I don't do videos of people in there."

Thank God for that.

"Watch, I move the camera to the kitchen to see what the maid was doing. Check it out. I bet that is delicious." Jared said as he pointed to a cake Phyllis was decorating. He pointed to the pantry door. "Now, watch here."

I watched knowing I was about to exit the pantry.

Jared brushed his hand through his hair and glared at the screen. "Bam! She comes out there." He whips his hand in the air waiting for me to high five him.

My mouth was open.

This is not good.

I moved the computer closer to rewatched the video. I asked, "Is this your only copy?"

"Yeah, I don't have a flash drive on me now to copy it for you, but we could go grab one," Jared replied.

I turned the computer where he could not see me delete the file, I handed him back his computer.

Thank you, Jacob, for teaching me how to completely remove the file.

In a stern voice, I said, "Delete all traces of any files you have about the Davis International Investigative Service and get out of here. We are done. Our other meeting is cancelled." I opened the door.

He started yelling at me, "It's gone. Why'd you delete it?"

I slammed his door as I watched him frantically trying to find the file. I slipped behind a bush and became invisible.

Jared jumped out of the car, revealing his Irish temper. "Lady are we still meeting?" He frantically spun around and screamed, "I need to get paid!"

Tucked behind a bush, I gazed into my mirror and teleported back to Eddie and Nadine invisible. "You've done an outstanding job. You can go home."

I returned home.

Wow! That was amazing.

I stood in front of the full-length mirror.

Who should I be now?

I concentrated on Phyllis.

This is fantastic.

Now Greg. I was even taller.

So odd. I look good.

I bit my lip as I thought about what I could do with this skill, but it was like God whispered, "Don't abuse the gift."

God had convicted me. I changed back to myself, and I asked Him for forgiveness. I returned to packing.

About fifteen minutes later, there was a knock on the door. I unlocked it and discovered Phyllis standing in the hall with my towels.

She marched into the bathroom saying, "Karen's going to be hanging around here for a while training with me. Is that okay?"

I waited for her to exit the bathroom to answer. "Yes, if she's wanting to get into your line of work, who better to learn from?"

"I figured I would take advantage of everyone being gone to train her properly," Phyllis informed me.

"That's probably a good idea," I admitted. Once my door was shut, I called Allison on the phone she gave me. I provided her with the information about the meeting and sent her a picture of Jared. She thanked me. Allison suspected she would be able to catch April unexpectedly with an agent dressed as Jared.

I hung out with Phyllis for a while. We discussed the changes in our lives over the past few years. She told me she and Hal were so happy they had their own home. She was planning a housewarming party after we returned from Italy. There wasn't much to do around the house, and she needed things for her and Karen to do so I sent her home early. I was rather bored because Mechelle and Austin were shopping for a few last-minute things she might need in Italy, Greg was working on his lawn, and Juliet and Jacob were doing whatever it is they do.

I teleported down to my grandmother's secret room to read a bit more of her journals. It amazed me the many things I was able to learn about her. I only wished she could have told me the stories herself. I ran my fingers along the journals as I often did to randomly select one. One day I hope to read these in order, but my life was too hectic for me to attempt it now.

May 20, 2003

Phyllis and I are back from our trip to Ireland. She really is the best companion for traveling. The Slieve League Cliffs were stunning. But nothing was more beautiful than the Dingle Peninsula at sunset. We spent time going through local shops and pubs in a nearby town. I think I'll be done with potatoes and cabbage for a while. We've had our fill of them during this trip. However. I'll miss the Irish stew with lamb. It was outstanding.

May 21, 2003

I tried to see if I could discover things the stone is capable of. Sadly, I was unsuccessful. One day, I'll find the cradle and its true potential will be revealed.

What haven't I discovered about it?
That had me thinking. I returned the book to the shelf and teleported myself to my room. I stared into my full-length mirror at the stone.
Okay, stone. What else can you do?
I began thinking about superheroes.
Let's see there's strength, speed, and heat vision.
My house was not the place to test these. I teleported to the wooded area by the cabin Kevin had shown me.

I moved over to a large tree. I said, "Bloom of Dreams please give me superhuman strength." I waited a moment before using every ounce of force in me to push the tree. Nothing happened.
Disappointing.

I said to the tree, "You couldn't even move a little. You're mocking me aren't you." It was a good thing no one was around because they may have thought I believed the tree was communicating with me.

What was the next one? Oh, yes. Speed.

I rolled my eyes. I was certain this one was not going to work. "Bloom of Dreams, please make me have superhuman speed." I thrust forward and gave it my all. As I slowed down, I realized I would never have a lightning bolt across my chest like the Flash.

As I thought about heat vision, I became concerned. This sounds incredibly dangerous.

What if I were having a dream and suddenly awoke with lasers flying out of my eyes? I would be burning up my room and the more I shifted my eyes around the more I burned.

I asked the stone for the power and focused on a fallen rotting tree a few feet away. Nothing. I shook my shoulders and tried again. With eyes narrowed and focusing on the knot on the log I concentrated. Still nothing. Feeling defeated, I lowered my head. I had enough and went back to my room.

I collected my phone and noticed a missed call from my mother. After a shower, I returned her call.

"I know you're busy getting ready for your flight, but I wanted to tell you to enjoy yourself and to have fun," Mom said.

"Thanks. I believe I have everything packed but my toiletries," I said proudly.

"Did you remember your Bible?"

I hesitantly said, "No."

"Brooke…"

I could almost hear her rolling her eyes through the phone. "I'm putting it in my suitcase right now," I said plopping the Bible on top of my pajamas.

We chatted a bit about how my business was going and the cruise she and Susie were going on to the Bahamas. Her call was interrupted by her boss.

My stomach announced its desire for food. I teleported to the pantry to see if there was anything to eat. Phyllis must have emptied the refrigerator since I was going to be gone. It mainly contained condiments, bottles of water, and a couple of yogurts. I opened the drawer containing all the delivery menus and perused them. I had narrowed it down to two when Mechelle sauntered in. "Hey there. Where's Austin?"

"He's headed home. His mom has a dinner planned for him," she said.

I held up the two menus and asked, "Are you interested in Italian or Tai?"

Mechelle picked up the rest of the menus and flipped through them. "I don't think Thai would be the best thing before a long trip on a plane. How about a pizza?"

We settled on a sausage pie. I helped her take her things to her room and watched her finish her packing while we waited for the pizza. "Austin will be here at 9:00 pm to pick me up. I think he's nervous about being on the plane so long," Mechelle said as she zipped up her suitcase. She held out her hand and asked, "Would you mind helping me get this downstairs?"

I picked up her suitcase, while she slung her purse over her shoulder and snatched up her carry-on bag. Once she had a good hold on my arm, I teleported us to the pantry. As we exited, I heard the doorbell chime.

"I'll get us some paper plates," Mechelle hollered to me as I rushed to the door.

I returned to the kitchen and found Mechelle grabbing two bottles of water from the refrigerator. She and I gabbed about things we would like to do on the trip. I offered to clean up while she went up to brush her teeth. I wandered out to the trashcan to dispose of the pizza box and was nearly blinded by Austin's truck as it pulled up.

He hopped out and asked, "Is my little lady ready to head out?"

"Absolutely. She ran up to brush her teeth, but you can grab her bags," I suggested.

Austin was loading them when she joined me in the kitchen. She narrowed her eyes. "Is Austin here?" She meandered to the window and peered out.

"Yes, he's loading your things. Would you do me a favor?" I raised my eyebrows and gave my best puppy dog eyes.

"Perhaps," Mechelle said as she tilted her head.

"I think April might be tracking me. Would you mind bringing my phone with you on the plane?"

She held out her hand and I placed my phone into her hand. As she walked out, she hollered, "See you tomorrow."

I spent the rest of the night watching television.

173

Twenty-Three

The guys arrived at 7:00 am and gathered in the dining room where Phyllis had a coffee and juice tray waiting for us. She provided strict instructions that we were not to go into the kitchen.

Juliet asked, "What time is it in Italy now?"

I replied, "2:00 pm."

Jacob asked, "What do you think Mechelle and Austin are doing?"

Greg replied, "I suspect she's showing him around the villa."

Phyllis appeared in the doorway of the dining room. "This morning, we are serving Shrimp Eggs Benedict with a mixed fruit bowl," she announced as Karen came in and passed out plates.

With a furrowed brow, Greg asked, "Did you make this Karen?"

Karen replied, "I did. I hope you like it."

Greg led us in saying grace, "Father, we thank You for this food You have provided. Thank You for meeting our physical needs of hunger and thirst. Please forgive us for taking this simple joy for granted and bless this food to fuel our bodies. We pray we'll be energized. In Jesus' name, Amen."

Everyone said, "Amen."

Karen and Phyllis stood by waiting to see our response. My plate was like a piece of artwork. I sliced it into it and watched the yoke of the egg cascade to the plate. As the food hit my tongue, I was greeted with the savory hollandaise sauce that had a touch of Old Bay seasoning. The shrimp was perfectly cooked. Wide-eyed I turned to Karen and said, "This is fantastic!"

She started to blush. Everyone ushered in compliments.

Karen topped off our drinks.

Phyllis and Karen left us to enjoy our meal. There was little conversation as we ate. I suspected everyone wanted to eat and be on our way. We were finishing up when Karen and Phyllis returned.

Karen asked, "Why didn't you'll fly over with Mechelle and Austin?"

Jacob replied, "We have work that needs to be done at the office."

Good catch Jacob.

There was a little more chatting before everyone said their goodbyes.

Karen asked, "Who's driving to the airport?"

My eyes darted over everyone. I am sure we all wanted to supply her with an answer. It had not occurred to me that someone could see our vehicles were not gone.

"We're getting an Uber." Jacob said.

"That's silly. I can drive you," Karen spurted.

Phyllis spoke up, "I'm sorry Karen you have work to do."

"Thank you for the offer but I'm ordering one right now," Jacob stated as he tapped on his phone.

Jacob turned to me. "Brooke, are your bags ready to go?"

"Yes," I mumbled.

What's going on?

"I'll fetch them," Greg said. He hurried off toward the stairs. I joined him to make sure nothing was left behind.

When we entered my room, I asked, "Do you know what's going on?"

Greg replied, "I suspect we're taking an Uber to the airport."

I rolled my eyes. Greg picked up my suitcase and I picked up my purse.

Everyone was in the foyer waiting for us. I asked, "Does everyone have their passport?" There was a lot of head bobbing.

"We've got our boarding passes too," Jacob added.

I hugged Karen and thanked her for Breakfast. As soon as I released her, Phyllis pulled me in for a hug.

"Have fun," she said loudly. Phyllis whispered, "Be alert. Not all the Granaldi's and their allies are in prison."

I nodded.

"Uber's here," Jacob announced.

Everyone grabbed their bags and stuffed them into the trunk of the Uber. Greg sat upfront while Jacob, Juliet and I squeezed into the back seat. Jacob provided the driver the address to our office. As the driver unloaded, he shook his head.

He's probably trying to figure out why we moved a bunch of suitcases a few blocks to a business.

The guys brought the bags in while Juliet and I closed the curtains.

I hope no one noticed us coming in.

I announced, "Boarding passes, please."

Greg stepped forward and planted a kiss on my lips.

Juliet commented, "Greg's holding our passes too."

Greg kissed me again, then I teleported us to my room at the villa. Bags were piled up by the window. I called the front desk.

"Good afternoon, Brooke," Isabella said.

I greeted her. She let me know Leonardo would be coming with a key. A few minutes later there was a knock on the door. Greg opened it and we found Mechelle and Austin gazing into each other's eyes.

Mechelle peaked inside. The room was crowded. She handed Greg my phone. "Juliet, I have your key. You're bunking with me," she announced.

Austin chimed in, "Greg, you're with me."

Juliet pulled her suitcase behind her as she squeezed through everyone to the exit. Greg followed.

"We'll meet you at the reception area in twenty minutes," Mechelle announced as she and Juliet left.

Leonardo strolled up as they were leaving. Jacob, here's your room key. Let me show you to your room."

Jacob asked, "I get my own room?"

Leonardo nodded. "Brooke thought it best because of the late hours you keep. She figured the privacy would help too if you needed to work."

"Thanks, Brooke," Jacob said as he fetched his bag.

I've got twenty minutes.

I teleported to my secret room in the wine cellar and updated the journal with my latest discoveries about the power of the stone. I was about to write about the shape shifting.

Every evil person in the world could use this to better themselves. No.

I shook my head. This will be a secret of the Blooms I'll keep to myself. I closed the journal and returned it to the safe.

I popped back into my room to grab my purse. One last inspection of my appearance in my full-length mirror before I strolled to the reception area. Greg and Austin were waiting when I entered the area. Isabella was working on her computer.

I asked, "What do you want to do in town?"

Greg pulled me in by the waist, "Whatever you want to do." He kissed me and gently released his hold on me.

I turned to Austin, "How about you?"

"I'm just here for the ride," he stated.

Juliet and Mechelle arrived.

Juliet asked, "Where's Jacob?"

Several of us shrugged our shoulders.

Mechelle said, "I hope you don't mind but I have planned a nice day for us."

"How exciting," I said.

Jacob meandered over to us, "Sorry guys, I wanted to set up my computer before we headed out."

"We're all here. Let's get going. I have a car for us," Mechelle announced.

We were led to a black van with dark tinted windows. Mechelle drove. Jacob rode in the front seat with her. He needed leg room. Greg and I were in the middle row and Austin and Juliet were in the back row.

We drove for a bit before parking. Sounding like a tour guide, Mechelle announced, "We are in the historical center of Florence, and it dates to 1873. You are about to experience vibrant colors, flavors, and fragrances. This is one of the first religious buildings to be built here."

Mechelle was right. We wandered through what appeared to be a flea market with clothes, leather goods, florists, bakeries, meat, pasta, cheese, seafood, and vegetables markets. We sampled a variety of cheeses and salami. I picked up a small bouquet for Isabella. It amazed me how many different types of fresh pasta were available. We spent several hours shopping.

We drove the short distance to Fortezza da Basso. As we approached the building Mechelle said, "The Fortezza da Basso is from the fourteenth century. It was inserted into the walls of

178

Florence. Its official name is the Fortress of Saint John the Baptist. Today conferences, exhibits and concerts are held here."

It was stunning. Also, larger than it appeared in pictures.

"We best get back and get ready for dinner," Mechelle said as we returned to the van. "Chef Giovanni has something special planned for dinner."

I gave the flowers to Isabella on the way to my room. Everyone showered and dressed. It was strange seeing Austin in a pair of slacks. Isabella said, "It's a beautiful night. I've arranged a table for you outside." She led us to it.

Once seated, Isabella said, "The chef is preparing a special meal for you. He hopes you enjoy it." She spun around and walked back toward the villa.

The server came by and wrote down our drink order.

A man at the next table said to his wife, "Why's the chef making a bunch of kids a special dinner?"

His wife stared at us. "Perhaps they're famous. Quick snap a photo."

"No. I don't want to be act like the paparazzi. They'll think I'm some crazy person," he responded.

The waiter served the first course of cheese and crackers.

Mechelle commented, "This is aperitivo your first course. I recommend you don't overindulge yourselves. There are six more courses to go.

"Seriously, that's fantastic," Jacob said enthusiastically.

Juliet and I rolled our eyes and laughed.

A short while later, Antipasti was served. It had the perfect blend of cheese and meat.

Austin asked, "What's the difference between Antipasti and aperitivo?"

"Aperitivo means before the meal. The Antipasti is a little heavier," Mechelle answered.

The gentleman at the other table asked, "Do you think these kids are going to run out on their check? That meal's going to cost them a fortune." He leaned back in his chair. "Seven courses for six people" He shook his head as he stabbed a piece of pasta.

Mechelle said, "The next course is the first official course in a traditional Italian meal. It's called primi piatti."

We were served Ravioli with baccala and carrot sauce.

Jacob asked, "What is baccala?"

179

The woman from the next table hollered, "It's salted cod."

Jacob whipped his head toward her and awkwardly said, "Thank you. He leaned over to Juliet. "Are they eavesdropping on our conversation?"

Juliet shrugged her shoulders.

Austin said, "It's sounds strange, but I'll try anything."

I agreed. Each of us bit into our food. We all commented that it was delicious. When the waiter tried to take my plate, I told him to leave it. If I had room for more, I planned on devouring it.

The waiter announced, "The second piatti is almond crusted plaice with asparagus, pea, and spinach avocado cream. We also present you with Broccoli Romano for Contorni."

Juliet commented, "This is a crazy amount of food."

Wow.

She was right. "I think my palate's being over stimulated," I commented.

Greg asked, "I've lost count. How many more courses?"

"Who cares, bring on the food," Jacob replies.

Mechelle turned to Greg, "The salad is the sixth course."

She was correct. It was a light dish served with oil and vinegar and sprinkled with salt and pepper.

Juliet asked, "What's the seventh?"

"Dolce. It's dessert," Mechelle answered.

I was getting full, so I only picked at the salad.

The woman at the next table asked her husband, "Aren't you going to pay the bill?"

"Not yet. I want to see what these kids do when they get the bill," he announced to his wife.

Many of us ordered coffee before the dessert was delivered. Before the server left, I asked him to get Isabella.

I pushed my salad away. Half hoping the dessert would be horrible so I wouldn't be tempted to eat it. Everyone was chatting about the day when Isabella strolled over.

She asked, "Is everything okay?"

Everyone commented on how fantastic the food was. I excused myself and pulled her away from the tables. I said, "Would you please pay for their meal from my account?" I motioned to the couple next to us.

She asked, "Are you sure?"

"Yes," I said and returned to my seat.

The waiter returned with Panna Cotta.

"Gorgeous," Juliet announced.

"This is my favorite. It's an Italian custard with jam on the bottom, then the custard and topped with fresh fruit. Sometimes you can find them with caramel," Mechelle explained.

I glanced over and saw Isabella speaking with the couple at the next table.

The man asked Isabella, "Why would you give it to us for free? Do you think I can't afford to pay?"

She replied, "No sir it's not that."

"What then?"

"Sir, the owner's here and has asked us to cover your meal. No reason was given," she said.

He shrugged and his wife narrowed her eyes. He glanced back at us and replied, "The owner? Who's the owner?"

Isabella peeked over at me and seemed unsure if she should reply. I excused myself from the table and joined Isabella.

The wife slapped her husband's arm and pointed at me.

I turned to the gentleman and said, "This is my fault. I never meant to offend you. I noticed you and your lovely wife enjoying your meal. I was led to do something for you."

He seemed to be inspecting me. "You're just a child."

I chuckled, "I assure you I'm older than I look. Please let me do this for you."

The wife asked, "Young lady, are you saying you own this place, or your parents do?"

Isabella spoke up, "I assure you; she owns the place. We are blessed to have her and her friends here for a visit."

The lady pried more, "You're American. May I ask your name?"

"I would rather not disclose that. The more who know my financial situation the more piranhas there are to fight off. I'm sure you understand."

"Well young lady, thank you for dinner. You have a beautiful place here," the man said.

"That's thanks to Isabella, Leonardo and their wonderful staff," I commented.

"I really must return to my friends. Enjoy your stay," I said before I returned to my seat.

Juliet asked, "What was that about?"

"Nothing really," I said as I placed a spoonful of the dessert into my mouth. "Oh my... incredible."

A few moments later, Chef Giovanni checked in on us. "I hope everyone enjoyed their meal. He was bombarded with complements. After thanking us, he told us to enjoy our visit before checking on the other guests.

Mechelle and I stood up.

Jacob said, "We haven't gotten the check?"

Mechelle leaned over and whispered, "Brooke's covering all expenses."

Austin said, "Thanks but why?"

Greg wrapped his arm around Austin and as they went back inside, and whispered, "Brooke owns this place."

I glanced over and noticed Austin's mouth was open and his eyes were nearly bulging out of his head. I felt the same way. It seemed unreal how much I was worth.

Lord, I know. I needed to stay humble.

Once Austin was able to compose himself, he asked Greg, "Dude, how much is she worth?"

Greg shot his eyes at me. I smiled to let him know he was fine explaining. "I don't think she really knows, but it's a lot. She's a modest person but generous. Oh, and you're not to discuss this with anyone outside of the Bloom Keepers. Her mother doesn't even know."

"She's awesome," Austin said.

"Isabella set up a private room for us to hangout in," Mechelle said leading us to it.

The six of us hung out until midnight. Most of us weren't tired because it was still early evening. We needed to try and sleep to get our bodies adjusted to the new time zone.

Greg walked me to my room. "I guess this is where I say goodnight."

I wrapped my arms around his neck. "It is," I said with my lips just inches from his.

He wrapped his arms around me. "Are you sure?"

I moved my mouth a little closer and softly said, "It is?"

Greg leaned in and gently touched my lips to his. This stirred my body to want more. I unlocked the door and we nearly fell through the doorway.

Greg pulled me to him and sensually kissed me. My entire body was stirred. I pulled him to the bed and fell back pulling him with me. Our eyes locked on one another. I wanted to touch his skin. He leaned in and began kissing me deeply as I felt his arm run up the side of me pulling my blouse with it.

The breathing was becoming heavy as my heart rate increased. I pulled him closer, sliding my hands under his shirt and up his back.

Greg moved to my neck. His hot breath could be felt under my shirt as he kissed me. Chills ran down my left side leaving me wanting more.

As I arched my back; his right arm slid under me. He held me tightly against him as his lips returned to mine.

My hands moved up and down his back wanting more. "Oh Greg," I muttered.

I started to pull his shirt off. He lifted himself to help and stared down at me. "I love you," he whispered.

I pulled harder on his shirt.

I'm ready.

Greg gripped his shirt to prevent me from pulling it off. He rolled off me to the other side of the bed.

Immediately, I felt ashamed and embarrassed.

Greg rolled back toward me. "Babe, I want you so bad."

"I feel the same. If you hadn't stopped us, I would have let you," I said.

"I suspected that. We made a vow. I can't break it," he said flopping back on to the pillow.

Tears filled my eyes. I laid my head on his chest and cried. He held me in his arms and consoled me. Until we both fell asleep.

Twenty-Four

I woke up in Greg's arms. It was nearly time for my alarm to go off, but I was not ready for it. I was so comfortable cuddled up next to him. The thought of being his wife and doing this every day was how I wanted to spend my life. I found myself staring at him. He was even beautiful as he laid there with drool creeping out of his mouth. I apologized to God, but I was grateful Greg stopped us.

My flesh is so weak when it comes to him.

The alarm went off causing Greg to stir. He opened his eyes and seemed confused to see me. Suddenly he jumped up.

"Brooke, I'm so sorry. I must have fallen asleep," Greg said nervously. He sprung from the bed. "I need to get to my room before Austin notices I wasn't there."

"Greg, please stop. God knows nothing happened," I said as I sat up. "Should you have stayed here? No, but we could have done something…" I lowered my head in shame. "But we didn't thanks to you."

"Brooke, you are the one. Do you understand? I don't want anyone thinking you are anything less than the amazing woman you are. God truly blessed me when he brought you into my life." He leaned forward and kissed me. "I'm sorry, I need to go. I love you," he said as he rushed out.

His words kept running through my mind like a song being played repeatedly. I was on cloud nine.

Thank you, Lord, for such an amazing man.

I leapt out of the bed and showered. Mechelle had told us last night we would need a bathing suit for part of the day. I wore it under my outfit and made sure to pack some under garments in my purse along with a plastic bag for my bathing suit if I changed. In the mist of braiding my hair, someone knocked on the door. I hollered, "Just a minute." I finished the braid before opening the door.

I was pleasantly surprised to see Greg standing there less frazzled. "Wow, you're gorgeous." He came in and gave me a kiss. "Good morning."

"Yes, it is a good morning," I agreed. I picked up my purse. "I know it shouldn't have happened, but it was wonderful waking up in your arms."

"I agree. I wish I didn't have to leave, but I know you understand why I did."

"I do and I'm glad you can keep me in line," I said rolling my eyes. "It would be a lie to say I don't desire to be with you," I said feeling my cheeks get warm.

"One day you will," he said just before kissing me. "We need to go before this gets out of control again." Greg opened the door and motioned for me to exit.

On our way to breakfast I asked Greg, "What do you think Mechelle has planned for us today?"

"There's a water park here," Greg commented.

"By the way, did Austin see you come in this morning?"

"I don't think so. It's difficult to wake him up. I messed up my bed and jumped in the shower before his alarm even went off," Greg informed me.

We ran into Jacob and Juliet on the way. Juliet asked, "Do you mind eating outside again?"

Greg and I glanced at each other and shrugged our shoulders. "Sounds good to us," Greg answered.

Leonardo was speaking with a guest as we passed him. I waved as we headed outside. We had the same table which overlooked the vineyard. I spotted Kyle. I excused myself and strolled over to talk to him.

I asked, "Are things still going well for you here?"

"Absolutely. When I lost my phone, I lost my daughter Lyndee's phone number, and we had no way of contacting each other.

Leonardo helped me locate her. She was able to come here and see me. She's my everything. When things are safe for me. I'm going to go visit her and her family."

"That's wonderful. I hope you'll be contacted soon. Have a good day." I returned to the table and discovered Austin and Mechelle were at the table.

Along with our drinks, coffee for me of course, we received a tray containing Cornetto, which is the Italian version of a croissant filled with custard, chocolate, or jam. There was also a tray of biscuits with a variety of jams. Totally different from a southern biscuit from home. There was also a platter of bread, cheese, and fruit. I pulled a piece of my Cornetto off as I sat back in my chair admiring the wonderful view.

Austin commented, "It's too bad they don't have a pool here."

"That would take away from the charm of the place," I said.

We finished up breakfast and set out on our adventure. Mechelle brought us to the Arno River to kayak. Everyone was excited to get started. Even Jacob. It amazed me how much confidence he had gained since I first met him. We piled our things in a locker and set out on the river.

The guys had several splashing battles going on throughout the morning. It was amazing gliding through the water seeing the city along the banks of the river. Once everyone was back on shore, we collected our things. I changed out of my bathing suit. Each of us checked our phones as we made our way to the van.

"Brooke, Allison left me a message. She wants to speak with both of us," Jacob announced.

Greg suggested Jacob and I get in the middle seat and teleport. We piled up in the van. Jacob and I leaned over and arrived invisible in Allison's office. She was on a phone call.

She said, "Yes, that's correct. How long till they get there?... Thanks." Allison slammed the phone down.

"Hello. We're here," I announced.

"Thank God!" She picked up her phone and pretended she was on it. "Agents are about to go into that videographer's apartment to collect the videos he did for April. When we sent our agent in pretending to be Jared, April told the agent she wanted the videos he had seen that had peculiar things in them. I suspect the Bloom Keepers might be on them. You need to get over there and deal with them. I only have a photo of the front door, but they could be there at any minute."

Brooke asked, "We don't have time to change. Do you have some gloves?"

Allison opened her computer case and gave a pair of rubber gloves to Jacob. "I only have this one pair. You need to go!"

I examined the photograph and immediately teleported Jacob and I there invisible. I pulled us through the front door. No one else was there. I glanced around searching for the equipment while he put the gloves on. It appeared everything was on a desk in the living room. I pointed at it and moved to the front window to see if there was any sign of the authorities. There wasn't.

I went to the bedroom and used the bottom of my shirt to touch things as I tried to find more evidence. There was nothing. I returned to the main room.

Jacob had the computer up and running. He opened the drone to pull out the SD card. He whispered, "There's another SD card in the computer." He opened the drawer on the desk. There were five more SD cards.

I kept a small corner of the blind open to see out. Suddenly, three black SUVs pulled in front of the building. "We need to go," I commanded.

"I don't have time to search everything," Jacob said shoving the SD cards into his pocket.

"Just take everything," I ordered.

"I am," he said as he cradled the computer in his arms. Just as we had begun to teleport, the front door was flying open. I brought us to the secret room at the villa. We put the SD cards and the computer in the safe along with the gloves and teleported them back to Allison.

Allison was staring at her phone as it sat on the desk.

"We believe we have everything," I announced.

Allison flew back onto her chair. "You scared me," she said catching her breath.

"Your men are there now, we didn't have time to delete everything, so we took it," Jacob informed her.

"That's good. Jared will just think he's been robbed, and my agency will conclude someone else must have known what he was doing for April. Oh, I forgot to tell you, April's in custody."

Jacob and I smiled at one another and bumped our fists into each other.

Allison's phone rang. She held up her pointer finger. "Agent Dunara," she announced. She listened to the caller and smiled. "Are you sure?"

I was tempted to see if she was talking with one of the men at Jared's apartment.

Allison asked the caller, "Have you found him?" She leaned back in her chair as they answered her question. "No. Without the videos his testimony about what he may or may not have seen will be irrelevant. He could testify April hired him, but he never provided her anything." She listened. "You're right. The evidence we already have will put her away for a long time. Just close it down." The phone went dead.

"Well done. There's no evidence of anything unexplainable going on with you. No one's going to be searching for Jared.

I enthusiastically said, "That's fantastic!"

"I love you kid, but you need to get out of here. I have a meeting in five minutes," Allison said.

We said our goodbyes and teleported back to the van.

Mechelle commented, "Where have you been?"

Jacob described the details of the mission along with the new knowledge about April being in custody. After a few questions for more clarification, Jacob said, "I'm starving. Can we go get something to eat?"

Mechelle drove us to Pizza Napoli 1955. Each of us had our own pizza and the chef even made some of them heart shaped. It was delicious. The remainder of the day was spent at the Plaza Hotel Lucchesi in their rooftop pool. Mechelle explained Leonardo had connections and was able to permit us an afternoon there. We returned to the villa to shower and rest for a bit from the day.

Our plan was to head to town for dinner and check out the nightlife. We decided on Yab, a popular nightclub and waited in the long line.

The dance music along with the atmosphere provided the club-like feel of things seen in movies in New York. None of us had been to a nightclub. To me, it was a bit intense. Perhaps I'm an old soul. Mechelle, Austin, Greg, and I went out on the dance floor.

It was astonishing how many people were squeezed together. Whether you wanted to or not, you were going to be intimate with the people next to you. I constantly felt people bumping up against me.

Mechelle and I excused ourselves for a much-needed bathroom break. There was a long line, where we had to wait for nearly five minutes to get in. When I came out of my stall Mechelle was applying her lip-gloss. I was washing my hands when I shivered as I felt like someone was staring at me.

I glimpsed toward the doorway and a young woman stood there waiting for a stall to open.

Where do I know you from?

A stall door opened, and an intoxicated woman stumbled out. The woman in line rushed to the stall and locked the door. I had a bad feeling about the girl. I leaned back and let the stone rest on my skin. It surprised me it had not warmed up.

Using telepathy, I asked Mechelle if she recognized her. She did not know who I was referring to. I proceeded to describe her as we exited the restroom. It was difficult to find everyone in the crowd.

Mechelle and I held hands as we squeezed our way through the swarms of people. Mechelle suddenly jerked away and shoved a blond man wearing a black shirt.

She directed her attention to him and yelled, "Don't you dare lay another hand on me, mister!"

The man appeared drunk as he placed one finger on her shoulder. Mechelle thrust her fist upward into his groin and paralyzed the man. She then gently pushed him, and he fell to the floor.

Good job Mechelle.

She clutched my hand and started leading me through the crowd.

We saw the others standing along the side of the dance floor. Mechelle motioned for them to join us. "What a creep," she said.

I asked, "What happened?"

"He grabbed my butt."

When we were all together, Mechelle asked, "Would you mind if we left?"

Juliet tried to say something, but I could not hear her over the music. I yelled, "What?"

"I'm all for it. Everyone talks about how much fun it is going to clubs but it's not really for me," Juliet hollered toward us.

Greg motioned for us to leave. The blaring music faded as we approached the van. Everyone agreed; this was not as fun as we would have thought. I never said anything about the man Mechelle brought down. That was her story to tell if she chose to.

We were near the van when the stone heated. "Guys stop," I ordered.

Greg asked, "What's wrong?"

I glanced around, "I'm not sure. The stone is heating up, but I don't think we should go to the van. If there's danger here, they'll be able to discover the villa owns the van."

Mechelle whispered, "Yeah, let's not do that. I don't need people to know where I work. We can get the van later."

Jacob asked, "Wasn't there a hotel down the road?" Jacob pointed south.

Greg commented, "Great idea. Lead the way."

Everyone started going but I waited. Greg stopped.

I said, "Stone, reveal the danger." A glowing line went up to a vehicle on the other side of the parking area. I could not see who was inside. We caught up with the group as we paraded down the paved street toward the hotel. We passed many motorcycles parked along the road. It astonished me how narrow the roads were. We were nearly at the intersection when we came to some bicycle parking. I really could not see the hotel.

Jacob crossed the intersection with Juliet on his arm and started moving east on Via Porta Rossa. The Hotel Davanzati was on the right. Suddenly a black car raced around the corner and began shooting at us. Everyone ran up the stairs toward the hotel lobby as bullets flew. I ducked behind a car and was able to catch a glimpse of the passenger. It was the lady from the restroom. I could not place where I knew her from.

I raced up the stairs and found Jacob sitting on the couch, blood had dripped down his pantleg. Greg had removed his shirt and had it pressed on Jacob's leg.

"Move out of the way," I barked.

I placed one hand near his wound and held the stone with my other. The stone heated. I asked Jacob, "Are you doing, okay?" The bullet had gone clean through his leg.

"I am now," he uttered.

The stone cooled. "We need to get out of here." I glanced around before asking, "Can you get up?"

Jacob jumped to his feet. No one was in sight. I took him and Juliet to my room at the villa. "You can't be walking around here with blood on you. Call Isabella and have them bring you some pants. Oh, and make sure you clean yourself up before you head to your room. We'll talk tomorrow," I said before returning invisible to the others.

Greg was pinching his nose with one hand while he held the bloody shirt in the other and was talking to someone in a hotel uniform. "Honestly. It's just a bad nosebleed."

"Come. Come," the gentleman said pointing inside.

Everyone piled inside.

"Go there. Cleanup," he said in broken English, pointing Greg toward a bathroom.

Using telepathy, I told everyone to go back outside. They did as I instructed. Once the coast was clear, I teleported Mechelle and Austin to my room.

Immediately, I returned to the lobby to get Greg. He was still in the men's room as I came through the door. Greg was drying his hands. Without saying a word, I placed my hand on his shoulder and returned to my room with him. Everyone was sitting except Jacob, who was in my bathroom.

Austin asked, "Who do you think that was?"

I replied, "I'm trying to remember where I know her from. I saw her in the lady's room at Yab."

"Perhaps she is one of the Granaldis," Jacob shouted from the bathroom.

There was a knock at the door and Juliet opened it. Leonardo strolled in and said, "Wow, we have a full house in here." He handed Greg a pair of pants. "Those are for Jacob."

Jacob's arm slid out from the bathroom as snatched the pants from Greg.

Mechelle filled him in on the location of the van and why we didn't feel it was safe yet to retrieve it.

"Brooke can take me to it. I'll bring it back. Just let Isabella know so she doesn't worry," Leonardo instructed.

Mechelle handed him the van key.

I dropped him off and swiftly returned to the others.

Could it be one of the Granaldis?

I ran the list of people I could remember. Suddenly, I was reminded of the attack in the school bathroom. Anthony Granaldi's niece. I shouted, "That's it!"

Everyone's eyes shifted toward me. I said, "The lady is Anthony's niece. I don't know her name." I shook my head. "It's been a few years but it's her."

We decided to call it a night. Greg kissed me and sauntered out with everyone else. I still had blood on me.

Time for a shower and straight to bed.

Twenty-Five

Leonardo confirmed that the woman that shot Jacob was Cara Granaldi, the great-niece of Anthony Granaldi III. The Bloom Keepers decided it was best to keep a low profile if I was in town because it was apparent Cara was very much like her great-uncle.

We made it to the Chianti area for a wine tour and Val d'Orcia both areas had breathtaking views of the Italian countryside. My final day there was spent on the beach in Livomo. The water was crystal clear. It was the most relaxed I had been in a while. The next day we said our goodbyes to everyone. Austin stayed another week to be able to get to know Mechelle's parents better, who arrived that day. There had been no sign of Cara since the night she shot Jacob.

We returned to the office and after a short while Jacob drove us back to my house. He and Greg carried our bags in.

Such gentlemen.

Karen was in the kitchen chopping up food when we entered.

Greg asked, "What are ya doing here?"

She lifted her eyes for a moment and said, "What does it look like? I'm making the girls dinner." She stood tall and asked Greg, "Will you boys be joining them?"

Jacob replied, "Sure."

Greg raised his eyebrow and leaned forward. He asked, "Is Mom cooking?"

"Nope. She and Dad have plans with the Slumans'," she answered.

Jacob and Greg inhaled and slowly exhaled at the same time.

Greg said, "Yes, I'll be here." He followed Jacob out of the kitchen with my bag.

"Don't mind him. He's having a hard time with you growing up. Give me a call when we need to come down," I said.

Juliet and I marched up the stairs. The guys were just about to head down when they saw us approaching. We both thanked them.

Juliet said, "I'm going to call my mother and unpack. See you in a bit."

Jacob followed her to her room.

"I guess you're with me," I said jokingly.

Greg laid across my bed playing on his phone while I unpacked my bag.

He glanced up from his phone. "I'm guessing grilled cheese sandwiches for dinner. What do you think?"

"Be nice. I think you are going to be surprised when you see what she has prepared."

"I hope you're right. She does make a good grilled cheese sandwich," he chuckled.

I tossed a soiled shirt from my suitcase at him. He retrieved it and hurled it back at me. Everything had been put away. I zipped my suitcase and placed it by the door.

I sat next to Greg on the bed. "Do you think Cara is anything we should worry about?"

"She is a Granaldi, and you did break her entire family apart when you helped Tony escape and put Joseph and Anthony in prison," Greg answered.

"I suppose you're right," I said biting my lip.

Juliet said, "Right about what?" As she entered my room.

I said, "That I should worry about Cara. I should probably worry about Anthony's wife too."

Jacob commented, "I'll check into them and see what I can find out. I doubt she knows you live here. She might be able to find out though."

"I'll pop in and see if I can find anything out. See if you can find out where Cara lives," I told him.

Karen called us to dinner. The table was set beautifully. Each place setting had a Caesar salad. I was surprised when Jacob asked me to say grace. The smile on Juliet's face showed she was pleased about it. Although all of us were Christians, Greg and I were always the ones leading us in prayer.

The salad was quite good. Karen collected our plates when we had finished and returned with a plate of mushroom gravy on top of steak, served with garlic mashed potatoes, and asparagus. Once the last plate was placed, she left the dining room.

She stood on the other side of the wall. "Smells amazing," I said cutting into the steak.

"It's more than amazing," Jacob belted out.

I asked, "What do you think Greg?"

"Well, I must admit. It's as good as anything Phyllis makes," he said plopping another piece of steak into his mouth.

I glanced up at Karen. She smiled and turned toward the kitchen. There was nothing left on our plates when we were done. Karen cleared the dishes and returned with individual Raspberry Baked Alaska. She even lit them one by one.

"Karen, you should be proud of yourself. This meal was outstanding," I complimented.

"Thank you, Ms. Brooke," she said with a nod.

I asked, "Ms. Brooke?"

Karen smiled and said, "You are the lady of the house." She smirked and pranced away.

I couldn't help but chuckle. Karen cleaned up when we finished. Everyone was exhausted. Juliet went out back to say goodbye to Jacob, while Greg and I meandered to the front door.

"You should brag about her food in front of your parents. It'll make her feel good," I suggested.

"It'll give her a big head," Greg said with his brow lifted.

I rolled my eyes.

"It was good," he said pulling me to him. He tried to kiss me, and I turned away. "Okay, you win. I'll tell my parents when she's around."

I bit my lip and smiled.

Greg leaned over and gently kissed me and said, "Good night."

I watched him through the window as I locked up.

Karen was still washing dishes when I came in. "Thank you for everything. Dinner was superb," I said bringing my fingers to my mouth and kissing them as the Italians do.

Karen raised her gaze and smiled as her cheeks became rosy. She turned back to washing, and said, "I should be thanking you." She scrubbed a spot on the plate with her nail. "Phyllis has taught me so much. I didn't get the job I wanted, but there will be others. In the meantime, she's going to keep training me so one day I can run a house like this."

"Do you want some help?"

Karen brushed a strand of hair from her cheek. "No, I've got this." She placed the plate in the dishwasher. "Tell me about Italy."

I sat at the bar and told her everything I could. When she was done cleaning up, she told me about the things Phyllis had been teaching her. It felt like she left no detail out as she enthusiastically talked about methods of folding towels, different cleaning products, and organizing her day. Karen was developing into an amazing focused young woman.

"Brooke did you hear me," Karen said loudly.

I was starting to doze off.

Karen pulled a key from her pocket and placed it in front of me. "You need to go to bed. That's the key Phyllis gave me," she said. I had her go out the front door so I could watch her go home. At a snail's pace, I ambled to my room.

Should I change into my pajamas? No...Yes, huh?

I knew I would not sleep well in my clothes, so I changed. I fell asleep soon after my head hit the pillow.

The next morning, I could not believe I had slept nearly nine hours. That was not like me. Greg and I had promised to go to church with his parents and have lunch with them afterward. After eating a bowl of fruit, I found and enjoyed my morning cup of coffee, I dressed and rushed over to Greg's house for church.

Karen answered the door. "Greg's still getting ready. Come on in," she said motioning for me to enter. "Mom, Dad, Brookes here," she yelled down the hall.

Andrew came out. "Good morning. I hear you had quite the time in Italy."

"Yes, sir we did."

He tilted his head and asked, "Was Greg on his best behavior?"

Before I had a chance to answer, Joann entered the room. "I'm so glad you're joining us today."

"I am too. I've missed you all," I said.

Once Greg came out, we set off to their church. Greg, Karen, and I rode in Greg's truck.

Pastor Lewis's sermon was titled, 'The 8th Deadly Sin'. He discussed our fascination with gossip. Yet he warned us of its effects after reading Proverbs 18:8, 'The words of a gossip are like choice morsels; they go down to the inmost parts. To quote him, "Gossip is like cancer."

After church, we went to Cluckers for lunch. Andrew ordered us the Hand-Breaded Cauliflower as an appetizer. Everyone but Joann ordered wings. The cauliflower had an outstanding flavor. While we waited for our wings Greg, and I told them about Italy and how my company was doing.

Greg told his parents, "Karen made us an amazing meal and presented it well. You should hire her for your next dinner party."

Karen blushed.

Joann said, "Really? That's wonderful. What did you make for them?"

Karen explained in detail what she did to prepare for the evening.

The wings came and had the perfect balance of vinegar and cayenne pepper. They were perfectly cooked with crisp skin.

I felt my phone buzz, but my hands were covered in wing sauce. Greg handed me another napkin; I was already on my third. I had received a text from Jacob.

JACOB: Got the info you wanted. I'll be home all day.

I flipped my phone to show Greg.

BROOKE: At lunch. Give me about an hour.

I devoured the rest of my wings. "Greg, why haven't we been here before? These are probably the best wings I've ever had."

Greg shrugged his shoulders and continued eating. I thanked them for the meal before we set off to see Jacob.

I strolled up to the door and nearly entered before remembering this was Jacob's home also. I rang the bell.

Jacob answered the door with a bag of chips in his hands.

Does he ever stop eating?

He dropped the bag of chips on the counter and gulped down his soda. Greg and I sat at the bar.

Jacob started, "Cara and Anthony's wife, Maria have been spending a lot of time together. In fact, Cara's having dinner at Maria's house tonight.

Greg asked, "What time?"

"9:00 pm, which means Brooke needs to get over there soon," Jacob answered.

Greg said, "He's right. Do you want me to go with you?"

"Actually, I think Jacob should. He can go through Maria's computer while I find out what they're up to if anything?"

Jacob says, "Cool. Let me get dressed."

I kissed Greg. "We could be gone a while. I'll call you when we get back," I told him.

Jacob and I teleported to Maria's bedroom.

Man, I never thought I would be back here.

I left Jacob to find out where everyone was. Maria was in the kitchen ordering the staff around. Cara did not appear to be there. I watched as her staff rushed to do what she commanded.

The door chimed. I was surprised to see Maria answer it. Where's the butler? I followed her to the front door. The door opened and revealed Cara and I believed her brother.

Maria said, "Riccardo, I'm so glad you could join us." She hugged them both. She directed them to have a seat in the dining room as she scurried off toward the kitchen. I stayed in the dining room.

Riccardo whispered, "I thought you were kidding."

"I think it's just her maid and the cook," Cara whispered back.

Maria returned and sat in the chair across from me. The maid brought out plates of macaroni and tomatoes with a little cheese sprinkled on them. In the corner of the plate was a single piece of bread.

Cara and Riccardo gazed at their plates for a moment before making eye contact with one another. Their eyes were wide.

Maria scrunched her eyes and asked, "What?"

Cara took a deep breath. "You shouldn't be eating like this." She glanced at her brother and back to her aunt. "None of us should be eating like this."

Riccardo spoke up, "What I think Cara is trying to say is… Our family is going through a tough time…"

Cara interrupted him. "Stop trying to sugarcoat this. What I'm saying is Tony is scum. He's worse than scum. How could he do this to his family? If our father were still alive, he would hunt him down…"

Maria interrupted her. "I agree with everything you're saying." She brought the glass of wine to her lips and lowered her gaze. "What should we do about it?"

Cara stabbed a piece of pasta with her fork. "That girl, Brooke, with that fancy necklace. If Uncle Anthony wanted it so badly, it must be worth a lot. I say we go after it."

Maria swallowed her bite. She placed her fork on her plate and leaned forward and whispered, "I don't see how we can afford to. Surely, she has already gone back home. I'm broke. My staff doesn't even know they are being dismissed at the end of the month. I can't afford them. I'm even behind on the payments for the house."

Cara's mouth dropped open.

Riccardo commented, "We had no idea it was this bad."

"No worries children. We're Granaldis. We'll bounce back," She bit into carefully brought the bite of pasta to her mouth.

Cara asked, "What should we be doing?"

"For now, we need to concentrate on building back our finances. Revenge will come later. Now eat up before your food gets cold," Maria ordered.

I returned to Jacob. The computer was off. I whispered, "Are you ready to go?"

Jacob nodded. I led him back to the office.

I asked, "What did you find out?"

"She's broke. Maria has been reaching out to many of Anthony's contacts. I guess to see if they can help her out financially or to see if they have suggestions on how she can raise some money. They appear to be avoiding her. I suspect this is because the police are aware of the family's criminal ties. There were termination notices recently saved for two ladies. Oh, and she has been talking with a realtor about possibly renting out her home. She's trying to avoid selling it," Jacob announced.

"That seems consistent with what I found out. Cara wants the necklace. I suspect she doesn't know of its power. She knows Anthony likes expensive things, and he wanted it. Maria told her there were no funds to finance a trip here. They're going to concentrate on building back the family finances," I said.

"Sounds like we won't need to worry about them for a while. I'll keep an eye on them. I have access to her computer now. I need to get a few things done before dinner. Juliet's parents are having us over," he informed me.

We said our goodbyes. I called Greg and we decided to spend the remainder of the day at Parkour. It had been a while since we had been there. Gloria was glad to see us. She commented on how much I had improved.

We spent the evening watching movies and eating pizza. When I laid down, I thanked God for everything. I fell asleep thinking about how excited I was about seeing Phyllis in the morning.

Twenty-Six

It was nice slipping back into our normal routine. Everyone worked out together before work. Greg and Austin were searching for a place to rent near the office because the drive for Austin had become a burden. Their goal was to find an inexpensive place because they both knew they would not be spending a lot of time there. Also, Greg wanted to be able to save some money.

Mechelle loved her work at the villa. She even admitted she was intrigued by working with people who dealt with the black market. It also terrified her. Austin visited so frequently causing the staff there to think he was rich to be able to come so often from the states. He said he would laugh and tell them he was a simple farmer. No one believed him. He always used my room when he visited unless I was there.

Karen was around frequently. She was gaining valuable skills from Phyllis. Her business was starting to take off. I paid her for the night she made us dinner and she agreed to help on the weekends or if Phyllis needed time off. Fortunately, she wasn't around enough that it was causing us any concern about her discovering my secret.

Jacob and Juliet were doing well. Oddly he seemed to have developed a bit of OCD about everyone keeping things clean and organized at the office. If he was around and you were not near your drink, the glass might find its way to the dishwasher. Juliet seemed to be the one most disturbed by this new tick of his.

Juliet's parents would show up at the house unannounced. They were having a hard time letting her grow up. She promised them she would try every week to have dinner with them on Sunday night. She had stepped into her role as CFO. She was taking additional classes and working on her master's degree.

We received a hefty check from Allison's agency for our work. She assured us she would let others know how pleased she was with our company. Allison even sent a reference letter that Jacob posted on our website.

Nadine and Eddie had proven to be an asset. We planned on hiring them to do surveillance on many of our cases. They were quite good at it. Juliet and I still liked having fun with them. However, the more we visited, the less scared they seemed to be.

I went to see Kevin and told him about my adding an entry to the journal. He still wanted it to remain in the safe at the villa. He seemed like he was doing a lot better.

The Bloom Keepers decided on the first Thursday of each month, we would train with Asahi and Akio in Japan. Everyone was excited about it. Asahi said he had a variety of training planned to help us develop our skills.

Greg and I would be testifying against the man that kidnapped Annie. Occasionally, I ran into them at the park when we trained there. Her father told us she wanted to do martial arts like us, so he signed her up.

Jared had been keeping in contact with Greg and Austin. He mentioned to them about someone breaking into his apartment and suspected the feds removed his things.

Jacob and I are going to keep my eye on him.

Jacob said there were other things on the videos that he witnessed. I question his motives. Only time will tell what they are.

Jacob informed me Zahara, Eleni Kostopoulos's daughter, planned on attending college in the states. He's still trying to figure out which college. I loved how he kept track of these things.

Greg has settled into his position well. He has delegated some items to Austin to take care of. Everyone had found their niche at the company, and we worked well together.

I was finishing up my notes for our Monday morning meeting when Mom called.

"I just wanted to say I love you. I'll have my phone with me, but calls are expensive, so I won't be checking in with you while I'm gone.

Gone? Oh yeah, the cruise.

I replied, "No worries. I have a lot going on here. We have two potential clients coming next week. One wants us to work undercover for some famous person because they suspect someone on staff is poisoning them."

Mom asked, "That's scary. Who's the famous person?"

"They haven't disclosed that yet, but it sounds like an interesting case," I commented.

"You be careful. We don't want anyone finding out what you're there for and trying to poison you. This job of yours makes me nervous," she said.

Ding Dong!

"I think Susie's here. Yes, it's her. I need to go. I love you, sweetheart. Give everyone a hug," she said before the phone went dead.

I was printing the agenda when Juliet came in.

She asked, "Are you about ready?"

Frequently we rode in together. The clock read 4:32 pm. Phyllis and Hal's housewarming party was at 6:00 pm. I glanced at my income emails. Nothing there. "Yes, just give me a minute to clean up."

My phone rang as I turned my computer off. It was Mechelle. "How's it going?"

Mechelle replied, "Good, I just wanted you to know Allison came for Kyle. She assured me he would be back soon. Leonardo and I want to offer him a full-time job as the manager of the orchard. Do you have a problem with that?"

"Absolutely not. If both of you feel he's qualified. Mechelle, you don't need to run everything through me," I told her.

"That's what Leonardo said, but I felt this one was one you should be aware of," she explained.

I continued, "I trust you completely. Oh, when will you be ready for me to pick you up?"

"I'm in your room, now. I really don't need much. I left toiletries and clothes there. It's going to be nice spending the weekend with everyone," she said enthusiastically.

"Everyone or Austin?" I chuckled.

"I'm definitely excited about seeing him."

I closed the blinds and teleported over and picked her up.

Juliet was surprised when we both exited my office.

Everyone greeted her. Mechelle asked, "Where's Austin?"

"He was running some errands for us. He should be back any minute," Jacob informed her.

The door burst open. Austin stood there with a box of copy paper and a bouquet of flowers on top. His eyes widened when he noticed Mechelle. He placed the items on the reception desk and hugged her. He said, "I thought I was picking you up at Brooke's house."

"You still can, if you've things to do," Mechelle informed him.

"Nope. I'm all yours," he said planting a kiss on her. He turned back to the supplies and snatched the bouquet. "I was going to surprise you with these when I picked you up."

Mechelle smelled them. "Thank you so much."

Juliet announced, "Brooke, we need to get going or we'll be late."

Juliet brought me home, while Mechelle stayed with Austin. We agreed to meet her at the party.

Jacob picked us up. I think the only reason Greg agreed to let him drive was that it was only a few blocks away.

Phyllis greeted us when we arrived. Hal was busy speaking with other guests. She led us on a short tour around the home. It was beautifully decorated with hints of modern mixed in with the antiques. As expected, there was a large array of goodies to eat. I was surprised when Karen came in dressed as a server.

Phyllis leaned over to me and said, "I hired her. She made several of the dishes here."

Impressive.

Phyllis wouldn't have her if she wasn't doing a good job.

I sat on her back patio for a moment away from the chatter in the building. The warm summer breeze caressed my skin, while lightning bugs filled the garden.

Thank you, Lord, for everything. I am not worthy of everything you have given me and entrusted me with.

I closed my eyes and just listened to the crickets in the distance.

Was I even aware of all the power the Lord had entrusted me with? Doubtful.

One thing was certain, I should not reveal everything I knew about the stone, and I suspected the Bloom of Dreams had more secrets it had not disclosed to me yet.

Cheddar Spinach Frittata with Bacon

Ingredients

- 8 slices of bacon
- ½ pound fresh spinach (rinse and dry before using) cut into pieces about an inch squared
- 8 large eggs
- ½ cup whole milk
- Kosher salt and ground pepper, to taste
- 1 cup grated cheddar cheese
- 2 tablespoons bacon grease

Directions

1. Preheat oven to 400 degrees Fahrenheit.
2. Cook bacon in a cast-iron skillet over medium heat until crispy. Place on paper towel to drain. Reserve 2 tablespoons of bacon fat in the pan. When bacon is cool roughly chop to desired size. (Recommend ¼ inch)
3. Add diced onions to 2 tablespoons of bacon grease and sauté until translucent. (2-3 minutes)
4. Turn off the heat and add spinach. Stir until the spinach leaves are wilted. Add the chopped bacon to the pan.
5. Put the eggs milk and salt in a bowl and beat until frothy.
6. Pour egg mixture into the skillet and stir to disperse the ingredients equally.
7. Place the skillet over medium low heat for approximately 5 minutes. Do not stir. Eggs will begin to set.
8. Sprinkle the grated cheese evenly across the top of the eggs and place in oven. Bake until the eggs are fully cooked. (10-15 minutes.) Serve in the pan to keep the meal warm.

Lemon Blueberry Muffins

Ingredients

- 3 ¼ cups all-purpose flour
- 4 teaspoons baking powder
- 1 teaspoon baking soda
- ½ teaspoon salt
- 1 ⅓ cups white sugar
- 1 ¼ cups milk
- 1 cup sour cream
- ½ cup melted butter
- 2 large eggs
- 1 tablespoon lemon zest
- 1 ½ cups frozen blueberries

Directions

1. Preheat the oven to 350 degrees Fahrenheit.
2. Line 16 muffin cups with paper liners.
3. Sift flour, baking powder, baking soda, and salt together in a bowl.
4. Combine butter, eggs, lemon zest, milk, sour cream, and sugar in a large bowl. Beat with an electric mixer on low speed until well blended.
5. Fold into the flour mixture until batter is just moistened. Fold in blueberries; avoid over mixing because batter will turn purple.
6. Fill muffin cups 3/4 full of batter.
7. Bake in the preheated oven until golden brown, 30 to 35 minutes. Let cool for 10 minutes.

Strawberry Lemonade

Ingredients

- 1 cup granulated white sugar
- 1 cup water
- 1/2 lb. strawberries washed and sliced
- 7 large lemons
- 6 cups cold water

Directions

- Make a simple syrup by pouring 1 cup water into a medium sized pan and place it over medium high heat. Bring the water to a low boil, then add in 1 cup of white granulated sugar. Whisk until the sugar completely dissolves, then remove the pan from heat, and let cool.
- Clean and slice 1 lemon and set aside.
- Clean and slice strawberries and place in blender. (Set a few slices aside for a garnish.)
- Add the juice of 6 lemons to the blender and blend until liquified.
- Pour the strawberry and lemon juice mixture into a large pitcher, along with 6 cups of water and the cooled simple syrup.
- Stir until well blended.
- Serve with ice, lemon, and strawberry slices.

Bill Dwinell's Spicy-Sweet Barbecue Sauce

Ingredients

- 3 cups of water
- 64 oz ketchup
- 1 ½ cups Worcestershire sauce
- 1 ½ tbs Hot Hungarian paprika
- 1 tbs black pepper
- 1 tbs garlic salt
- 1 tbs white vinegar
- ½ tsp garlic powder
- ½ tsp cayenne
- 3 ½ tbs onion powder
- 2 cups light brown sugar

Directions

1. Combine all ingredients. Stir frequently.
2. Bring to a boil over high heat.
3. Reduce heat. Simmer uncovered for 60 minutes, or until it reaches your desired thickness, stir frequently.
4. Let cool before bottling unless you are canning. while stirring (Yields 2.5 Quarts)

Discover other titles by D.A. Dwinell

Guardian of the Stone Series
The Bloom of Dreams – Book 1
The Bloom's Cradle - Book 2
Bloom Keepers - Book 3
Path of the Guardian – Book 4
Bloom of Secrets – Book 5

Available on Amazon
https://www.amazon.com/stores/DA%20Dwinell/author/B09D
TPVWCF

Connect with D.A. Dwinell
If you want the latest news on D.A. Dwinell or interested in
connecting on social media, please visit the following site:

Facebook:	www.facebook.com/DADwinell
Instagram:	d.a._dwinell
Twitter:	DA Dwinell @da_dwinell
Clapper:	Dana_Author_Florida
TikTok:	dana_authorfl_jesus #DADwinell

Acknowledgement

I would like to express my gratitude to my editors which include Bluefield Mountain Editing & Proofreading Services.